Savage

Gerry

Savage
Gerry

A Novel

JOHN
JANTUNEN

Purchase the print edition
and receive the eBook free.
For details, go to ecwpress.com/eBook.

Published by ECW Press
665 Gerrard Street East
Toronto, Ontario, Canada M4M 1Y2
416-694-3348 / info@ecwpress.com

Cover design: Michel Vrana

LIBRARY AND ARCHIVES CANADA CATALOGUING IN
PUBLICATION

Title: Savage Gerry : a novel / John Jantunen.
Names: Jantunen, John, 1971- author.
Description: Series statement: The Tildon chronicles ;
book 2

Identifiers: Canadiana (print) 20200383418 | Canadiana
(ebook) 20200383434

ISBN 978-1-77041-560-7 (SOFTCOVER)
ISBN 978-1-77305-690-6 (EPUB)
ISBN 978-1-77305-691-3 (PDF)
ISBN 978-1-77305-692-0 (KINDLE)

Classification: LCC PS8619.A6783 S28 2021 | DDC
C813/.6—dc23

The publication of *Savage Gerry* has been generously supported by the Canada Council for the Arts and is funded in
part by the Government of Canada. *Nous remercions le Conseil des arts du Canada de son soutien. Ce livre est financé en partie
par le gouvernement du Canada.* We acknowledge the support of the Ontario Arts Council (OAC), an agency of the Government of Ontario, which last year funded 1,965 individual artists and 1,152 organizations in 197 communities across
Ontario for a total of $51.9 million. We also acknowledge the contribution of the Government of Ontario through the
Ontario Book Publishing Tax Credit, and through Ontario Creates for the marketing of this book.

PRINTED AND BOUND IN CANADA

PRINTING: MARQUIS   5   4   3   2   1

For Drake

The past is never dead. It's not even past.

William Faulkner

*F*our Harleys led the way. Their riders were clad all in black leather and had shaven heads, their faces painted as white as bone and their mouths tattooed with the imprint of skeletal grins so that they more resembled ghouls than men. They rode two by two under a star-fraught sky carrying hell's own thunder along this country road, its two lanes enshrouded by spruce and pine and cedar trees broken at intervals by scattered settlements — groups of four or five houses clustered around gas stations and country stores and shuttered motels, their gravel driveways and unmowed lawns enclosing domiciles as dark as tombs. At their approach twitches, like nervous ticks, parted the drape of curtained windows, revealing prying eyes widened in muted horror as if these were but the vanguard for an army of the vengeful dead, or the crest of a wave they expected to rear up at any moment and whelm them under.

Onwards they rode ever north, espying none of the palpitations spurned in their wake, blind to the world beyond the scour of their headlights upon the blacktop ahead. At last they passed a lone bungalow moored some ten feet above the road upon a granite ledge. *The house was fashioned out of wood panels the colour of honey and roofed with cedar shake and had an expansive porch cobbled together out of chinked logs. From its rails hung crudely embossed signs — Folk Art and Mennonite Furniture and Live Bait and Ice Cream and Cold Drinks and Fireworks! — and above these there perched a smattering of woodland creatures: a brace of squirrels upraised on their hinds and chipmunks poised in furious ascent along its vertical beams, a martin caught mid-slink and frogs mid-croak, racoons rearing with expressions of curious bemuse from each of its posts. Amongst them their creator sat hunched over in a pine rocking chair. He was an old man, clean shaven and wearing a long-sleeved plaid flannel shirt and a wide-brimmed hat made of straw and banded by sweat. In his right hand he held a hook-bladed carving knife and was using this to tease his latest creation from the block of rock maple in his lap, neither that nor the shavings scattered about his slippered feet giving any clue as to what it might become. Another chipmunk perhaps, or maybe a squirrel (and why not?). As the motorcycles sounded their trumpet, he looked up with the idle contempt of someone who's seen everything and wouldn't at all have been surprised if the devil himself had appeared at the foot of his stairs proffering to him his heart's content, which at that moment wouldn't have amounted to anything more than an ice-cold bottle of beer.*

The Harleys had barely passed when there arose a splash of light and a rumble from beyond the southward bend in the road. These heralded the approach of a transport truck hauling a flatbed trailer on which loomed an excavator of a size amenable to moving mountains. Lounged upon its treads were a half dozen men and there were others sitting in precarious recline on the roof of its cab, all of them cradling rifles of a military grade and drawing on cigarettes with the plaintive deliberation of soldiers being carried off to war. Hitched behind that was a second trailer. It was smaller than the first and lit with spans of Christmas lights strung between the steel posts affixed to its corners. Within their festive glow the old carver could see it had been furnished to resemble a parlour now set to rocking and reeling with a motley assemblage of musicians: two men with fiddles on a couch and a man with a banjo sitting in an easy chair, another hammering at the keys of an upright piano and one plucking at the strings of a stand-up bass, a sixth astride a three-legged stool, pounding out a chaotic rhythm on a snare drum and cymbal. They were all garbed in the vestments of simple country folk — dungarees, coveralls and plain white T-shirts or bare-chested — and one of them was singing, the old man could not tell of which. All he could make out of the song itself was a single line, sung thrice with the exuberant lilt of an old-timey barn hall jig.

Raise a little hell, raise a little hell, raise a little hell!

The voice and the music were both then swallowed by the gust of wind spurned by the trailer's passing and the old man turned towards the bend in the road again, seeking out with plaintive eyes any wonders this night might yet still behold. A moment later there was another splash of light and this heralded the approach of a white cube van, unremarkable except that it was followed by another grim rider, a perfect duplicate of the ones that had come before save for the flagpole affixed to the back of his seat. From this there billowed a standard emblazoned with a green and leafy tree cast upon a hilltop against a diffusion of reds and oranges such as might colour the sky approaching dusk.

The old man knew then whence this strange caravan had come and the only thing left unresolved was the matter of where it was going. He barely had a breath to ponder on that before he heard the crackling scorn of his wife's voice straining through the screened window at his back.

What in the devil was that all about? she asked and her husband turned northward, scanning the road and probing deeply of its dark, searching out any and all of its possible ends.

I do believe, he said at last, they're headed for the prison.

He awoke with Millie's voice still ringing in his head.

Gerald! she cried, startling him awake from the dream and into the dark, his hands flailing, reaching out as if he meant to comfort her and finding only a cement wall, its cold and hard so at odds with her warm and soft that he was at a sudden loss to explain where he might have been.

His head ached as if it had been pressed into a vice and his tongue throbbed like a slug baking in the sun. When he inhaled, the air was enlivened by the stench of rotting meat, so rank he could hardly breathe, and only then did he remember where he was: locked in a prison cell with a dead man. He could hear the thrum of flies, and the traipse of them over his cheeks and within his bushman's beard spoke to him of his own future, no different than Orville Gates's, all two hundred and eighty pounds of whom lay stretched beneath a blanket against the back wall of the cell, dead now these past five days.

The stench of his putrefaction had soured the air with such a pungency that it seemed to have impregnated Gerald's lips and his tongue, his very skin, curing him like a gutted pig strung from the rafters in his grandfather's smokehouse. As he rolled over, burying his face in his pillow, he clung to this memory, conjuring in his mind the subtle waft of porcine-infused smoke seeping from its chimney, recalling how his grandfather always used white oak when smoking his hogs. There weren't a wood that burned cleaner, he'd told Gerald no more than a week after he'd come to live with the old man on his farm at the end of Stull Street, Gerald then a boy of seven. His grandfather explaining, Everything else would be like if we used swamp water to make lemonade. The old man swore he could tell by the subtle variations in the smoke's flavour the exact moment the meat was cured and when the time was drawing nigh he'd circle the smokehouse following its drift, his nose upraised, stopping every now and again to flick his tongue against the cleft in his top lip with the deft precision of a lizard, as if when the meat was ready he'd be able to taste it.

Gerald peppering this reminiscence with a myriad of details as if through sheer force of imagination he might be able to trick the stench into abeyance. The swish of timothy grass against his legs as he followed his grandfather's endless circling. The crunch of pebbles beneath his shoes as he traversed the pile behind the smokehouse, left over from when the old man had dug the new well. The taste of clover which Gerald would suckle from the flower's multiform spikes, same as his grandfather, who'd told him that the sweet perfume of its nectar cleansed the palate. Grasshoppers knocking against his legs and the pinch of their claws when one landed on his arm. The electric whine of cicadas from the woods and the *trollop* of frogsong from the ditch along the road, the restless fret of chickens scratching for grubs in the yard. How, whenever his grandfather stopped to take a whiff, his right hand would come to rest on the butt of the Smith & Wesson revolver holstered on his belt, which he always wore though it had been years since he'd retired from the RCMP. His left hand would scratch at the scruff of his beard and he'd look ever so much like a sheriff catching a whiff of trouble on the horizon in one of those old westerns they used to watch.

On and on he went but no matter how he inhabited the memory he couldn't inure his thoughts to the embalming force of Orville's decay. His right hand, in the meantime, had slipped beneath his undershirt and had come to rest on the plastic laminated shell encasing the picture hung around his neck on a shoelace. He had the sudden urge to pull it out but was stalled in this, as he was whenever he felt the sudden urge to chance a look at his son, by the recollection of a piece of prison wisdom a sixty-year-old lifer had imparted to him during his first week at the Central North Correctional Centre.

There is nothing more painful than days of joy recollected in days of misery, he'd said and if truer words had ever been spoken, Gerald had never heard them.

But it was the endless stretch of the three life sentences ahead of him that had lent the adage its veracity. He hadn't seen a guard for going on a week and it was by then painfully clear to him that his present future didn't add up to more than a couple days, three at most. Not that it really mattered since the cell was about as dark as a coffin and he wouldn't be able to see the photo anyway. So he left it were it was, biding his time drumming his fingers on its shell and conjuring into his mind the image of his son on the picture that his wife, Millie, had taken to mark the boy's fifth birthday, one of the thirteen she'd taken every June fifth since he'd been born. They were all snapped from the same spot, her standing on the front porch of their cabin and Evers on the boulder at the end of the outcropping of rock that stretched thirty feet into the lake.

Gerald himself had given her the idea on the day Evers had turned one.

To mark the occasion, they'd hiked the two kilometres from their house to Beausilake (what his grandfather had called it since the lake had no designation on any map and the family name was Beausoleil). Seen from above, the lake resembled an elongated foot imprinted in the granite, ringed red with iron deposits leached from the rock, its heel calloused by the ridge — some fifty feet high — that banked the northern edge and its toes forming a series of coves nestled amongst the firs crowding the shoreline to the south. It was around the biggest of these that his great-grandfather had built seven one-room cabins, one for himself and his wife in the middle and three for his daughters on the left and three for his sons on the right. None of them, nor their offspring, had been to the lake for years by then and the middle cabin, which Gerald's grandfather had claimed for his own, was the only one that hadn't been let fall into ruin.

Millie had just come out of its front door after stowing her pack inside. Evers was standing on the boulder, slapping his knees and shouting, Bah!, which he always did to express his joy. Gerald, who'd just put him there, was standing a few feet off, ready to spring to the rescue if it looked like he was about to fall. The picture she took was the only one of the thirteen with Gerald in it. She'd just surprised him by shouting, Say cheese!, and he was looking directly at the camera with an expression that had always seemed strangely lost and forlorn and at complete odds with Gerald's memory of that day, which he'd always counted as one of his happiest. Evers's expression was one of reckless abandon. His right foot was upraised, about to take that one step over the edge, heedless of the four-foot drop onto

4

bedrock. The moment after she'd snapped the picture, Millie had screamed, Evers!, and that had shocked Gerald back to life. Panic gripped, he lunged for the boy, catching him as he fell, holding him then cradled in his arms, Evers giggling like some sort of infant lunatic, unaware of the fright he'd just caused his parents.

Millie had later framed the photo and put it on the mantel in their living room. Every year thereafter she'd added another and each spoke to one facet of the boy so that it had come to seem to Gerald that when he was looking at them all together he could almost catch a glimpse of the man his son might one day become.

His favourite of them all was the one she'd taken when he was five.

He'd carved Evers a bow out of rock maple and had given it to him as a present along with the best twelve arrows he'd rooted out of his grandfather's supply in the shed. Millie had stitched him a quiver out of her old purple suede jacket, the same jacket she'd been wearing the night she'd followed Gerald home from the Legion in Capreol, a year to the day after he'd buried his grandfather. She was plenty drunk and he drunker still. Seeing the coat hanging from the back of the chair in his bedroom upon awaking the next morning had come as much of a surprise to him as had been the woman cooking eggs in the kitchen after he'd finally stumbled downstairs.

In the picture, Evers was up on the rock, the quiver slung over his bare chest, the arrows' feathers lashing against his cheek, and he had the bow raised up over his head in his right hand. His mouth was open in a bestial roar and his eyes were narrowed to slits and he'd never look more fierce or wild than he did standing on the boulder just then. The picture spoke to Gerald better than any of the others as to the man he hoped his son would one day become and whenever he passed by the picture on the mantel he couldn't resist the urge to reach out and touch it, whispering a quiet invocation to himself, *May he never lose that spirit.*

He was doing the same now, exhaling the words with the solemn determination of a dying man speaking his last, and those apparently rousing his other cellmate, Jules.

You say something? Jules asked in a hushed voice, though that seemed like an antiquated sort of luxury, held over from a time when talking after lights out might earn the censure of a guard, all of whom, as far as Gerald knew, had long since abandoned them.

Gerald!

His voice had risen a notch, veering towards panic, but Gerald wasn't in the mood for talking and responded by holding his breath as if playing at a game of hide-and-seek, a vain effort locked as he was in a cement box, six feet by ten.

After a moment he heard Jules's rasp as he inhaled through the door's slot. The last guard they'd seen, a man by the name of Foley, had left it open in clear violation of prison protocol, though it seemed a tender sort of mercy now. Beforehand, he'd slipped each of them a plastic-wrapped emergency ration and a bottle of water — their last — and Jules, for about the hundredth time over the past four weeks, had asked if there was any news about why the prison's main power had gone out. Foley seemed reluctant to talk about that, or had been ordered not to, and answered as he always did by saying, That's a mystery all right. But don't you worry about that. It'll be back on any day now.

He'd turned to leave and Orville had called after him, asking for his insulin shot.

Shoot, Foley'd said, I forgot about that. I'll be right back.

He'd added, Don't you go anywhere now, his good humour while he said it meant to assure Orville that it was just a mere oversight, nothing to worry himself about. Except Foley hadn't returned and a few hours later the emergency lights in the hall had gone out too so Gerald knew the prison's emergency generator had finally quit. Orville had died that night, panting like a sick dog and then passing without a sound except for a faint hiss like air leaking through a pinprick in an inner tube.

The next morning Gerald had awoken to the buzzing of flies and the day after to a crunching noise like caterpillars ravaging a tree, though he'd only wished it was that. The room had shortly become overwhelmed with the acrid stench of rotting meat and ever since Jules hadn't moved an inch from the door's open slot, idling his time drinking deeply of the air from the unit's common area.

Gerald, Jules prodded again. Are you there?

Exhaled in a carefully measured stream, the air whistled a strained harmony through Gerald's nostrils.

Yeah, he said, though it only felt half the truth. I'm here.

I can't take it anymore. The smell. I can't, I can't— I can't fucking take it anymore.

A couple more days.

What?

It'll only be a couple more days.

What do you mean? Until someone comes and lets us out?

If they was gonna let us out, they'd've done it by now.

So they're just going to let us fucking die in here?

They already have.

Jules must have been thinking about that for it was a moment before he spoke again.

How long do you think it'll be? he asked.

A couple more days, like I said.

I can't do two more fucking days of this.

Ain't much I can do about that.

You could kill me.

How's that?

I said, you could kill me.

I ain't going to kill you.

It'd be easy. You could smother me with my pillow.

I ain't smothering you with a pillow.

But why not? You killed three men already, haven't you? What's one more?

Gerald opened his mouth about to say, That was different, they deserved it, but bit his lip before the words could form.

Truth was, Jules deserved it as much as any of the men Gerald had killed. He'd been an investment broker in his previous life and had swindled the savings out from under his nearest and dearest — his friends and family. His skin was the colour of wet clay except for the flays of red like volcanic rivers carving tributaries through the dull pallor of his cheeks and those had told Gerald he'd spent a good deal of his previous life raising toasts to his good fortune. He'd often kept Gerald up all night crying over the two men — one his own brother — who'd taken their lives when they found out they were broke, and he'd never once looked either of his cellmates straight in the eye. If he hadn't ended up as the third man in a cell built for two he wouldn't likely have wasted even a single breath on such a lowly creature as Gerald knew himself to be.

But none of that was why Gerald wouldn't do him this simple mercy, though it went a good way to accounting for why he didn't feel overly compelled to explain to Jules why that might have been.

You could tie my sheet into a rope, Jules was saying. Strangle me.

My killing days are long past, Gerald answered in a sharp tone that he hoped would put an end to the matter.

It didn't.

Please. I can't— I can't take it anymore.

A desperate whine had crept into Jules's tone and Gerald felt the familiar surge of anger welling in his chest as it often did when he spoke to his cellmate.

Won't you just kill me? Get it over with. Please, please. I'm begging you.

Gerald rolled back over, burying his face again in his pillow and muttering under his breath, more to himself than to Jules,

You keep it up, I just might.

Y ou hear that?

    Gerald was lying on his back, half dozing. Jules's voice rose as a tremulous whisper, no more than a ghost might have made. Beyond that Gerald could hear a distant rumbling.

Sounds like thunder, he said.

It doesn't sound like any thunder I ever heard. It sounds like—

Before Jules could finish, a splash of light blanched the ceiling's grey — a sudden intrusion more like one cast by a passing car than a bolt of lightning. In its bright Gerald could see that Jules was standing beside the bunk, one hand grappling with the frame for support. His head swivelled, tracing after the fleeing luminescence, probing of its glare as if trying to make sense of where it might have come from. All reason was then lost to a vociferous crunching given over to the dull clatter of buckling concrete and the sharp *ping!* of rebar snapping.

Jules stumbled back as the wall crumbled inwards, smothering Orville's deflated hump. The cell's inner dark was vanquished by an outer bright casting Gerald in shadow against the far wall, his hands in a desperate clutch at the bed's frame as if he expected, at any moment, to be washed away by a sudden deluge. It was a fleeting thought dispelled by the guttural roar of an engine and the sudden waft of air pungent with diesel fumes and cement dust.

Shrouding his eyes with a visored hand, he turned towards the chasm opened out of the toppling wall. There was a giant hand raking its rubble, and Orville too, in one outward sweep. It was ringed with an aura of almost otherworldly light and Jules stood with mouth agape like maybe he was waiting to hear the voice of God calling out to him in its rapture. But the hand departed having uttered nothing but the hiss of its hydraulics, and the light departed shortly thereafter.

Gerald's eyes hadn't yet adjusted from their slumber and all he could see in its wake was a blur of yellow streaking past the hole. It was accompanied by a lumberous creak and he'd just got in mind what that might have meant when there appeared another light, no more than a spot, prying through the haze. All of this so far away and so much like a dream that Gerald froze stock still, afraid that if he dared move or breathe he'd awake again, alone in the dark, perhaps terminally this time. Every tha-rump of his heart thereafter served to shatter the illusion but even when a barrel-shaped man appeared scrambling over the rubble the excavator had left behind, he still couldn't conjure the will to more than peer back at him.

Orville, you in there? the barrel-shaped man called out.

Through the dust and the flicker of flies, his flashlight found Jules coughing into his arm.

You ain't Orville.

No, Jules choked out. I'm—

But he was cut off by the man before he could continue.

God, don't it reek in here!

Gerald could see that the barrel-shaped man was short, shorter even than his own five foot eight, and wore a beard a shade longer, its brackish curls straggling over a belly so big and round it'd be a miracle if he could touch the pads of his fingers together in front of him. He had one arm crooked over his mouth to guard against the stench and all Gerald could see of his face were his eyes, black pits blinking against the dust.

Smells like something died, the barrel-shaped man was saying and that snapped Gerald out of his daze.

That'd be Orville, he said.

The moment he spoke the flashlight searched him out, striking upon what must have appeared to the other a strange and gnomic cave-dwelling creature cowering on the top bunk and squinting against its glower.

What'd you say?

I said, That'd be Orville.

He's dead?

Five days now.

You kill him?

There was a hint of accusation in his voice and that and the way the man's free hand had searched out the stock of the automatic pistol slung on a strap over his shoulder had Gerald vigorously shaking his head.

No, he said. They never came by with his shot.

The flashlight had taken to darting about the cell, chasing the dark out of its corners. Finding no evidence of Orville's remains, it again sought out Gerald.

What'd you do, eat him?

Last I saw he was lying on the floor, about where you're standing now.

The barrel-shaped man looked down to his feet. The flashlight lit over a stain the colour of motor oil. He seemed to get the point and turned back to the gaping hole in the wall. The beam scanned over the pile of rubble a few yards beyond and the man was just moving after it when Jules finally found the will to speak again.

You want to tell us what the fuck's going on? he asked.

Well, what do you think? the barrel-shaped man said, turning back and flashing them an impish sort of grin.

It's a goddamn jail break!

Gerald and Jules emerged from the hole, clutching each other around the waist and gulping great mouthfuls of air laced with diesel fumes, heaven-sent compared to the cell's putridity.

The excavator had moved on and was launching a fresh assault on the wall twenty paces hence. In the peripheral glow of its headlights Gerald could see the barrel-shaped man talking with a tall stick-like figure. The both of them were staring dolefully at the bloated arm jutting from the pile of rubble that had been his cell's outer wall. Each was wearing a matching denim vest over a bare chest and on their backs was embroidered the picture of a hilltop tree cast against the setting sun. Beneath its billow of leaves, from the lowest branch, there hung a singular reddish globe — what looked to be an apple but what Gerald knew to be a drop of blood.

He'd seen the picture plenty of times before.

A good number of the prisoners had it tattooed on their arms and back, Orville included, but even before he'd come to Central

North, Gerald would have had to have been living on the moon not to have known it was the insignia of The Sons of Adam Motorcycle Club. They'd had a compound in Chelmsford, a small town less than a half hour from Capreol, where he'd lived with his grandfather. Both Chemmie, as the locals called it, and Capreol had been amalgamated into the City of Greater Sudbury long before Gerald was born. The Sons' colours were outlawed there but they defied the spirit, if not the exact letter, of the law by wearing cuts embroidered with the tree, and sometimes brazenly displaying a standard with the same affixed to the back of their bikes as they cruised the network of country highways connecting the half dozen communities on the outskirts of the city proper.

Whenever he and his grandfather were out on an errand in the old man's antiquated Ford F-150 and a group of them approached, his grandfather's hands would tighten on the wheel, his teeth would clench and his eyes would narrow to slits. For a moment it would seem to Gerald that his grandfather was fighting a life-and-death battle to keep himself from swerving into the oncoming lane, run the whole damn lot of them under his bumper, his ill will towards them not so much a result of the thirty-odd years he'd spent with the RCMP as it was because he blamed them for the death of his only daughter, Gerald's mother.

His grandfather never spoke of them otherwise, a towering silence that led Gerald to suspect he blamed himself for what had happened to her as much as he did The Sons. It wouldn't be until he was well into the fifth year of his incarceration that Gerald would discover that his mother's death was the least of their crimes.

It had been Jules who'd filled him in.

The Sons had dragged the investment banker out of his cell one evening, his third at Central North. When he'd returned, some hours later, his head had been shaved, which The Sons did with any prisoner they'd claimed as their property. A stubbling of nicks leaked blood from his bald crown so it was clear that whoever had done it must have used a dull blade, and Jules was walking with a lopsided hobble so Gerald knew they'd also branded their tree on his ass. Orville hadn't returned until just after the horn had sounded lights off, at eleven, and Gerald had been left alone with Jules in the cell, listening to him crying and cursing, Fucking animals, evil motherfuckers, into his pillow.

He'd been at it for what seemed like hours before Gerald had finally told him to shut up, he was trying to sleep.

You shut the fuck up, Jules had spat back at him with the petulance of a bratty child.

Boy, you sure do swear a lot for an investment banker, Gerald had replied, thinking if he wasn't going to get any sleep, the least he could do was have a little fun.

They fucking branded me, Jules whimpered. Fucking animals. Evil motherfuckers.

They never bothered me none.

Never bothered you— What the fuck does that have to do with anything?

I'm just saying.

You're just saying?

Live and let live I always say, Gerald added, which seemed a sensible way to go about his day-to-day, in prison or otherwise.

Live and let live? Jules blurted, aghast. After what they did? The whole fucking lot of them should be rounded up and shot.

I wouldn't know about that.

You wouldn't know about what?

Gerald was regretting having said anything and clamped his mouth shut.

You'd have to have been living on the fucking moon not to know what those evil motherfuckers did.

Well, maybe I was.

You really never— I mean—

Jules was plainly exasperated dealing with such an imbecile as his new cellmate was proving himself to be. On any other day Gerald would have relished befuddling Jules but the mention of being branded had recalled to Gerald how his own mother had proudly worn the same brand behind her left ear. He hadn't thought about her in years. Now, against his will, he found himself remembering the time when he was seven and he'd been awoken in the middle of the night by the sound of smashing glass. When he'd come into the kitchen his mother was doing a little remodelling with a baseball bat. There were broken dishes all over the floor and as he stood in the door, wiping the sleep out of his eyes, his mother was launching an attack on the stove. Her feet were all torn up and there were deep slashes up and down her arm, maybe from the paring knife sitting in a pool of blood on the table. He'd seen his mother freak out before and did what he'd always done: run back to his room to hide in the closet, wait for her to wear herself out.

But on that night, she never did.

One of the neighbours must have called the cops because soon he heard sirens growing louder. A few seconds after they'd quieted in front of his house, someone was pounding on the front door and a man's voice was calling out, Is everything all right in there, ma'am?

There was a moment of silence and then Gerald had heard a wailing shriek, his mother perhaps, and then someone, a woman this time, was yelling, She's got a knife!

She'd barely spoken when five gunshots rang out: *Bang! Bang! BangBangBang!*

Forcing that memory from his mind, trying to concentrate

on what Jules was saying now about The Sons and only catching parcelled bits, the majority of which had to do with their involvement in the spread of a drug called Euphoral.

You've heard of Euphoral, haven't you? Jules asked when he first mentioned it.

Gerald grunted, giving no indication either way, but the truth was he really would have had to be living on the moon — or at least somewhere other than Central North — not to have heard of Euphoral. Half the inmates were there on charges related to the drug, the latest escalation in the opioid pandemic sweeping the planet. Its high promised the user euphoria and its low a violent psychosis, the only cure for which they'd found so far being death. Speculation on the range as to its origins was split between those who blamed the Chinese for creating it, to control their excess population after automation put a half billion of their people out of work, and those who blamed the Americans, who'd possibly developed it as a means of destabilizing foreign countries prior to attack. The only thing both sides agreed upon was that it was developed in secret and that it was a secret that didn't last long. Its dissemination was rapid and cataclysmic. Within a few short years Euphoral had become so widespread that when Gerald was growing up he'd often heard his grandfather say that it posed more of a threat to global stability than climate change. Gerald had long suspected that it was the main reason the old man had kept him sequestered from the rest of the world and also why the one time he'd asked his grandfather why he didn't have internet, he'd answered, Bad enough the world's going to hell without me having to hear about it every damned second of the day.

Any of this ringing a bell? Jules had asked after providing Gerald with a rough précis of the same.

Ding, ding.

But maybe what you don't know, Jules said, is it was The Sons who brought it to Ontario. They'd started off cutting it into whatever other drugs they were selling, getting people hooked. There was some even said they were making it themselves and just giving it away for free. That they knew what would happen and that was their plan all along. That they were a bunch of fucking religious nuts, a doomsday cult stockpiling weapons in secret compounds spread throughout the north, and that Euphoral was their means to bring about The End.

Now there's some who'd blame the government, he continued. That it was Nora that caused all the problems.

Nora? Gerald asked. Who's that?

Not a who, a what. You know, N-O-R-A. The Northern Ontario Repopulation Act?

He had heard of that. It was the reason Millie had always given him why she'd come to Capreol. She too had been born in Sudbury, or rather Scuzzbury as she always called it, most often hocking a spit at the ground right after as if its mere mention left a bad taste in her mouth. She was eighteen when she'd finally fled to Capreol, first living in the basement of the bungalow her sister owned with her husband up on Beech Crescent, and then with Gerald on the farm at the end of Stull after she'd followed him home from the Legion that one night and had never left. Over the years she'd relayed to him parcelled bits of information about the city of both their births and so he'd come to know that long before he was born, the automation of Sudbury's only real industry of merit — mining — had devastated the local economy. It would have dealt it a death blow too if it hadn't been, in Millie's words, someone's "bright idea" to repurpose the city as one of four northern social services hubs for the growing masses of unemployables residing in the cities to the south.

NORA, as Jules called it, offered substantial relocation incentives to anyone on social assistance and expanded the province's vagrancy laws, allocating municipal councils sweeping powers to round up anyone unfortunate enough to find themselves living on the street for immediate transport up north. By the time Millie had fled to Capreol, five years later, Sudbury's population had swelled from just under a hundred thousand people to over three, thus providing, if Jules was to be believed, The Sons with an ever-expanding pool of the down-and-out from which to draw converts to their cause.

But it wasn't the government's fault, Jules contested. They were trying to help those people. Give them a place to go, get their lives together. It was the fucking Sons who preyed upon them, exploited their weakness. Got them hooked on Euphoral. Some even said they'd put it in the fucking water and hell, I wouldn't put it past them. Those evil sons of bitches.

The RCMP finally raided their main compound, just outside of Thunder Bay, arresting dozens of their members. The Sons' reaction was swift and calculated: they cut off all supply of Euphoral to the cities above the forty-sixth parallel as a warning to those living down south. And that's when we learned, the hard way, that the only thing worse than a fucking Euphie was ten thousand of them in withdrawal. And boy did we ever fucking learn that.

Hearing Jules recounting the epidemic of outrageous violence that had followed immediately called to Gerald's mind memories of watching *The Road Warrior*. It was one of several hundred DVDs his grandfather had inherited from his older brother when the latter died, leaving his younger the family farm. Most of the other movies were old westerns and over the years they'd watched the whole collection three or four times after the evening chores, a rare concession to a world the old man no longer seemed to want any part of. Those nights invariably ended with his grandfather falling asleep in his armchair except, that is, when they watched *The Road Warrior*. Then his grandfather would sit craned forward through to its end, peering in furtive contemplation as the story unfolded. He'd be shaking his head and clucking his teeth, same way he did while he was watching the evening news on their one and only channel, as if the movie was simply the logical extension of what he saw happening there.

Some said it was maybe even the start of a civil war, Jules said by way of a conclusion. The army was called in but by then Euphies had already burnt Timmins to the ground. The flames spread to the surrounding forest, igniting the largest forest fire in the province's history. They still haven't released the death toll from that but it was in the thousands at least.

Timmins was a city three hundred kilometres north of Sudbury. It too had been designated a northern social service hub and at its mention Gerald remembered that he'd also heard something about what had happened there, not from Millie, who'd been dead two years by then, but from Barry Woods, who everyone in Pod 2 called Zip. He was a skinny little runt with a face that looked like someone had punched it clear through the back of his head. Between his eyes and his mouth there was a mess of scar tissue like lips puckered sour and the skin beneath that receded inwards over toothless gums. He'd got his nickname after he'd tattooed the teeth of a zipper inked in a Y from the crest of each of his cheek bones. Where the two lines came together, roughly at the height of his missing nose, he wore a silver hoop of a kind that might be called a bull ring though it had always reminded Gerald more of a door knocker.

Gerald had never found out what had brought Zip to Central North nor what had happened to his face. He did know he was a Son, which didn't come as much of a surprise since Pod 2 was where they kept most of The Sons of Adam at Central North. He'd been the unit's *lugger*, prison slang for a person who could procure pretty much anything you wanted inside. He reserved these luxuries for his fellow Sons and his biggest seller was Zip juice, what he called his own special blend of concentrated THC and psilocybin. Once a week he'd drop by the cell to give Orville his allotment and he'd often stick around, sometimes for an hour or more.

He was a real talker and what he liked to talk about most was his prowess as a hunter. So Gerald and him might have had plenty to talk about except Zip always treated him with a certain diffidence, rarely communicating anything to him besides the odd nod in his direction should they pass in the unit's common area. It was how most of The Sons treated him, like what he'd done — killing two cops — had earned him their respect or because it was known amongst their ranks that he was a literal son of one of them and that had placed him outside the scorn they reserved for almost anyone who didn't wear their patch.

In all the years he'd been dropping by, Zip had never spoken to Gerald, confining his conversation to Orville, whose only reply to his tales of hunting derring-do would be to shake his head and say, Explain to me again, what it is you got against grocery stores? He'd said it so often that Gerald began to suspect it was for his benefit alone that Zip was really telling stories of his prowess as a hunter.

The only time he could recall Zip deviating from his hunting stories was after a riot had erupted in Pod 5, which everyone called Club Euphie since it was where they kept most of the junkies. Six guards had been killed along with fifty inmates and Zip'd had plenty to say about that.

You think they'd have learned their lethon after they burned Timminth, he'd opined in his distinct nasal lisp. Only way to deal with them, ith you got to thoot 'em on thight.

Fuckin-A. Shoot 'em all, Orville had chimed in. Fucking Euphie-fucks.

22

Orville, by then, was already six drops into the Zip juice and it was lucky he could even muster that much to say.

You know I wath born in fucking Timminth, Zip continued with enough scorn in his voice to infer that it was Timmins that had taken his face. I mean Timminth, it'th, it'th fucking Timminth, all right. I ain't trying to defend Timminth here. Timminth wuth a fucking thit-hole. It wuth a thit-hole when I wuth born, it wuth a thit-hole when I left and if they ever get around to rebuilding it, it'll thtill be a fucking thit-hole then. Timminth can kith my fucking ath, and you can write that on my tombthtone.

Fuck Timmins!

Word man, tha'th the fucking word.

There was a pause then, long enough for them to have bumped fists.

Weren't anyone happier to hear they'd burned fucking Timminth than me. But if they'd jutht thot all them Euphie fuckth right off the bat it never would have happened. And then they got the audathity to blame The Thonth of Adam? That'th fucking bullthit. Half the fucking world going craythee and the other half trying to pretend it'th bith'nith ath uthual. It wuth jutht a matter of time before thump'in had to give. And boy did it ever fucking give in Timminth!

Seeing the patches worn by the barrel-shaped man and the skinny stick figure now, Gerald was thinking that that same something must have given all over.

A sliver of dread had wormed its way into his gut, tempered only by the sudden wonder he felt peering up into a sky so fraught with a blaze of stars that it seemed they must have somehow stolen every bit of man's bright. Scanning the horizon and seeing nothing beyond the outline of treetops, dark and ragged, on the far side of the prison fence, recalling how when he'd first come to Central North and couldn't sleep he'd often stand at the cell's window, coveting the thin wedge of sky he could see through the bars in the tempered glass. He'd be lucky if he saw a single star prying through the hazy diffusion seeping out of the cities to the south. A hundred million lights (or more) like a slow rolling tide washing over a great black beach and the stars but dulled pieces of quartz encrusted in the sand. Here, now, with only the excavator to challenge the night's dominion, he knew something truly terrible must have happened.

The two men commiserating over Orville's body would have known what that might have been, if anyone did, but whatever that was seemed to have caused them about as much concern as did the fate of their friend.

And I thought he smelled bad when he was alive, the barrel-chested man was saying and to that the tall man laughed and shook his head.

I always told him them Jelly Bellies'd be the end of him.

He'd eat 'em by the pound.

Shit, he'd eat 'em by the truckload.

The tall man said something else and the two men laughed again.

But Gerald was no longer listening. He'd just caught a whiff of cooking meat. It seemed to be coming from around the right side of the building. Jules had smelt it too.

Smells like . . . barbecue!

Their eyes locked for a fleeting instant, registering the significance of that. And then their legs were setting off in a stumbling flurry, chasing over the uneven path churned up in the excavator's wake as if heaven itself awaited them around the bend.

When he came around the corner of Pod 2 they were met with a most curious sight.

The Central North Correctional Centre was comprised of five hexagonal "pods" and in Gerald's mind had always looked more like a lunar colony than a prison. The building was buffered on all sides by an expansive lawn and in the middle of the yard between Pod 1 and the perimeter fence there was now a small flatbed trailer wound with Christmas lights and furnished to resemble a parlour. Two men with fiddles lounged on a couch while a third reclined in an easy chair, plucking a banjo. Another stood between them with a stand-up bass, a fifth was seated at a piano and a sixth sat beside him, pounding out the beat to an old-timey country jig on a snare drum and cymbal. The band was whooping and hollering and two old men in prison greys were dancing in circles with interlocked arms in front of a bonfire. Flames lapped in feverish delight and sparks belched from their mire, flickering incandescent against the star-speckled night. A dozen other men ranged around it, some calling out in joyful welcome to the men hobbling away from the prison or locked in the desperate embrace of brothers, or lovers, they feared they'd never see again, others sitting in the grass or squatting on hunched knees drinking from tall cans of beer and bottles of water in between bites out of submarine buns oozing with thick slathers of meat.

On the far side of this revelry there was another, larger, trailer. It was the one they'd brought the excavator in on and it was from this that the simmer of grilling meat wafted. Five men stood in a queue extending up the rear ramp, all of them wearing the same prison greys, gaunt-faced and with beards as full as Gerald's, though his was bushier than most and of a redder hue than any. At the front of the line, on the trailer's platform, there was a fifty-gallon steel drum cut almost in half and filled with freshly stoked charcoal. A fatted hog was roasting on a rotisserie above and every man in line was peering at the bounty with fevered eyes.

A boy — couldn't have been older than thirteen — was turning the crank on the rotisserie and a man — seventy if he was a day — was cutting great swathes from the hog with a butcher's knife. Could have been the former was, like Gerald himself, the son of one of The Sons and had come to help his father with the jail break. He had a shaven head and was wearing a plain black muscle shirt in defiance of the boney ligature to his arms and a fierce scowl belying his tender age. The latter had the familiar tree emblazoned across his back and was clean shaven and naked from the waist up except for an apron that read *You Can Kiss The Cook If You Want (But I'd Rather Have A Blow Job)*. As each of the men shuffled up to the front of the line, he goaded them with the exuberance of a grandfather cooking up a feast for a brood of grandkids he hadn't seen in years, teasing that they weren't nothing but damn skeletons as he lathered thick strips of barbecued pork onto the buns and exulting as he handed them over, This'll put a little meat on your bones!

As the men exited down the second ramp another boy, as similar to the first that they might have been twins, handed them each a bottle of water and a beer from the two coolers at his feet. Passing them by as they stumbled towards the bonfire, dousing their thirst with the bottles and their hunger with a frantic gnashing of teeth, Gerald could see beads of sweat glistening on the cans' aluminum. It had been years since he'd had a beer and the thought of downing an ice-cold one had him licking his lips as much as the simmer of grilling meat had his stomach tying itself into knots.

At the foot of the ramp was a man with a submachine gun slung on a strap low at his waist. He was wearing the same denim vest over a bare chest as the others and was tall and thin, with a cadaverous face dusted with whiskers of the same grey as the long bob of his thinning hair, which was pulled back into a ponytail. As Gerald and Jules approached he affixed them with a stern glare, not unlike the guard who'd provided Gerald with his two one-piece jumpsuits, a bar of soap, a toothbrush and a tube of toothpaste on the day he'd arrived at Central North. That was enough to put a slight hitch in Gerald's step, such that it was Jules who made the ramp first.

Where do you think you're going? the cadaverous man snarled as Jules tried to push past, his eyes locked in a mortal grip on the hog. The man grabbed him by the arm and used his other hand to jam the barrel of his gun into the hollow just below Jules's ribs, Jules glaring back at him with widening incredulity, the same way his previous self might have gaped at a maître d' at some fancy restaurant who'd just told him he couldn't find his reservation.

What do you mean? he asked. I'm going to get some food.

Do I know you?

Jules Blake, he said, holding out his hand as if to shake. Pleased to meet you.

The man looked at his hand as if it might have been holding a fresh turd.

I'm going to need to see your invitation, he said.

My invitation? I don't—

Eyes widening further still, head on a drastic swivel, looking past the man at the hog as if it might be able to provide him with a suitable answer. Looking then back at the man and seeing that he'd forsaken the rifle for a large hunting knife, its blade tapering to a fine point just beneath Jules's right eye.

Now wait just a—

Jules made a backwards lunge but the man held his arm in his other hand, locked at the elbow and twisting upwards, causing Jules to emit a sudden squeal.

Wait, wait! he cried out. I just wanted something to eat. I haven't eaten in five days!

But the man wasn't listening. He'd inverted the knife in his hand and in one downward slash he cut a hole in the jumpsuit from Jules's chin to his groin. Resheathing the knife, he grabbed at Jules's shoulder and wrenched the fabric, tearing it over his arms and down to his waist. Giving then a cursory glance at his back and at the sag of his biceps. Seeing only folds of skin hanging in loose flaps over the outline of ribs and shoulder bones, he released Jules, who gasped and buckled over, peering up at the man with ill-contained malice.

No invitation, no food, the man said.

Swivelling then towards Gerald, his eyes narrowed to slits of careful scrutiny. Gerald couldn't think of anything to do except smile wide and so he did that. It seemed to do the trick, for after a moment the man said, I do know *you*.

The trace of a smile shortly flickered at the corners of his mouth, the same way the inmates at Central North had so often reacted when they'd recognized Gerald for who he was. Sizing him up and finding him lacking, not just in stature but in the same exaggerated grin he wore now and had been wearing for the past five years as his only defence against trouble, looking ever so much like a simpleton and only exacerbating that by how he'd stick his hand out in formal greeting.

Gerald Nichols, he'd say to whoever had come over to meet him. How'dya do?

The other getting the joke or not, either way taking his hand in tenuous embrace, watching him with hovering amusement as Gerald gave it a perfunctory shake, grinning like he was meeting the prime minister. He'd then turn his eyes skyward if they were in the yard, or towards the TV if they were in the common room, and offer, They's saying it's going to rain. Don't much feel like rain, you ask me. But then I didn't grow up around here. What do you say?

The simple country courtesy of his upbringing about as out of place at Central North as an evening gown so that more often than not they'd only answer him with a mocking leer and a nod, leaving him to himself thereafter, maybe studying him from a distance for a time, trying to reconcile the man who did what they said *he*'d done with the man standing over there.

But Gerald was too tired and hungry to bother with any of that now and let his eyes wander back to the hog. It might as well have been a picture in a magazine for all the good it did him.

Well go on then, the cadaverous man said.

Gerald turned abruptly for fear that he was about to repeat the rough treatment he'd visited upon Jules. He'd barely made a step when he felt the sharp censure of the man's hand on his arm.

Ain't you hungry? he asked and Gerald looked back at him like he must have been having him on. He found only a thinly veiled delight in the man's eyes.

I'm damn near starved.

Well go on then, the man repeated, get yourself a feed.

G erald ate sitting on a flat span of concrete, as big as a queen-sized bed, jutting from within a pile of rubble in front of one of the holes in Pod 1's wall, all the while trying to ignore Jules, who was standing a ways off, holding the lapels of his slashed jumper sutured with a clenched fist and keeping a rueful sentry on his ex-cellmate like a beat dog waiting on scraps beneath its master's table.

Between bites of the sandwich measured with carefully parcelled sips from his bottle of water, Gerald watched the parade of eager inmates lumbering away from the prison in a heady rush to join the party. Other men were walking amongst them, two by two, carrying the bodies of the dead or dying, he couldn't tell which, and the whole scene recalled to him a similar one he'd seen in one of those old western movies: of soldiers retreating from a battlefield during the Civil War.

The scene with Jules replayed itself at the trailer a few times, the uninvited sent on their way with slashed jumpers and one who'd protested a trifle too much with a deep gash on his cheek leaking blood between the slits of his fingers, pressed tight, trying to stem the flow as he stumbled off towards the other outcasts. The lion's share of these were huddled in a small crowd at the western edge of the perimeter fence. To a one their heads bobbled in suspicious backwards glances as if they were engaged in some vengeful plot or perhaps worried that some vengeful plot was being enacted against them. As to what had drawn them to that particular spot, it wasn't much of a mystery. It was the gaping hole in the fence not twenty paces south from where they'd gathered. The wire mesh had been trampled under the excavator's tread and all that lay between the yard and the outside world was five men standing at intervals beside an equal number of Harley-Davidson motorcycles of a variety some might have called choppers. All were clad in black leather and had shaven heads and held assault rifles in crooked arms with fingers resolute on their triggers. Four had their backs turned and only the middle one was looking towards the prison's yard. His face was painted white and within the respiring glow of a cigarette's cherry Gerald could just decipher the outline of a skeletal grin imprinted over his mouth. If the time he'd spent waiting to die in a cell with a dead man and the manner of his deliverance and the strange celebration under a star-fraught sky which had greeted him in the yard hadn't been enough to tell him that something had seriously gone wrong with the world outside the prison walls, these grim riders surely were.

He pondered on that until he was washing down the last bite of his sandwich with the last sip from the water bottle without coming to any definite conclusion except that whatever had happened must have been pretty bad. The food had barely put a dent in his hunger and as he cracked the tab on the tall can of Old Style Pilsner he turned back to the pig roast, wondering if maybe they were handing out seconds, and catching a whiff of skunk.

Thinking he'd just as soon have a taste of that, he tracked its drift back to the bonfire's revelry. Sure enough, he could see several cigar-sized tubes of rolled paper being passed amongst the throng of men, each of them taking a heady drag and passing it to the next, holding the smoke in and exhaling only when another of the cartoonishly oversized joints came their way.

But it wasn't on them that his gaze finally settled. It was on Jules.

He was now standing just outside the perimeter of the bonfire's illume and appeared to be pleading with another man. The latter was a gargantuan six foot eight and as well built as your average professional wrestler except that his left arm ended at the elbow and in place of the joint there sprouted a hand no larger than a baby's. It was the arm as much as his stature that told Gerald the man was Mathew Del Papa, whom everyone called "Pops" because of his name and for a couple of other reasons besides. As to his affliction, it didn't seem to bother him too much. Mostly he treated it like it was a big joke, calling the baby hand Junior and telling anyone who'd listen that it was Junior's fault he'd ended up serving five for aggravated assault, since Junior had all the discretion of a two-year-old and held his liquor about as well. If Pops caught someone staring at Junior in the yard, he'd go right over and introduce himself and Junior too. Junior would be reaching out, patting the other's shoulder or poking him in the ribs, sometimes prodding at the other inmate's face like a blind man's would, his Pops all the while apologizing for the little rascal, *But what are you going to do? He won't listen to a damn word I say.*

At least he ain't got a temper like Senior does, he'd then offer, holding up his right hand. There was a patchwork of scars latticed over its knuckles — a record of how many teeth it had reduced to bloody shards — and those would make his point clear enough so that after he'd introduced someone to Junior they rarely ever gave him a second glance.

It had been Orville who'd introduced Jules to Pops, the very same day a guard had led the investment broker to their cell, the latter carrying a thin foam mattress rolled up and clutched to his chest. Orville had raised a stink, complaining that the cell was hardly big enough for two men much less three (at which the thought had crossed Gerald's mind that it was hardly even big enough for one man, if that man was Orville Gates).

The guard had promised that it'd only be a few days, a week at the most, they were just waiting on a bed to become available in one of the medium security prisons. That had been six months ago. A bed had never become available or someone up the ladder was making an example of Jules or maybe they'd just forgotten about him. Regardless, he'd never been transferred and the only person who'd come out ahead in the deal was Mathew Del Papa.

Jules's trial had made the national news as the largest case of investment fraud in the nation's history so it wasn't a surprise he'd have registered as a cruise ship–sized blip on the big man's radar. All of his assets had been seized but anyone with even a passing knowledge of this breed of malfeasance must have suspected that Jules had a rainy-day fund somewhere, in the Cayman Islands or another suitably safe haven, all the while earning him interest over the course of his sentence.

It wasn't more than a few minutes after Jules had been assigned to their cell that Orville had taken him under his prodigious wing, offering to introduce him to someone who'd give him "a little hand on the inside," the obvious pun lost on Jules until he was standing outside Pops's cell a few moments later.

Gerald would shortly learn from Jules that Pops was a Sergeant-at-Arms in the Thunder Bay chapter of The Sons of Adam. It wasn't much of a surprise then that he'd now been let out by his brethren and that Jules would search out the big man to get another little hand up. In response to his pleas, Pops was frowning and shaking his head as if the story Jules was telling him had all the earmarks of a great tragedy.

They wouldn't give you any food? he was saying, his voice of such an elevated pitch that only a deaf man wouldn't have known that he was having Jules on. Jules though didn't seem to notice the sarcastic tone and nodded solemnly, looking about as pitiful as he could without actually resorting to tears.

Well, we'll just have to see about that.

If there was one thing Gerald had learned about Pops after all these years, it was that the friendlier he got the more likely it was there'd be trouble for someone down the line. And Pops was being plenty friendly right now, setting his good arm over Jules's shoulder, Senior giving him a pat on the back for good measure. Jules must have got a hint that things had taken a turn for the worse too, for instead of leading him on a straight line towards the trailer's ramp Pops had taken a sharp left and was hustling him towards the darkness enshrouding the semi's front grill. Jules's head was arched in a desperate crane towards the fleeting promise of food and he must have said something in protest because Gerald could just make out Pops's voice raised in joyful declaration, Don't you worry about that, we got something *special* planned for you!

Exactly what that might be would have to wait. Just then Gerald heard a sharp voice, almost a squeak, calling out, Gerald Nichols, as I live and breathe!

He jerked around and saw a figure striding towards him. The lank of his form was reduced to ribbons by the blaze of the bonfire at his back such that at first glance the man looked like a floppy-eared puppy's head had been impaled onto a scarecrow's body. As he came closer, Gerald saw that what had first appeared as floppy ears was a furred cap — he'd have guessed rabbit — with mangy flaps hanging to the man's shoulders. He also saw that his face resembled more a rat's than a puppy's except for his eyes, eager and beseeching, which did indeed remind him of the border collie his grandfather had owned when Gerald first moved in with him, though Whiskey was already an old dog by then and the man standing before him couldn't have yet been twenty.

He'd cut off the sleeves to his jumpsuit at the shoulders, exposing his rail-thin arms, and while he spoke he shuffled nervously from one foot to the other like he had to pee or was standing on hot coals.

I saw you sitting over here, he was saying. Shoot, I said to myself, that looks like Gerald Nichols. And here you are!

The scarecrow then stuck out his hand like he was practising a quick draw.

Clayton, he said. Clayton Crisp.

Gerald had learned over his stint at Central North that any perceived slight, such as refusing to shake a proffered hand, could mean a knife in your back and also that often the most harmless-looking sorts ended up doling out the most grief. And the scarecrow certainly looked harmless enough, if a little off, so Gerald played it safe by offering his own hand. Clayton gave it a vigorous shake such that his whole body seemed in danger of coming apart at the joints.

Shoot, he said, here I am shaking Gerald Nichols's hand!

Once he'd released his grip, he stood a moment staring down at his hand as if he expected it to be glowing, shaking his head like he couldn't believe his luck, and Gerald wishing he was any-where but here.

I didn't know you'd joined The Sons, the scarecrow said after a moment.

I didn't, Gerald answered, searching out the trailer for signs of Pops or Jules and seeing neither.

How'd you get the food then? They say only Sons is allowed to eat.

First I'm hearing about it.

A queer look came over the scarecrow's face, that of a child who'd just caught his father in a lie. After a moment, he shook his head and went back to smiling in his lackadaisical way.

Well, he said, I guess it's true what they say.

And what's that?

It pays to be famous.

Gerald had never considered himself such but then it wasn't much of a mystery to him why Clayton might think he was. It was that damned book! Gritting his teeth, shaking his head and silently cursing Jordan Asche, the journalist who'd written it, Clayton Crisp just one more notch in the belt tabulating all the reasons he'd have to kick that son of a bitch's ass if ever they should meet again. The bile was rising in his throat even thinking of him and he took a sip from the can in his hand to wash it back. The beer had gone warm. It tasted little better than piss being poured into the bottomless pit that had become Gerald's stomach and his eyes wandered back to the hog.

Its ribs were showing and the cook was down to sawing off meat from its shanks.

The scarecrow was looking at the same thing and his tongue was rolling around inside his bottom lip, imagining, no doubt, getting itself a taste.

Listen, he said, leaning close and lowering his voice to a conspiratorial whisper, I know where there's an apple tree. I saw it when I was on a garbage detail down on Gilwood Park Drive. That ain't more'n a ten-minute walk. All we have to do is get past them.

He motioned towards the grim riders with a slight jerk to his head and Gerald glanced their way. They stood beside their bikes as before and there was a man, one of the uninvited who'd broken off from the group, standing in front of the one facing into the yard. He was maybe three paces on this side of him and cast in the shadows. Gerald couldn't see much about him except that he was tall and had long dark hair, almost to his waist, but something about the subtle mockery in his slouch reminded Gerald of Wayne-Jay, his only real friend back home. Wayne-Jay was an Ojibway from Wahnapitae, the reserve north of Capreol, and over the course of their acquaintance they'd also discovered they were distant cousins, seven or eight times removed. So this man could be an *Indian* too. It was a term that Gerald didn't much like to use since it always came out sounding like a slur, the last thing he'd have wanted, but as there was no one likely to be reading his thoughts right then, he let it stand at that.

The man's head was cocked to one side, as if he was sizing up the grim rider. He took a tentative step closer. If the grim rider saw him he made no sign, staring straight ahead like one of those palace guards in London. This seemed to give the man a measure of courage and he inched closer until he was standing right in front of the rider, staring into his eyes, daring him to make a move. When he didn't, the man flopped his head backwards and let fly a caterwauling ululation, a war cry it sounded like.

Still not a hair's breadth of movement from the grim rider and the man turned back to the crowd of uninvited.

Fucking chickenshits! he yelled then made a quick dash past the man and his bike.

When he'd made it into the field, he whirled around, flashing both middle fingers and yelling, Thanks for nothing, assholes! Then he was spinning back around and starting off at a hard run towards the woods on the far side of the field, letting fly his war cry again.

The crowd of outcasts at the fence replied by shuffling a little closer to the hole, none quite yet willing to get within ten feet of the five ghouls who stood between them and freedom. For their part, the four grim riders facing out responded by mounting their bikes as if maybe they were planning on running the man down. Instead, they set the barrels of their rifles on their handlebars, hunkering low and taking beads on the forest across the field through their scopes, the green tint of the lenses giving Gerald every indication they had night vision. The middle rider, facing inwards, had also mounted his saddle and was flashing his headlight three times. This had the immediate effect of silencing the music and reducing every man within view to a silhouetted statue, leaving the bonfire's shimmer the only shade of movement in the entire yard aside from a few stragglers on the fringes — those still hurrying to join the party — and Clayton striding towards the hole in the fence.

Come on, what you waiting for? he called back over his shoulder as a spot of light appeared from between the trees at the edge of the field, no more than a flicker, almost like a . . . a firefly. And though it was too bright to be that, and also of a whiter hue when Gerald well knew that fireflies shone yellow, the mere thought was enough to freeze Gerald where he stood.

His eyes flitted about the glade as if at this, the moment of his release, it would only seem right that a flurry of these winged creatures would appear before him, the insects having played a not insubstantial role in his capture those five years ago. A fleeting thought interrupted in the next instant by a sharp *pop!* ringing out from across the field, calling Gerald to full attention even as it snapped the fleeing man's head back, same as if he had just run into a span of wire strung nose high. His legs flew out from under him and even before his body had been absorbed into the field's dark Gerald was pitching to the right, diving behind the pile of rubble as a barrage of similar *pop!*s rang out with the urgency of hailstones on a tin roof. These were almost at once drowned out by a barrage of machine gunfire.

Face buried in the grass, his hands clamped over his head, waiting for the onslaught to relent. But it went on and on and on. When he finally found the will to look up, he saw Clayton unmoved and peering towards the forest on the far side of the field with a mix of curious wonder and morbid delight even as a shot ricocheted off the cement slab not a foot from where he stood. Another tufted a divot at his foot and yet that still wasn't enough for the scarecrow to glean that someone was plainly shooting at him.

. Get down, you damn fool! Gerald hollered up at him from the ground. You're going to get yourself killed!

I s it the cops shooting at us?

The scarecrow hadn't moved an inch from where he'd sprawled onto the ground beside Gerald. He was lying prone with his hands clasped over his head, clutching at his rabbit-skinned hat as a trench-soldier might clutch at his helmet while the mortar shells flew, though it seemed unlikely that the people across the field, whoever they were, would be equipped with artillery such as that. Gerald had since crawled to the far corner of the cement slab, where he now crouched peering out from behind its cover, trying to get a sense of how the battle — if that's what it could rightly be called — was playing out.

Could be, he answered.

Maybe it's the army.

It ain't the army.

How do you know?

If it was the army they'd have blowed us all to shit by now. It's probably just a buncha locals.

You think?

If you're so hell-bent on finding out, why don't you come on over and see for yourself.

The scarecrow opened his mouth but didn't seem to have an answer to that and Gerald turned back to the field.

After the first barrage of *pop!*s, the battle had become a decidedly lopsided affair. The grim riders had roared off into the field's dark, releasing bursts of machine gunfire, and these provoking only a few more staggered *pop!*s from whoever it was hiding in the trees.

From Gerald's vantage he couldn't see the hole in the fence and thus couldn't tell the fate of the uninvited who'd huddled together a few feet away from it. The only evidence he could make out of the men who'd been engaged in the festive revelry were the vague outlines of crouched legs between the wheels on the far side of the trailer and the no less docile forms of others who hadn't made it that far, lying face down and likely dead within the halo of light cast by the bonfire.

An almost ghostly silence had settled over the prison yard, buffeted by the distant rumble of motorcycles on the war path and broken shortly by an intermittent beeping. Red lights flared from behind the trailer as a white cube van backed slowly into view, a group of four men creeping along behind on the mincing tiptoes of cartoon villains. They were all holding assault rifles and one had a cylindrical object propped at a slant on his shoulder, its size and shape making it immediately recognizable to Gerald as being some form of rocket launcher.

As the van passed from view behind the sheet of concrete, the man with the cylinder stepped away from the others, moving on a quick lateral towards the hole in the fence and also disappearing from sight. Pushing himself up and steadying himself with one hand on the crumbling edge of the cement slab, Gerald peered over its top, watching the man raising the front end of the tube, taking aim at the trees.

Is it over? Clayton asked.

As if providing its own answer, the launcher gave out a sudden *whoosh!*

The rocket leapt from the tube, the sight enough to propel Gerald to his feet, watching with muted apprehension as it flared through the hole in the fence and across the field. It struck just inside the treeline, exploding with a ball of fire and lighting the field with the sudden incandescence of a flash bulb, searing Gerald's vision and making him avert his gaze. When he looked back, flames were sweeping up a copse of spruce gathered within the blast zone, their sun-blanched needles turned to embers and set aloft against the star-riddled sky, splinters of wood and leaves flittering about with the lassitude of feathers. Two of the spruce were leaning forward, toppling into the field, and even before they hit the ground a frenetic pounding, like a jackhammer's, erupted from the back of the cube van.

All he could see of what was making the noise were spurts of flame belching pinpricks, darting through the dark. They hit their mark with a thrash of treetops moving right to left, crushing the smaller trees in their wake and causing the larger ones to shimmy and shake, Gerald but one of a few dozen men watching the path of destruction in dumbfounded awe.

Those Sons sure don't fuck around!

Clayton had gained the courage to stand and was doing so now beside Gerald, calling out over the pounding with an undisguised glee matched by the joyous grin of a child witnessing the miracle of fireworks for the first time.

How many locals might be hiding in the trees and were no doubt then being pulverized to a mush, it was impossible for Gerald to even guess. For all he knew, it could have been all of

Penetanguishene, the town upon whose outskirts they'd built Central North. It seemed likely that someone had sounded the alarm and a hastily contrived posse had descended on the prison, carrying whatever weapons they had — mere hunting rifles most likely. Gathering in the woods to the east of the prison which for the past fifty years had provided jobs for some five hundred men and women, many of whom lived in Penetang, as it was commonly called: a great boon for any town in which the predominant industry — tourism — lasted only a few months out of every year. All those men and women, whose only crime had been a desire to protect their families from the ravaging hordes of prisoners likely to be unleashed on their town by an excavator as large as the one they'd been told was toppling the walls of the Central North Correctional Centre, now being reduced to a bloody pulp while Clayton and the others to a one — minus only Gerald himself — cheered and called out with wild gestures of encouragement.

Their cheers were shortly eclipsed by a rumbling noise, growing louder with the celerity of a flash flood and turning Gerald towards Pod 1 as the semi-truck surged into view from behind. It must have turned around in the open space on the far side of Pod 5 to get up speed for the dash across the field, and was picking up greater speed still. Its lights were off and the only thing to illuminate it was the distant glow of stars and the lap of flames from the bonfire, towards which it was racing on a collision course. It struck with an explosion of sparks and their sudden flare revealed the figure of a man tied with arms outstretched over the front grill — none other than Jules Blake. Firelets spattered over his jumpsuit and singed in his hair, Jules all the while screaming against their ravage as the truck sped past, its wheels gnashing at the soft soil and spattering earth in great sodden clumps.

Fifty-odd men were crowding the trailer's bed, clinging to wheel hubs and to each other, and there was a lone man standing amongst them. In the dark, all Gerald could make out of him was that he was holding fast with one hand to a chain affixed to the truck's cab like a charioteer and that his other arm was upraised and ended at the elbow. A baby's hand sprouted from its stump and rather implausibly supported a machine pistol emitting sporadic bursts of flame into the night sky.

The trailer's still-lowered ramps were bouncing over the heavily rutted ground and down this tumbled the makeshift barbecue. It was spitting embers and spewing sparks and careening towards a man chasing after the truck, stumbling on a lame foot and calling out in vain pursuit, Wait for me! Wait for me! His eyes widening in alarm, he dove out of the way, the half barrel blundering past and the white van swerving to avoid it as it spun in a loop, coming up fast behind the trailer.

Letting off a last burst of gunfire from its box, the van breached the gap, passing in heedless slight both the too-slow and the uninvited, quartering right, angling across the field in pursuit of the truck, its trailer flanked now by four grim riders, two on each side. The fifth hung back until the van had passed then roared after with its banner flapping behind and every man still standing in the yard was gazing with abject longing after the motley caravan bumping over the curb and onto the road, disappearing in an instant behind the cluster of trees that shrouded the prison from the houses on Fuller Avenue.

There arose in its passing an anguished chorus from the locals secreted in the woods, desperate voices and distant screams, as remote to Gerald as the starlight. Shortly, flickers no less bright began to appear amongst the shadowed pillars of the tree trunks. Their spectral beams cut through the fringes, growing brighter as the survivors clambered into the field, and Clayton clutched Gerald's arm, worried maybe that they'd start shooting again. But the fight had clearly gone out of them and their good intentions had been reduced to a straggle of shadowy forms in frantic flight towards the road.

There were men running the other way now too. First a couple then a few more and then all the uninvited and the too-slow were swept into a mad dash back towards the prison. It was as if what they'd just seen spoke to them of the sanity of four walls and a bed, a quiet place to wait out the end, and Gerald was thinking much the same. But it wasn't their cells they were bound for, it was the overturned barbecue. What remained of the pig's carcass was lying beside the barrel. The men converged on it like a pack of hyenas, tearing loose its bones and gnawing at the meat, breaking fire-brittled ribs and femurs and sucking at the marrow.

Behind them Pod 1's hexagon loomed large. It had since come to resemble a monstrous birdhouse pocked with holes, and those spoke to Gerald only of the men still trapped inside. The prison population ran to over two thousand and there couldn't have been even a hundred of those sprung free. All the rest must have been still trapped in their cells, the already dead making it a living hell for those unfortunate enough to find themselves yet drawing breath. It seemed like he should have been able to hear them — a second chorus of voices calling out from their doom — and more so that he should have felt something, knowing it was just the luck of the draw that had spared him. But he felt little beyond the resilient pang of hunger in his belly coupled with a faint apprehension as to what might happen next, and all he could hear was the frenzied gnash of teeth and the stifled crack of bones from those ravaging the pig.

A man had wrenched its head free. He was scurrying away with the pig's head tucked under his arm and two others were chasing after him. The two were then tackling the one and all were lost into the yard's shade, the one crying out, This is mine. Get your goddamn own!

Gerald heard the thud of clenched fists pounding at the man's head even as he felt the clutch of Clayton's hand on his sleeve, dragging him on a hard right towards the hole in the fence.

Come on man, he was yelling, whatya waitin' for? We're free!

T he apple tree is just down there.

They were peering, one on either side, around the trunk of an oak tree. All that stood between them and their past lives as wards of the state was the twenty-or-so-acre forest of spruce and pine at their backs. Any and all of their possible futures found perfect expression in the two lanes of asphalt stretching in either direction not ten feet away, though it didn't so much resemble a road as a tunnel, cast as it was in utter black.

Clayton was pointing right and Gerald stepped out into the ditch. Leaves crunched beneath his feet and he stopped at their sound, peering again down the road as one might at a fast-flowing stream whose depth was uncertain. Clayton though had no such misgivings. He was hustling past, scrambling up the loose gravel of the ditch's incline and starting down the road.

Come on, he called back, you ain't never seen apples like these!

He set off at a jog but his legs didn't quite seem up to his haste. He hadn't got more than a few strides before he slowed to a fast walk and Gerald had trouble even keeping up with that, his own disused legs feeling like two logs cramped at the bottom of a wood pile.

On their side of the road the forest broke at intervals into spacious yards, some cluttered with the vague outlines of children's playsets — swings and slides and one an extravagant fort with a bridge between its two towers — but most empty except for the odd maple tree or willow looming against bungalows and simple two-storey houses, cars and pick-up trucks, sometimes three and four, in every driveway. Gerald glanced anxiously from these to dark windows, looking for any sign of movement from within as he passed, but Clayton only had eyes for the other side. The houses there, to a one, were palatial. They were guarded by fences, eight feet tall and mostly made out of wood slats, though there was also a span of black wrought-iron pikes between which pressed the clipped boughs of a cedar hedge, and further on a two-hundred-foot span of cobbled stone, also eight feet high and rimmed with what appeared to be thorny rose stems growing out of its mortar.

The stone wall ended at a vacant lot, a hundred feet across and lightly wooded with the thin trunks of poplars and the even slighter stalks of aspen. Gerald's grandfather would have called them junk trees and they told Gerald that the lot had been clear-cut in the past few years, for poplar and aspen grew about as fast as weeds. A slight breeze murmured through the leaves of the poplars, a delicate rustle that carried with it a faint hint of algae which suggested to Gerald that what the fences were really guarding was access to the private beaches encircling Georgian Bay.

When he'd come to the far edge of the lot, Clayton turned back and whispered over his shoulder, It's this one here.

He scurried across the road, following the strip of loose gravel shouldering it from the far ditch until he'd come to the corner of another of the wooden fences. Ducking low then for no reason except it fit the part of an escaped prisoner, skirting along a wall as if trying to evade the probe of a spotlight, stopping only when he'd come to the gate, halfway along. It was fashioned out of wood slats of the same light hue and the only thing that differentiated it from the fence at all was that it had a diamond cut into it to serve as an eyehole. Into this there'd been fitted a metal grate, its bars made in the image of cross-thatched vines.

Clayton crouched even lower before that, looking backwards and searching out Gerald, spotting him across the road and giving him a frenzied sweep of his arm, motioning him over. He then raised himself so that his head was even with the eyehole and snuck the quickest of peeks through it. He mustn't have seen anything to cause him undue concern and took a longer look and was still doing that when Gerald came up beside him.

He could see now that what he'd thought were vines was actually the body of a snake coiled in a criss-cross with its head hanging below as a hook or maybe a handle since the door didn't have one of those. It had neither a latch nor a lock and the only way of ringing the house was a blank vidscreen secured in the post beside it.

There it is, Clayton whispered and shuffled sideways so Gerald could have a look too.

He did so, steadying himself by gripping the snake's head in one hand and pressing his face to its coils, the significance of those hardly lost on Gerald as he peered into what could only be described as someone's little piece of paradise. Two storeys of glass framed the house, its roof flat and this ornamented with a lattice draped with vines, potted plants hanging below, a patio perhaps. Tracking left then into the expansive yard and finding at once the tree cast against a murky black, the subtle lap of water against a dock telling him that must have been the lake. All the while he was staring through the hole, he was thumbing the snake's head, or rather one of its fangs. The point was almost sharp enough to draw blood without any help from him so that when Clayton slapped him on the arm, saying, Come on, we'll go around the other side, he felt a sharp stab and jerked his hand back.

His thumb pad was already beading blood and as he trailed after Clayton he sucked at it, thinking it'd be a lucky thing indeed if a prick in his thumb was all he suffered following after such a damn fool as Clayton Crisp.

I 'll give you a boost.

  They'd threaded through the poplars and aspen crowding the empty lot until they were about halfway to the water. Clayton was squatting down at the fence and cupping his hands into stirrups between his legs.

  I don't need no boost, Gerald said.

  Clayton looked from him to the top of the fence and back again, his doubt that Gerald would be able to reach the top, much less climb over it, writ large in the dubious curl to his lips.

  Well, can you give me a boost then?

  Squatting low, Gerald cupped his own hand. Clayton stepped into that, hoisting himself up and over, and Gerald stood there a moment, telling himself he'd be better off on his own and that this was as good a chance as any to rid himself of the scarecrow. He'd gone so far as to take a step towards the road before the grim riders he'd seen at the prison impressed themselves upon his mind.

If it really had become their kind of world, Clayton'd be lucky to last a day.

So what if he doesn't? You don't owe him nothing.

He nodded to himself but that didn't do him a damn bit of good and he turned back to the fence.

There were two poplars growing in front of it, four feet apart. Reaching to the limits of his arms, he took the trunk of each in either hand and pulled himself up with a shimmying motion until he was clear of the top of the fence by a good foot. Pendulum-swinging his legs backwards, he propelled them forward, letting go of the trees and thrusting his body over the fence, landing crouched with the ease of a cat.

When he stood, Clayton was looking at him again with unbridled adulation.

Shoot, he said, that's a helluva trick. I'm gonna have to try me that sometime.

They approached the tree, scouring the ground for any apples that might have fallen. Finding none, they peered up into the tree's lowest branches. There weren't any visible there either.

Shoot, Clayton said, it was full of apples last time I saw it. Maybe there's some higher up. Give me another boost.

Gerald obliged and Clayton clambered onto the lowest branch. He stood hugging the trunk, his head craned upwards, searching amongst the leaves.

I think I see one, he whispered down.

He climbed in his gangly fashion, disappearing amongst the foliage before he was two branches up, his whereabouts known to Gerald afterwards only by a sporadic rustle and leaves falling with the wistful drift of boats sailing on a calm sea. He was up there for some time, Gerald all the while keeping sentry on the house for any flicker or shadow moving about within its dark glass case, seeing nothing beyond the outline of a table and chairs.

Bombs away!

Gerald looked up a fraction too late to dodge the globe as big as a softball parting the space between the branches. It struck him in the shoulder and bounced into the shadows. He scurried after it with down-stretched arms, his fingers prodding in grass gone to seed and almost as high as his knees.

Sorry, Clayton said, dropping back to the ground. That one got away from me.

His jumpsuit was spilling over with the fruit. One arm was crooked under a bulge that would have put him into his eleventh month if he'd been pregnant, and as he chomped on the apple in his other hand, three or four apples were pressing outwards from the V of his half-opened zipper.

Ain't they sweet, he said after taking his first bite.

Gerald was already on his fourth.

Ain't never tasted sweeter.

God, I can't remember the last time I had me a fresh-picked apple. The ones they gave us at Central North always tasted like Styrofoam.

You don't have to tell me.

Gerald was by then nibbling at the core of his. Pitching it into the lawn, he eyed Clayton's cleavage with a depraved sort of wantonness.

Go on, Clayton said, offering up his bosom, have another.

Don't mind if I do.

Hell, you can have as many as you—

Shhh.

Gerald had stopped mid-chomp. He could have swore he heard—

What? Clayton whispered. What is it?

A gentle swish then, like a sliding door opening and then he heard it again — a low growl — except this time it was louder and left no doubt in his mind as to what it was. The growl was immediately followed by the frenzied rake of nails on wood, the dog's claws trying to find a grip on the back deck as it lunged out through the opened door, swinging a hard left. There then was an instant of utter quiet, the dog maybe leaping down a set of stairs, and then a bristle of fur was tearing out from behind the corner of the house, letting loose a snarl as mean as a bear's.

Gerald and Clayton spun as one and the both of them set off in panicked flight towards the fence. The grass battering against their legs might as well have been sand, for the way it sucked at their feet. To Gerald, it felt like they were running in slow motion and the fence a mile away, though it wasn't more than twenty feet from the apple tree.

Clayton was screaming, Jesus! Fuck! Christ!

Gerald leaping and getting both hands on the fence's top, his sneakered toes finding purchase on a slat, pushing him upwards and over. His left knee knocked against the wood as it cleared the fence, spiking a sharp pain up his leg and sending him reeling into an awkward plummet. His hands flailed in front of him, trying to couch his landing, but it was his face that struck first. Something tore into his cheek, a sharp stick gouging from his temple to his chin, snapping his head back. The sudden agony erased all sense of the impact and the world went black, disappearing altogether except for the pain in his cheek, the rabid snarl of the dog from the other side of the fence and Clayton screaming, It's got my leg! It's got my leg!

Pushing at the ground, levering himself to his feet, looking up at the fence.

All Gerald could see of Clayton was his head and two arms — the boy holding on for dear life. His legs were thrashing in a frenzied assault against the other side of the fence and he was screaming, Get the fuck off! Get the fuck off me!

Gerald kicked hard at the wood slat directly below Clayton, striking it three feet up with the sole of his shoe. He heard the wood crack and kicked out again. The board split in two, the top edge of it buckling downwards and Gerald grabbing that, wrenching the board loose from its nails. Its splintered end was as sharp as a spade and he clutched it like a spear, jabbing it through the hole and striking something both hard and soft, hearing the dog yelp and knowing his aim had been true. Clayton was then tumbling over the fence, his body twisting as it dropped and his feet somehow finding the ground. One of the scant few apples he had left from his harvest tumbled out of his pant leg and rolled into the tall grass as he propped his back against the wood, gasping in great heaves, trying to catch his breath.

It would be a moment yet.

Loosing a vicious snarl, the dog's snout appeared between the gap, barking and snapping its teeth. It was a German shepherd and the slats on either side of the hole were bulging against the force of the dog's shoulders as it tried to bully its way through.

Clayton cried, Shit! and dodged away, tripping over a fallen tree before he'd gone two steps and sprawling into the dark even as Gerald strode towards the dog, sidestepping the snap of its teeth and driving the sharp end of the board into the hackles sprouting at the base of the dog's head. The dog let out a feeble whimper and there was a terrible crack, maybe the splintered end of the slat snapping off in the dog's neck or maybe the neck itself snapping as it was driven down onto the fence's crossbeam. Either way, the dog slumped limp, its eyes become quivering globes and its tongue lolling out of its mouth, a lone canine now parting its maw, stuck to its top lip. Its chest gave out a heave and Gerald raised the board again, waiting on the dog to make another move though it was clearly dead.

Almost took off my damn leg!

Clayton was back on his feet. He was bent over and tugging delicately beneath the tatters of his pant leg, wincing as his fingers prodded at the gash oozing blood beneath.

Setting a dog on us over a few apples. What in the hell's the world coming to?!

Peering then over at Gerald. He was kicking at the wooden slat beside the hole, breaking it in half and widening the gap, and Clayton's expression paled as if he thought maybe Gerald was about to make good on the malice he himself felt.

But Gerald had plans other than revenge.

He was grabbing the dog by its collar, yanking it clear of the hole.

What are you doing? Clayton asked.

Standing upright, Gerald wiped the dog's blood off his hands on his pants.

You're still hungry, ain't ya?

W e ain't going to eat it raw, is we?

Clayton had led them along a path that snaked through the patch of woods to the west of where Gilwood Park Drive turned southwards, away from the water. After a five-minute walk the trail opened into a small clearing where, he'd said, the six inmates and the two guards on the cleaning detail had eaten their lunch. He'd found a plastic Coke bottle in the garbage can beside the trail's head and had filled it from one of the muddied pools collecting in the hollows along the path, meagre remains from the last rain. He drained the rest of it now with the bracing swig of a drunk seeking one final ounce of courage before heading home from the bar.

No, Gerald answered, I got a match.

He'd carried the dog slung over his shoulder and was now setting it on the ground beside the bench in the middle of the clearing. He stood for a moment, solemn and grave, peering down at it as if he was saying a prayer for the dead, though that wasn't what was on his mind. He was remembering how, not more than a few hours ago, he'd told Jules that his killing days were long past and here now was the proof right in front of him that they clearly weren't.

It's just a dog, he reminded himself but that didn't do much to ease his conscience.

There was a dribble of blood draining over the tongue lolling out of its mouth and he couldn't help but think of Chuckles, the boxer his grandfather had given to him as a pup for his fourteenth birthday. Gerald had counted him as the best friend he'd had growing up, really more like a brother than a pet. When Chuckles was five, he had died coughing up blood on the porch after, Gerald suspected, that son of a bitch Ellis Wilkes had fed him a steak laced with iron filings. He'd been devastated then and felt a sudden shame now for murdering someone else's dog, a creature whose only crime had been trying to protect its family.

There's no use brooding about that now, he told himself and looked over at Clayton. He was stooped over at the bench, arranging his remaining apples in a line on its seat. There were six in all.

There's a birch tree a ways back, Gerald told him. Its bark'll do for tinder. Fetch me three or four good strips. And that dead spruce'll do for kindling. He motioned with his head at the skeletal remains of a tree on the far side of the clearing. After you fetch the birch bark, break me off as many branches as you can reach of that.

We just going to cook it whole, fur and all? Clayton asked.

You let me worry about that.

He watched after Clayton until he'd hobbled back down the path and out of sight. Only then did he unzip his jumpsuit, feeling beneath his undershirt for the picture of his son hung around his neck on the shoelace. Even thinking about it in prison had only served to prove the truth of what his old cellmate had said about times of joy recalled in times of misery and he hadn't passed more than a chastening glance at it in years. It was too dark to see more than an outline of Evers standing on the birthday rock and as he gazed down upon it he wasn't thinking so much of the day Millie had taken it but of its rightful place on the mantel in their living room along with all the rest.

How the photograph had come to be in Charlie Wilkes's possession he could only guess.

The Wilkes family had lived in the last house on Stull before the road switched from asphalt to the kilometre of gravel dead-ending at the Vermilion River. It was on the banks of this that Gerald's great-grandfather, Hubert Beausoleil, had built his brick two-storey house and a barn. Before then, he'd been a trapper for the CN and the story his grandfather had told Gerald was that he'd gone off to war and what he'd seen overseas had struck the killing mood right out of him. Capreol had been founded as a CN rail town and after he'd hung up his traps, he'd bought fifteen acres along the Vermilion from his old employer. He'd built a house and a barn and the only concession he'd given to his past life was to hang his old bear trap inside the front door of the latter, telling anyone who'd listen that it had always given him luck where every horse he'd ever owned had only caused him grief.

Somewhere along the way he'd fallen in love with Harriet Batiste, a young woman from the Wahnapitae reserve and Gerald's great-grandmother. Together they'd raised a brood of six kids and a hundred years later Gerald's grandfather would retire there following the death of his brother, his last remaining sibling.

The Wilkes family had moved to town a year after Gerald had come to live with him. Mrs. Wilkes must have seen the sign for *Fresh Eggs & Roasting Hens* Gerald's grandfather had posted on the community board at the Foodland in town because one Saturday morning she walked up their driveway and left a few minutes later with two dozen eggs and a chicken from the freezer. The next Saturday she'd brought her son along with her and that was how Gerald would first meet Ellis Wilkes, who he'd shoot dead twenty-six years later for the sin of killing Millie, before fleeing into the northern wilds with Evers.

Ellis was the same age as Gerald but that's where any and all similarity between them ended. At the time Ellis had been a frail little boy with skin like onion paper so that the first thing Gerald noticed about him was the veins running in blue tendrils up his neck and his arms. Mrs. Wilkes had placed an order for a fresh roasting hen the week previous and Gerald's grandfather was blanching the Wilkeses' headless chicken in boiling water, which he always did before plucking it. He sent Gerald off to fetch their eggs and Mrs. Wilkes asked if maybe Ellis might be able to help.

He can hold the pitchfork, Gerald had replied after some thought.

You collect eggs with a pitchfork? Ellis had asked when they'd come to the annex at the back of the barn where they kept their chickens and Gerald was reaching for the tool in question hanging between two nails beside the door.

It's for Max, Gerald replied, handing it over.

Max?

Our rooster. He can be right mean.

Gerald was unlatching the door and opening it enough to take a look-see.

He's over by the far wall, he whispered.

Then turning back to Ellis with the seriousness of a general commanding his troops into battle:

When I open the door, you'll go in first. Keep the prongs of the pitchfork between you and him at all times and whatever you do, don't never turn your back on him. You got that?

Ellis nodded though the quiver to his hands on the pitchfork's handle told an entirely different story.

All right, get ready, get set . . .

He'd then kicked the door open without saying Go! and ushered the other boy through, the pitchfork levered before him like a knight's lance.

Max was over by the exit door. He let out an ominous yowl that sounded more like a cat than a rooster and took a quick three steps forward, Ellis taking a step back and Gerald slipping past, hurrying to the boxed shelves where the chickens laid their eggs. The rooster was stalking back and forth along the far wall, uttering stuttered clucks that sounded like threats, and Ellis was trailing the pitchfork after it, struggling under its weight to keep the prongs between them.

All right, let's go, Gerald said when he'd emptied all the nests into his basket and was headed for the door.

As Ellis backed after him, the rooster seemed to have admitted its defeat, taking a quick three-step and flapping its wings, striking aloft and coming to a perch on top of the boxes. Ellis craned his head, searching out the door. His eyes weren't averted for more than a second before there was a fluster of wings and when he turned back Max was in full flight towards him, its eyes as grim as a crocodile's and its claws become razor-sharp talons aiming straight for Ellis's face. Gerald grabbed him by the shirt, yanking him roughly out and catapulting him over the stairs. He slammed the door shut and when he turned, Ellis was sitting on his ass gasping for breath and holding the pitchfork anchored into the ground, its prongs raised before him en garde against another attack.

I told you not to turn your back on him, Gerald said as he reached down to help him up. The whole thing had struck him as rather comical and so he might have been smiling when he said it.

But Ellis didn't think it was funny at all.

Blood was beading in three lines along his arm from where Max had slashed him and his lip was trembling. It looked like he was about to cry. He'd batted Gerald's hand away and yelled, Keep your fucking hands off me!

He'd then scurried to his feet and run back down the driveway, wiping at his eyes with the back of his hand and his mother hurrying after him, calling out, What's wrong? What happened? Honey, what's wrong?

For the next five years the only time Gerald would see Ellis was through the window of his grandfather's pick-up truck when they drove past his house on the way to town. Then, one hot August morning, he was wading in the creek that bordered their property, fishing with a butterfly net for minnows to use as bait, and he'd felt the sharp sting of a rock striking him in the shoulder. When he looked back, Ellis was standing ten feet away at the edge of the creek. He'd grown tall in the meantime and towered over Gerald, who'd hardly grown an inch. He was with two other boys, both of them bigger still.

If it ain't *Wee* Gerry Nichols, Ellis said with a derisive scowl.

He was walking forward and the other two were following at an even pace behind.

You know, he said to the boy on his right, I heard his mother sucked cock for a living.

Shit, I heard that too.

That true, *Wee* Gerry? Your mother suck cock for a living?

The other boys were chuckling a silent and mirthless laugh and Ellis was sneering at him, daring him to do something.

What's a matter, *Wee* Gerry? You look like you're about to cry.

And it was true, there was water beading at the corners of his eyes. Overcome then with a sudden rage, he'd snatched up a rock from the creek bed, throwing it with all his might and striking

Ellis in the middle of the face. His nose erupted in a gusher of blood and he stumbled back, his lip trembling again. Gerald picked up a stick about as big as a bat and stormed towards Ellis. He broke his knee cap with the first blow, two of his ribs with the second, and his jaw with the third. A defiant snarl at the other boys was all it took to make them turn tail and run.

It was later that day Gerald would first meet Charlie Wilkes, Ellis's father and the man who'd bring him to justice some twenty-seven years later. He'd just finished his evening chores and had come out of the barn with a full pail of milk. There was a Sudbury Police cruiser parked in the driveway and a man in uniform was talking to his grandfather on the porch. All he heard of what they were saying was his grandfather's voice raised in a menacing growl.

If you think you're goin' to take that boy away from me, he was saying, well I'll tell you one thing, I'da shore like to see you try!

His hand had settled on the butt of the old Smith & Wesson slung on his belt and Gerald felt sick, thinking about all the grief he'd just made for him.

Officer Wilkes had said something else and then turned, walking down the steps and catching sight of Gerald standing in the barn's door. He was as pale-faced as his son, sickly even, and was glaring at Gerald with a look of such piercing hate that Gerald would never see its like until he was sitting in court listening to Charlie spinning his lies and glaring at him with the same look all over again.

He'd only seen him one more time after that.

Six months into his sentence at Central North, he'd been told he had a visitor — his first — and when he'd come into his booth, it was none other than Charlie Wilkes on the other side of the Plexiglas. He'd aged considerably and facing the man who'd killed his son he didn't look so much full of hate anymore as old and worn out, tired of the whole damn affair. He was wearing a navy-blue suit and a white shirt and red tie, and what was left of his greying hair was slicked back. To Gerald he looked like a sinner might on his way to church, and Gerald had never been more aware of how he himself must have appeared — his hillbilly beard and his mad flop of hair and his eyes like tadpoles darting about in a shallow pond making him out to be some kind of lunatic.

Neither had said a word, nor made so much as a move to sit in their chairs, and after a moment Charlie had simply turned around and walked away. It would only be a few minutes later that Gerald would find out why he'd come at all. The guard who led him back to his unit gave him the photograph, saying only that his visitor had wanted him to have it.

Over the next few months he'd have plenty of time to reflect upon why Charlie Wilkes might have brought it to him, contriving in his mind a host of scenarios, all of them starting with Charlie spying the photographs on the mantel, tracing along to the one Millie had taken on Evers's fifth birthday and it speaking to him of something, maybe the same thing it had always spoken of to Gerald.

How many times had he whispered, *May he never lose that spirit*?

The last he'd heard, Evers had ended up in a foster home in Sudbury and Gerald knew enough about what happened to boys thrown into foster care to know that it would be a miracle if his spirit survived more than a few months.

Charlie Wilkes must have known that too. He'd given him the picture as a last stab at revenge, a harsher punishment than any prison wall and — so Gerald told himself — a fitting penance for the crime of forsaking his son in his hour of greatest need, though that wasn't entirely the reason he wore it on a shoelace strung around his neck.

On the day he'd come as a seven-year-old to live in the house on Stull, he'd ventured back downstairs after stowing his bag in the bedroom at the far end of the hall on the second floor, the one he'd been told was to become his. The stranger he'd been told was his grandfather was sitting at the kitchen table. In front of him there was a drawer, thin and wide, which Gerald would later find out was from the desk in the living room that served as a console for the TV.

This here's the accumulated wealth of the entire Beausoleil line, his grandfather had said, fanning his hands in a dramatic flourish over the drawer filled with a few dozen baubles and trinkets, most of them brass and all of them old and weathered so they'd looked more like junk than prized possessions. Gerald wasn't yet used to his grandfather's brand of humour and when the old man added, This is all going be yours one day but I don't see any harm in you claiming a piece of your birthright a little early, he'd scrutinized the motley collection with solemn deliberation.

You can take any two pieces, his grandfather added after it looked like his grandson might have been stumped.

After careful consideration, Gerald chose a brass Zippo lighter engraved with a picture of a howling wolf's head and a penknife with a handle made out of ivory and a blade that, he'd learn a few seconds later, had been sharpened to about half its original breadth.

Ever since, Gerald had never felt whole unless he was carrying both a knife and a lighter. Having one of either at Central North was enough to get you a month in the hole. While Gerald had resolved to do his time as quietly as possible, he couldn't resist the urge one evening, while manning a mop and bucket in the prison's workshop, to pick up a small triangle of scrap metal discarded beneath a work bench, a leftover from when they'd replaced the ventilation ducts. It was only an inch and a half on its longest side and of a grade a trifle soft for a blade good and proper. But after he'd whetted its edge with a stone scrounged from the yard, it was sharp enough to slice a callous off his hand and he'd kept it hidden in a spare bar of soap he'd bought from the commissary. A lighter was out of the question but stick matches, also prohibited, were easy enough to procure. It wasn't until Charlie Wilkes had given him the picture that he'd finally figured out a way to carry both about him at all times, the inconvenient truth that it would be his son who would make him feel whole again hardly lost on Gerald as he set about putting his plan into motion.

Of all the guards in Pod 2, it was Foley — the very last guard he'd ever see — who'd always been the friendliest. He was also the slightest, which was maybe why he always treated the prisoners on his watch with the utmost deference — his brain's attempt to ward off any trouble down the line that his lack of brawn couldn't handle. Gerald had felt plenty uneasy taking advantage of Foley's good nature but resolved that it couldn't be helped.

One morning when Foley was delivering his breakfast, he commented, Shoot, that's what I need.

And what's that? Foley had answered.

Gerald pointed to the laminated badge with the guard's picture and number pinned to the chest of his uniform. When Foley registered what he meant he smirked like it was Gerald's idea of a joke.

Well, it's not for sale, he'd said.

Not the badge. The laminate. They do that here or they send them badges out?

Foley smirked again, trying to figure out what game Gerald was playing at. The slack to Gerald's jaw and the vacuous sheen to his gaze must have told him it couldn't have been much of one.

After a moment he answered, They got a machine up in the office.

A laminator?

I guess that's what they call it. Why do you ask?

I got this picture of my son, Gerald answered. I keep it under my pillow, but it's got all wrinkled. Lucky it lasts out the year much less three consecutive life sentences. If I could laminate it . . .

The laminator is for official prison business.

Shoot, I figured as much. No harm in asking though.

That afternoon Foley had searched out Gerald while he was mopping the unit's common area. He told him that he'd got the okay to laminate the picture for him, which is how Gerald had laid even odds it'd play out. He fetched the photo, which he really did keep under his pillow, that much was true. He handed it to Foley and the guard didn't cast more than a cursory glance at the front before flipping it over.

What's this on the back? he asked, though it sounded more like an accusation than a question.

A piece of cardboard, Gerald answered, though it seemed obvious. I glued it there to keep it from getting any worse.

Foley picked at the corrugated sheet in a few spots, finding the cardboard well affixed, and then told Gerald he'd have it back to him the next day.

That had been two years ago and he'd worn it around his neck ever since though it'd be six months before he felt comfortable enough to cut a hole in the laminate big enough to worm his blade in under the cardboard. He added to that a single wooden match, which he'd sliced in half to keep the bulge from looking too suspicious. He'd sealed it with a strip of clear packing tape he'd also swiped from the shop. In the face of any real trouble, the match and the blade wouldn't have amounted to more than two grains of sand but it made him feel better just knowing they were there — a little part of himself he kept hidden from everyone else.

And it was with lingering thoughts of this in mind that he'd sent Clayton to fetch some tinder before taking the photograph from around his neck. He flipped it over now, scratching his thumbnail at the tape along its bottom edge and peeling it back. He then bent the photo between his thumb and forefinger, widening the hole and using his index finger to jimmy first the match and then the blade into the palm of his hand. He was using the bit of tape to glue the match back together when he heard the irregular pad of footsteps that told him Clayton was heading back.

I got five strips of the bark, he said, dropping them and an armful of branches at Gerald's feet. The branches are from a tree that was on the ground. They's good and dry.

Gerald stuck the match behind his ear and took the largest sheet of bark, setting it before him on the hard-packed earth and peeling the paper-thin outer layer of white from all four of the other strips, crumbling them like paper.

Ain't never ate dog before, Clayton said as Gerald piled twigs over the bark. He was looking down at the German shepherd, clicking his teeth together as if getting them used to the idea. What do you think it'll taste like?

Gerald had retrieved the match from behind his ear and was foraging about the ground, feeling for a rough stone upon which to strike it.

I guess we're about to find out.

Gutting, skinning and slicing the meat from the dog had dulled the blade. After he'd made a spit on which to roast the strips of meat, Gerald idled his time sitting on the bench and whetting its edge on one of the bench's steel legs.

Clayton sat beside him tending to his wound. In the orange glow from the fire his calf looked like it had been run through a thresher. Clayton had torn a two-inch-wide strip from his undershirt and was winding it around the bloody gash.

You're going to want to disinfect it first, Gerald said.

And how am I supposed to do that?

My gramps once told me urine is a disinfectant, on account of the ammonia.

You're saying I should piss on my leg?

I'm just telling you what my gramps told me.

Clayton thought about that.

I don't think I could manage more than a few drips.

You asking me to piss on your leg?

If it's all the same, I'd rather you not.

At least make sure you get all the pieces of pant out of the wound. Else it'll definitely get infected.

Clayton spent the next few minutes picking bits of cloth out of the gash. When he was done he wound the dressing around his leg and tied it off in a double knot then stood, taking a few cautious steps to test it. His expression had turned dour and Gerald thought he was worried about the leg.

He wasn't.

God, he said, I can't even remember the last time I took a piss. How long was it since the lights went out?

More'n a month ago.

Couldn't have been that long.

You talking about the main lights or the emergency lights?

The emergencies, them's the ones in the hall?

Yeah.

They's the ones I mean.

It's been five days since they went out.

Well, I ain't taken a piss since a day after that. And it was a day before then I last took a shit.

Grease hissed in the fire's coals and Gerald walked over to it. The meat was bubbling on the low side and he gave the spit a half turn. The meat was bottom heavy and flopped to its original position and he rotated it back and held it there, crouching in the waft of black smoke. It stung his eyes but smelled a little like heaven and he basked in its promise of a filled belly shortly to come.

And I was always real regular like too, Clayton was saying. He'd sat back on the bench and had picked up an apple. One at seven in the morning and another at seven at night. My mom used to say she could set her watch to it.

He took a bite of the fruit and chewed on that.

It's what done me in, you know? he said after a moment.

What do you mean?

Why they caught me.

They got you on the shitter?

No. But I was coming out of it.

And the cops got the drop on you?

No. It was Earl.

Earl?

He was the man my mom married after my dad died. I was just zipping my fly when he clocked me over the head with a rolling pin, or at least that's what they told me later.

Why'd he do that?

Clock me over the head? I guess it was because I'd shot him in his bed not five minutes earlier. Three times in the chest. If I'd just shot him in the head like that Ellis Wilkes fella you killed, I'd have been home free.

Hearing him say that, Gerald snapped his head around and whatever good mood the smell of grilling meat had lent to him drained from his bones.

What did you just say?

If I'd just shot Earl like the feller you ... His voice trailing off seeing the look of murder in Gerald's eyes.

What the fuck do you know about that?

Nothing. I mean— Only, only what they wrote in that book about you.

Gerald grit his teeth and shook his head, an involuntary twitch spurred by the memory of the eight hours he'd spent talking to Jordan Asche in an office in the prison's administrative wing.

At first, Gerald had only answered him with two and three words at a time, mostly just confirming or denying stories the journalist had heard from other sources. About his past, how his father, Wesley Nichols, was an enforcer for the Sudbury chapter of The Sons of Adam who'd put his mother, Dolores Beausoleil, in the hospital eight times with multiple broken bones, the last time with a fractured skull, and how Wesley had ended up at none other than the Central North Correctional Centre for his part in the shooting deaths of eight people, including three women and two children, at an isolated farmhouse just outside of Chapleau. He'd been killed in prison in apparent retaliation for the same. Three months later, when the police knocked at her door, Dolores, hooked on Euphoral, had answered brandishing a knife and was shot dead while her then-seven-year-old son was cowering in his closet.

Gerald had told him that he didn't know anything about that and Jordan had smiled, plainly not believing him but unwilling to push him any further so early in the interview. The journalist was sitting with his back to the window overlooking the parking lot and sunlight was glinting off the blond highlights in his perfectly coiffed hair as he consulted his notes.

When did you start dealing weed? Jordan had asked after a moment. Was it before or after your grandfather died?

Weed? Gerald had asked, feigning affront. It's illegal to sell weed without a licence.

So you didn't deal?

No sir, he lied, though it wasn't much of one. All he ever did was grow a few plants, selling buds from those by the quarter to people who didn't have a car or couldn't bother driving to the dispensary at the reserve or who'd rather buy from a white man or who'd as soon buy from anyone as long as it wasn't the government.

So Ellis Wilkes wasn't after your crop the night he broke into your barn?

Hell if I know what he was after.

But it wasn't the first time Ellis had broken into your barn, was it?

The truth was it was the third, or so Gerald suspected. The first two times he'd stolen the crop Gerald had hung to dry from the rafters and on the latter of these he'd left a freshly laid turd on the floor, his idea of a joke, as screamingly hilarious as what he'd done to Chuckles some years previous. But Gerald couldn't even think about that without wanting to punch something and so he'd simply said,

What can I say, I guess he must have liked his eggs.

Eggs?

They were about the only thing in the barn of any worth, far as I know.

Jordan had smiled curtly at that and then consulted his notes again.

What can you tell me about your grandfather's old bear trap? he asked after flipping through a few pages.

Hearing mention of that had been like an electric shock administering ten thousand volts with Jordan Asche's hand on the button. Gerald had been filled with rage at the mere thought of it and more so at the way Jordan was tapping his pen on his notebook and looking at him through preening eyes.

It weren't my grandfather's, he'd blurted out. It was my great-granddaddy's!

Such vitriol in his voice that he heard the creak of leather at his back and knew the guard at the door was reaching for his baton. Jordan too had reacted with alarm and was covering his unease by thumbing at his notebook.

Of course, of course, he'd said. Then looking back up again, smiling in a vain attempt to regain Gerald's trust. I understand he'd hung it over the door after he'd built the barn.

That's right.

Gerald's anger had subsided some and he was feeling embarrassed at his sudden outburst, his shame further compounded by how rattled he'd been at the mere mention of the bear trap.

Forcing a mawkish smile he'd said rather sheepishly, I remember the first time I saw it. Gave me one helluva fright, I tellya that.

Relating then:

It was the very first time I followed my gramps into the barn, on the very day I'd come to live with him.

When you were seven?

That's right. I was maybe five steps through the door when I heard this, it was like a, you know, a predatory hiss from a dark corner. When I turned towards it all I could see was a pair of yellow eyes and two white fangs. It was one of the barn cats. They were half-feral, a skittish lot. I'd never get within an arm's length of one the entire time I lived there but I didn't know that at the time. It seemed it was about to pounce. I spun on my heels to get the hell outta there, and that's when I saw the bear trap hanging over the barn door: a circle of teeth as menacing as a shark's bite. The barn seemed to come alive right then, like it was a creature unto itself. It was as if the restless clop of hooves on cement, the fretful clucking, the ravenous snort of pigs, were all *emanations* from the same beast, if that's the right word.

Jordan told him it was as good a word as any and Gerald continued.

And when I saw that bear trap hanging over the door it looked like the creature's gaping maw. It seemed like it was about to lunge — *snap-snapping* — off the wall and right then and there the barn'd swallow me whole.

Jordan had laughed good-humouredly. Gerald had shook his head, laughing too, and their laughter had become like a hairline fracture in a dam that brought the whole story pouring out.

And as Gerald told it he began to see another side to it he'd never seen before, or maybe it was just the way he'd wished it had gone. By the end of the telling it had become something entirely different than the way he'd always thought of it, like it had meant something more to him than merely a life sentence and his son forced into foster care.

L ooking back at the bench, Clayton was still gazing at him with quivering apprehension and Gerald felt bad, like he had with that Asche fellow, scaring him the way he had.

You really read that? he asked as a peace offering.

Hell yeah, Clayton answered. And it was mighty inspiring too.

I wouldn't know.

You never read it?

Gerald shook his head.

Two years after their interview Jordan Asche had sent him a copy of *Savage Gerry: Canadian Outlaw*. On its cover there was a photograph of mad-dog eyes peering out through a slot in a cell door — his own eyes, they were meant to be, though they were tinted green and not his hazel and the door itself seemed to have been culled from some Hollywood movie rather than the door that had stood guard over him. The latter was painted orange, not steel-grey, and also had a rectangle of reinforced Plexiglas for the inmates to peer out of, if ever they felt so inclined, though Gerald never had. It seemed as much of a lie as the one he'd told Jordan, as if there was any truth to be derived from how he'd killed three men and then fled into the northern wilds with his thirteen-year-old son except that he'd be in jail for the rest of his life and Evers would grow up a ward of the state, a feeling exacerbated by what was handwritten on the inside page.

To Gerald, it read in Jordan's almost girlish script, *Give my best to Everett.*

Below that was the address of the foster home where Evers was staying, all that Gerald had asked in exchange for the interview. He'd started a dozen letters to his son by then without ever figuring out what it was he'd really wanted to say. He'd thrown every last one in the garbage and that's what he'd done with the book too.

Well it was mighty inspiring to me, Clayton was saying.

And you didn't learn nothing from it?

Hell, I learned plenty.

Not enough to keep from getting caught.

Ah hell, that was just stupid bad luck. Clayton shaking his head with the memory, and then: I had the whole damn thing planned down to a T. I was going to set off into the woods just like you did, had a bag packed and everything. A rifle, plenty of ammo, a bow, a knife, flint, everything you took and a few things besides. I even had a pair of binoculars, which is the one thing you said you'd wished you'd brought. I was just heading out the back door with my pack when I felt it coming on. I looked at my watch, damned if it wasn't seven o'clock on the dot. So I turned around and the last thing I remember was coming out of the bathroom in our kitchen, zipping my pants. I woke up the next day in a hospital, handcuffed to a bed.

Taking another bite of the apple and tonguing the chunk into his cheek, sucking the juice from its meat, ruminating deeply, as if trying to make some sense out of his own story.

I'll tell you one thing I did learn, he said after he'd swallowed. That Earl, he sure was a tough old coot.

They ate sitting on the bench, pulling off pieces of the sinewy meat from the skewers. They were half-burnt and half-raw and almost too tough to swallow but they tasted similar to goat which Gerald had always liked, though he preferred it stewed.

Their previous conversation seemed to have opened the floodgates in Clayton and while they ate, the gnash of their teeth was interrupted at intervals by the idle wilds of his restless mind.

What'dya miss most about being inside? he'd started off by asking.

Evers was the clear answer in Gerald's mind but he didn't want to get into all that so instead he answered, Swimming I guess.

No shit?

On a hot summer's day, ain't nothin' better than a cool dip. You?

That's easy. A decent mattress.

That's a good one.

Clayton smiled like he'd never received a better compliment than that.

A girl I used to go with, he said, she had this king-sized pillow-top, you know? Most comfortable bed I ever laid in. I asked her one time how much her parents had paid for it. You know what she said?

What?

More'n you paid for your car, I bet.

Shoot, I said, that ain't saying much.

Then she asked me how much I paid for *it*.

I says, I asked you about the bed first and she says, The difference is, I don't really give a shit how much you paid for your car.

So I told her, I paid four grand for it.

You'd have to be an idiot to pay four grand for that piece of shit, she says.

I guess I'm an idiot then, I tell her and she says, You won't get no argument from me.

She broke it off a short while after. When I asked her why, she told me she was sick of being with such a damn fool. So I says, If this was about the car, the joke's on you, because I only paid eight hundred for it.

That was the last time I saw her. Weren't no big loss really, she was a real handful, more like four, you know what I mean. But I sure did miss that bed.

Then clicking his teeth:

I never did find out how much her parents had paid for it.

And sometime later:

You ever been to Marmora?

What's that?

It's a town. Where I'm from.

Never heard of it.

I ain't surprised. Ain't nothing but a spit, forty-five minutes on the other side of Peterborough. You heard of Peterborough?

Rings a bell.

Ain't never been there?

No.

Well, you ain't missing much. Only reason I ever went was I had a girl there.

The one with the bed?

No, this was another girl. She had a futon. You ever fucked on a futon?

Can't say as I have.

It was like fucking on a sack of flour, hers was anyway. But I was talking about Marmora. They had this old pit mine up there. It was seven hundred feet deep. All but the top hundred was filled with water from an underground spring. A while back — long time ago, before I was born — the owners tried to sell it to Toronto. They was going to plug up the spring, drain it, fill it with garbage. Bunch of environmentalists got together, you know what they did?

What's that?

Stocked it with fish. Lake trout, mostly. Snuck in there one night with a water truck filled with 'em. Hundreds, maybe even thousands. After that the government wouldn't let the company sell the mine. Said it wasn't fair to the fish.

Why didn't the owners just catch 'em all?

I don't know. All I do know is that there's a huge pit full of spring water and lake trout just outside of town. Used to think about it a lot when I was a kid, how if things got any worse — you know, end-of-times shit — I figured there wouldn't be a better place to live than Marmora.

Things must be pretty bad now.

And getting worse by the minute, no doubt.

So you heading back?

Ah hell, I ain't never going back to Marmora.

And lastly:

So what do *you* think happened?

You mean, why the power went out?

Yeah.

Gerald thought about it for a moment.

Ain't seen enough to know one way or the other, he finally offered. Then thinking about his grandfather and what Jules and Zip had said: Whatever it was, it's been coming down the pipe for some time.

That's what Virgil said, too.

Who's that?

Virgil Boothe. He was my cellmate these past six months. He was some high muckety-muck in The Sons.

Lucky for you.

Clayton raised his empty pop bottle as if in toast.

Cheers to that.

Then working at a strand of meat lodged in his teeth with a fingernail:

Virgil was a real prophet of doom, I tellya. He was always going off about how it'd be the damn Yanks who'd do us in. Said it was only a matter of time before they got sick of paying for our water. He said they had a virus could shut down our entire electrical grid. All it would take was the push of a button and the lights'd go out and that'd be that. They wouldn't even have to attack, he said. All they'd have to do is seal up their borders and wait. Ninety percent of the population wouldn't last the winter and they could just move right in. Said it'd be any day now.

The first time he told me this, I asked him, How can you be so sure? He says, Boy, ain't you been paying attention? I told him I never had much use for the news, which I figured is what he meant, and he laughed and clapped me on the shoulder. The news ain't got nothing to do with it, he says. All the news does is muddy the waters. That's its job, to keep you from seeing what's going on

81

right there in front of you. You got to use your own two eyes, boy, you really want to know what's going down.

He was getting all riled up, spit spraying out of his mouth and his eyes, I swear to god, like they were about to pop out of his head. Reminded me of this Euphie who was with me in remand. He never shut up the whole time I was there. You say boo while he was going off, he'd come at you. One time I saw him bite another man's ear clean off who'd told him to shut it. Virgil was looking that way too, so I just smiled and nodded, like he was speaking the god's honest truth, though at the time I thought he was as crazy as the rest of them Sons.

Just look around, he went on. You got front-row seats right here. Ain't no better barometer for the state of affairs than a prison. Cons, he said, are like those canaries they used in coal mines. Then he asked me, How many riots we had over the last year?

He was looking at me like it'd be my neck if I didn't answer so I says, I don't know. I only been here a few days.

He wasn't even listening.

Fifteen goddamned riots, he said. All because they've packed twenty-five hundred men into a jail meant for half that. The most of them drug addicts or nut jobs. And them building new prisons every day, like they can just lock all that crazy away, forget about it.

And if things are getting bad up here, they're ten times worse in the States, he said. It'll be any day now, the power'll just go out. You mark my words.

Picking up an apple, Clayton rubbed it on his pant leg before continuing.

As I said, I'd always thought he was crazy.

Raising the apple then to take a bite, shaking his head.

I sure don't now.

He ate the apple without saying another word and after he'd pitched the core into the woods he looked at his wrist, as if he was checking his watch.

What time you think it is? he asked.

Gerald was crouched by the dying embers of the fire and turning the end of a birch branch over in the coals. It was six inches long, about the width of his middle finger, and he was hardening its end in advance of attaching the blade.

Sometime past midnight, I'd guess.

Feels like seven o'clock to me.

When Gerald looked over at him, Clayton was grinning at the joke and that made Gerald smile, too.

Clayton wheeled around and Gerald went back to turning the branch. He'd just wheedled the blade into the slit he'd made in the hardened end and was tying it off with a strip he'd torn from Clayton's undershirt when the scarecrow came tromping back out of the bush, zipping his jumper and grinning like the goose that had just laid a golden egg.

Gripping the makeshift knife by the hilt, Gerald pressed the blade into the seam of his pant leg to see if it gave. It held just fine and he tucked its haft into the elastic of one of his socks as Clayton gathered up the last three apples, holding two in one hand and one in the other, his arms cocked as if he was setting to start juggling them.

Where to now, boss?

Gerald's hand had sought out the photograph slung around his neck and his thumb was stroking at its veneer as if trying to bolster his resolve from the boy's indomitable spirit.

Home, he said.

They came to a river as the first faint strains of light were leaking into the sky towards the east. Thick grey mist couched its banks, rendering the far shore an ill-defined and vaguely ominous slope leading upwards into a veil of nether white. The water beading in their beards and cooling on their cheeks was a welcome reprieve from the night's humidity and they stood for a time, tottering on the hollowed-out web of roots straining at the base of a cedar tree bowed at a precarious angle over the water.

The darkly ribboned stream below frothed into a dirty foam within the branches of a beaver-felled maple tree and caught within its net was a detritus of plastic bottles and pop cans, a single purple flip-flop and a pair of pink underwear snagged as if on a finger, riding the current in a listless pantomime of pleasures long past but hardly forgotten. Watching it with the eager remorse of a boy spying from a closet as his sister undresses, Clayton licked his top lip, covering his lechery by blurting out, We ought to fill up the water bottle.

He bent, about to lower himself down through a gap within the thicket of roots, and Gerald clutched at his arm.

This water ain't clean, he said. We'll find a spring elsewhere.

Gerald was already turning downstream and Clayton turned after him, pausing momentarily to look back down at the quixotic eroticism of the underwear's shimmy and that only firming his resolve.

You go on, he said. I got to take a piss. I'll— I'll catch up with you.

Gerald hadn't made it more than twenty steps when there appeared out of the mist a slightly darker shade of grey: the cement trestle of a bridge. The water passing beneath flowed languid and calm, a perfect counter to the restless fret of his mind as he looked up the gravelled embankment leading towards the road.

They'd spent the night in anxious cavort, skirting from one wooded refuge to the next as they followed Highway 12 south from the fringes. Its two lanes had led them on a winding path away from Midland — Penetang's sister city — guiding them along the shores of Severn Sound, a sheltered cove opening into Georgian Bay and scattered with small settlements, the main purpose of which was to service the tourists whose cottages lined the shore. They travelled under the cover of dark, seeing neither a soul nor a single light, Gerald all the while planning the journey yet to come.

The 12 would take them to the 400, a four-lane highway that would lead them on a straight shot north, connecting with the 69 this side of Parry Sound and that taking them into Sudbury. It was the short side of four hundred kilometres and on his own he figured he could manage thirty or forty klicks every day, which meant he'd be walking into Sudbury in less than two weeks, Capreol seven or eight hours after that.

Except he wasn't alone.

In the five or six hours since they'd roasted the dog they hadn't made even ten kilometres and Clayton had barely managed those, stumbling along on his wounded leg, huffing like a horse run too hard, each step seeming like it might be his last.

Glancing back the way he'd come, Gerald found Clayton emerging out of the fog, hobbling along with the use of a stick to take the pressure off his wounded leg, though it hardly increased his pace. His pant legs were wet to the waist and he was grinning with embarrassed aloof. Gerald let him pass and followed him up the embankment and onto the road. Dawn's first rays were struggling against the early morning mist, masking it in a hazy shade of grey. They couldn't see even halfway across the bridge, the fog was so thick, and Gerald stood a moment listening for what might lie ahead. He could hear a not-too-distant cawing of crows — maybe a few dozen — and the ominous tenor of their cacophony gave him little incentive to venture further.

Clayton, though, plunged straight ahead, disappearing into the grey. After a breath, Gerald slunk after him, holding his blade before him like a dagger and knowing it wouldn't be any better than a toothpick if someone spotted them crossing the bridge. When he'd caught up with Clayton, he was crouching down halfway across, peering at something, Gerald couldn't quite make out what.

You think he's dead? Clayton whispered.

Who?

Clayton motioned his head down the road and Gerald took a cautious look forward, seeing the vague form of a man emerging out of the haze. He was sitting propped up with his back against the cement barrier that guarded cars against a ten-foot drop into the river below.

He's dead, ain't he? Clayton asked.

It's a helluva funny place to take a nap, if he ain't.

As Gerald approached the body, he knew the man hadn't been dead for long, a few hours at most. He hadn't yet begun to smell and his skin hadn't turned grey, as Orville's had a few hours after he'd died. The man was wearing a pair of aviator sunglasses propped on a flourish of auburn hair and a blue collared golf shirt and tan khaki shorts. There were lesions, like squished slugs, eking out from within his collar and the cuffs of his shirt.

Gerald gave him a wide berth as he stepped around him. On the body's far side there was a smattering of muddy footprints imprinted on the sidewalk — several medium-sized dogs or maybe coyotes. Walking a few paces past he heard a sudden squawk and saw a black form — one of the crows — pitching upwards through the mist. There was a vague impression of another body lying prone on the ground just below where it had taken off, and he turned around.

Clayton had taken the pair of sunglasses off the man and was fitting them over his ears.

I wouldn't do that if I were you, Gerald said as he approached.

He ain't goin' to mind.

It's not that. You see them tracks on the ground there?

Gerald had come back to within five paces of the body and that was about as close as he was willing to get.

They look like dog tracks.

They're coyote. And they didn't want nothing to do with him.

So?

Clayton tilted the sunglasses up and peered down at the man.

The man was sick, Gerald said.

Sick?

Can't you see the sores on his neck? That's what must have killed him.

Clayton was staring down at the body harder still.

You don't think it's catching, do ya?

I ain't no doctor.

A culminating unease was curdling Clayton's lips and all of a sudden he jerked backwards away from the body, flinging the glasses off his head and wiping his hand on his pant leg, looking over at Gerald with fearful eyes.

Didn't your mother ever tell you not to touch dead things?

Without another word they followed the river downstream.

Their prison jumpsuits made them a pretty clear target. Worried that someone would see them as a threat and take a shot at them, Gerald thought it best if they sought shelter during the day and only travelled at night. The sun had yet to appear as anything more than a subtle lightening of the fog, and the less-than-subtle nag of mosquitoes battered at the back of their necks and faces with a frenetic buzz. They came to a copse of cedars along the bank and he told Clayton they'd hole up there for the day. Inside was a cubby as good as any cave, big enough for the two of them to lie down out of the sun, and the ground was well cushioned by fallen cedar fronds. Gerald broke off a fresh one from a low-hanging branch and crumbled it between his fingers, pressing the fragrant leaves to his nose and inhaling deeply of their scent, which he'd often done on his many wanders through the woods north of Capreol.

I think it's getting infected.

Clayton was hunched over his leg, sitting with his back against the cedar's trunk. He'd peeled off the dressing and was wincing at the mangle of torn skin hanging in jagged flaps over the two deep furrows in his calf. The mosquitoes had followed them into their shelter and Gerald swatted at one sucking at his neck while he looked over the wound.

Some staunchweed'd do it a world of good, he said, remembering the poultices his grandfather had used whenever he cut himself.

You got any handy?

It grows practically everywhere. Bound to be some around. Best thing for you now though is to get some rest.

Gerald lay down on the ground with hands behind his head and his eyes closed, though he was too wired to sleep.

Clayton stretched out beside him.

You think that man really was sick? he asked after a few breaths.

Sure looked it.

You think maybe that's what happened? Why the power went out? A sickness of some sort.

I thought you said it was the Yanks.

No, it was Virgil thought it was the Yanks. Could have been a sickness just as likely. Plenty of those going around.

You say so.

Could have been them Earth Firsters, too. They've been threatening to shut her all down ever since all those islands disappeared in the South Pacific. Ah hell, it might just as well been them nanopreds.

Nanopreds?

Nanoscopic predators. You never heard of nanopreds?

I'd tell you if I had, Gerald said.

They're these microscopic machines they, like, program to hunt vermin. Bugs and slugs and whatnot. They use them in farming and they also made these ones that target mosquito larvae.

Those ones mustn't have worked too well, Gerald countered, swatting at one of the bloodsuckers feeding on his cheek.

They mostly used them in Africa and South America, I think. To combat the malaria. You really never heard of nanopreds?

Only just now.

They even made a movie about 'em. Scary as hell too. *Nano-Fright*, it was called, which I always thought was a pretty shitty name. They should have called it *Nano-Bite*, you know bite, like with your teeth. That would have been a better name because boy, you should've seen what they done to humans when their safeties were switched off. Stripped them right down to their skeletons. It was like a tornado — a tornado of blood and guts, you know. I couldn't sleep for days after I saw that, thinking they'd be coming for me next. Mind you, I was only six. Earl let me watch it one night when Mom was at work. Imagine, showing that to a six-year-old. That son of a bitch never did have any sense. This one time—

Clayton, Gerald interrupted when it seemed like he'd never shut up.

What?

I'm tired.

Oh, sorry.

You should get some sleep too.

I'm too wired up to sleep. Hell, it feels like I ain't never going to sleep again.

They lay in silence for some time. Clayton's breathing took on an elongated rasp and Gerald knew he'd fallen asleep after all. Gerald though wasn't any closer than he had been before and while he lay with his eyes closed in static repose, his mind was a veritable cyclone. Images swirled up out of the dervish, mostly parcelled memories from the night before, fragments broken off from the whole and battering against each other like leaves in a gale as if by some miracle of recombination they'd form into a pattern that'd make any kind of sense to him at all. The jackhammer lash of that big gun pounding at the forest, Jules tied to the front of the truck, screaming his agony as it raced past, his voice then pleading against the dark of their cell, I want you to kill me, that crumbling under the grating rumble as the excavator tore a hole in the wall, a spot of light appearing through the haze of concrete dust and that leading him right back to where he'd started, seeing again the transient flicker appear from between the trees at the edge of the field across from the prison, almost like a . . . a firefly.

Knowing at once that it wasn't that and yet the recollection still culled to mind now, as it had then, the memory of how the spring after he and Evers had fled into the northern wilds on the run from the law they had come upon a lightly wooded glade enlivened by the migrant glow of thousands of the phosphorescent insects transforming the forest into an almost magical realm where anything might have been possible.

If it wasn't for those damn fireflies, Gerald muttered to himself now, knowing it wasn't really their fault him and Evers had been caught not six days later.

You want to blame anything, you might as well blame that old rooster, Max. He was the one who got you into this mess in the first place. And while you're at it, you might as well blame that old bear trap too.

He was sitting up though he couldn't remember doing so. He was breathing hard, impossibly so, and there were beads of sweat dripping over his brow. The salt was stinging the scratch on his cheek and he had the sudden urge to just get up and run, knowing even then he could never outrun the past.

It was running that did you in to begin with.

A fleeting enough thought, and one he knew was a lie.

The only truth is right here, right now, he told himself, taking a deep breath and trying to still the race of his heart. *It's you and this boy, that's all there is. Without you he'd have been dead twice over. And he's given you a reason to live.*

Another sentiment that struck him as not entirely the truth and he looked down at Clayton for some sort of affirmation, that it wasn't just chance that had thrown them together, but part of some greater design. He was lying on his side, his legs curled towards his chest and his head pillowed on his hand, its thumb twitching with the listless fret of a fishing bob tugging against the current. A mosquito landed on its knuckle. Gerald reached over to brush it off and was startled by the angry chatter of a squirrel, as sudden and loud as an alarm clock.

Looking up, he found it perched on an overhanging branch, some five feet above. It was a red and it was peering down at him with an eager sort of malice, nattering in angry bursts like he'd done it some great wrong just by sitting there. There was another identical squirrel on the opposite side of the trunk some two feet above it. It scampered in a frenetic downward scuttle as quiet as a feather's drift. If the other knew it was there it made no sign, continuing on in its unrelenting chatter, sounding more expository than angry now, as if it was relating to him a tale of great import — must have had something to do with nuts, the way it nattered on — and Gerald vacillating his gaze between it and the other. When the second came even with the other, it froze as still as a pine cone, only its tail twitching as if laying dire plans of its own.

You better watch yourself, Gerald warned the first. He's coming for ya.

At the sound of his voice the other disappeared around the

side of the tree, appearing a moment later behind the first and that one making a sudden leap two feet up the trunk, scuttling around it with the other in frenzied pursuit. As they chased each other in spiralling loops around the tree's trunk with the zeal of a circular saw spinning out of control, one of them, he couldn't tell which, emitted high-pitch reprimands that came out sounding like a dog's squeaky toy, Gerald all the while watching their playful scurry and muttering to himself, At least someone's having a good time.

G erald spent the rest of the morning trolling along the river, looking for some staunchweed.

He finally found a patch of the small white flowers at the edge of a meadow with the sun winking at him through the bristling leaves of a poplar tree on the western bank. It was the weed's leaves he was after. They grew in a feathering of lance-like sprouts along their stem that always looked to him like a chipmunk's tail. There were a dozen plants growing in a cluster and he stripped all of them clean, chewing the leaves and spitting out the bitter mush into a curl of birch bark he'd peeled from a nearby tree. He added to this a few camomile leaves to serve as a dressing and, to give it some cushion, a clump of moss that grew in sodden fields just inside the forest's damp.

When he'd come around a bend that brought the cedar grove back into view, he found Clayton down at the water, washing something in the stagnant flow. As Gerald passed the felled maple on the far shore, where they'd first come to the river, he searched about its branches for the ripple of pink that had marked it then. It was gone and he recalled the look of startled shame on Clayton's face when he'd emerged out of the fog, his pant legs wet and Gerald even then certain he'd known why.

Careful you don't drown her, he called out as he approached and Clayton jerked around, his hands in a sudden and secretive flounder tucking something into the folds of his jumper.

Drown who? he answered, genuinely confused.

Your girlfriend.

My wh— he started.

His jaw locked and his cheeks flushed red, getting the gist of what Gerald meant. The expression recalled to Gerald the same look of befuddled shame that Evers, then thirteen, had worn one morning at breakfast after Gerald had asked the boy, Your girlfriend not coming down to eat?

My girlfriend? Evers had asked, baffled.

You didn't have a girl up there with you last night?

No.

I could've sworn I heard someone up there with you. Sounded like the two of you was fixing to break the bed. What, she go out the window?

Evers looking at him with shameful disbelief and Millie kicking him under the table, glaring at him with ice in her eyes.

It's no wonder he doesn't talk to you anymore, she'd chided after Evers had gone up to take a shower.

What?

He's thirteen.

I was just having some fun.

How'd you feel if you were thirteen and your dad was making fun of you for — lowering her voice to a hush — jerking off.

My dad was dead six years by the time I was thirteen, Gerald said laughing, so I guess I'd have been pretty shocked.

96

Scowling, Millie had reached out and pinched him hard on the arm, which she often did when he'd said something stupid.

Now Gerald was flinching at the memory same as if she'd reached out from beyond the grave to pinch him again. Back then, it had always seemed that it was his good moods that had got him in the most trouble. And he'd been in plenty a good mood just a moment ago. It had crept up on him unawares as he wandered along the river, lost in its quiet gurgle and the scamper of chipmunks and squirrels, the dry rustle of the wind through poplar leaves and the sun dappled in bursts of warmth on his cheeks and above all the sanguine spice of the forest's musk, breathing it in as if in their decay the trees were releasing the essence of life itself, infusing his blood and bringing the loose amble back to his stride, feeling better than he had in years, a far worse trap than feeling bad.

I thought maybe you'd took off, Clayton was saying. He'd recovered from his shame and was clawing up the bank. Through the open flap of his jumper, Gerald could just make out a tuft of pink winking at him from the cleft.

No, he said. I was searching out some staunchweed.

Clayton's eyes brightened.

You find any?

Gerald held his package up.

You think it'll stop the infection?

It sure won't make it any worse.

Seeing only a worried trace of consternation in the other's eyes.

Come on then, he said. Let's go and get you fixed up.

They set off again only after the sun had settled beyond the trees.

Last grasps of its light straggled through the wisp of a cloud hanging low on the horizon, an ethereal fanning like cotton balls pulled apart by some mischievous child. Its frayed tufts were soaked in reds and oranges as if daubed in paint and darkened at the edges as if by ink. One last ray of a brilliant yellow parted the billow, alighting, by some divine refraction, in a lucent downward blaze, casting its glimmer in a roving band on the blacktop ahead.

It was the prospect of just that kind of sunset that would have sent his grandfather scrambling up the path leading to the ridge behind their barn so as to get a better look. He called it a ridge, or more precisely The Ridge, but to Gerald it always looked more like a mountain had crumbled leaving behind a jumbled conglomeration of granite ledges and boulders piled on top of each other with all the care of a toddler laying blocks. There was a flat-topped slab of grey granite, six-foot thick, perched precariously at its peak and within a seam of windblown dirt covered with moss at its base there grew a lone spruce tree. It was twisted by the paucity of its birthplace and seemed to be waging a battle against all reason, its trunk clambering in spiralling loops above the towering spires of the much grander trees below, though even the greatest of these could only dream of reaching a fraction of its elevation. His grandfather would use it to climb up onto the platform, where he'd stand in reverent contemplation until the last of the light had leaked from the sky.

For all his prognostications about the sordid fate of humankind his grandfather had never been morose and had relished every sunset as a man cleansed within the dwindling shroud of its light. As the last of its radiance now leaked out of the sky above, dimming the road and remaking its promise into a threat of what might be lurking in the evening's shade, it was with a desperate longing for his grandfather's resolve that Gerald recollected something he'd said to him when he was seventeen.

He'd thought his grandfather was dying at the time though he'd end up living another two years. The last memory Gerald would have of him was of the old man waving goodbye on a crisp autumn morning as he set off to check his trap-line. Gerald wasn't there to hear his dying words, if he uttered any, and took in their stead what he'd said the morning after he collapsed while he was chopping the winter wood.

Gerald had come out of the barn where he'd been milking their Holsteins and found him on his knees, trying to use the axe handle to lever himself back to his feet.

What's wrong? he'd asked walking towards his grandfather.

The old man turned with a look of stark fright in his eyes, though when he spoke his voice betrayed only the mild irritation of someone who'd, say, just stubbed his toe.

I don't know, he'd gasped. I'm having trouble breathing.

He then winced in pain and clutched his fingers in a spider-lock at his chest.

Lie down then while I call the ambulance, Gerald said, already heading for the house.

The ground'll have me soon enough. Give me your hand, help me up. If I can get to my chair, I'll be all right. Don't just stand there, boy!

Gerald had given his hand and eased him to his feet, clutching him around the waist, his fingers latching on the loose droop of skin over bare ribs, his grandfather sagging against his arm and it feeling like his skeleton was holding on for dear life while its flesh gave way around it.

I'm reminded of something my Pop-Pop once told me, he choked through spastic gasps as Gerald half carried, half dragged him towards the house.

Maybe you ought to save your breath, Gerald chided, though he knew there was about as much chance of that as him getting the old man up and into the pine rocker on the porch.

Pop-Pop, that's what we called my grandfather, the old man continued unabated, as if death might be too shy to interrupt a man while he was talking. I don't know if I ever told you that. One time we'd come to visit, I couldn't have been older'n five. I was chasing his black Lab along the driveway's gravel, about where we are right now. I tripped over something, my own two feet likely, skinned both knees and an elbow. I was sitting there crying and Pop-Pop, he just picks me up, sets me back on my feet. He says to me, Not much a man can hope for in this life except putting one foot in front of the next and when he trips to be able to pick himself back up. Always seemed sensible advice to me.

Coughing then, choking up a wad of mucus dribbling over his chin and taking up residence in his beard like a slug that had just crawled out of his mouth. They'd come to the porch and he peered up at the chair with a hateful scorn, as if it was in some way mocking him.

Just set me down on the steps, he said then added: I think maybe you oughta call an ambulance after all.

Gerald did and when he came back his grandfather had scrounged his pipe from his breast pocket and was engulfed in a mire of blue-tinged smoke, taking short draws and his chest convulsing with every puff.

Now I got the (hic)cups, he said, as if that was the worst of his troubles.

Then considering:

I never heard of a man (hic) dying from the (hic)cups. You reckon I might (hic) be the first?

The sardonic lilt to his eyes while he said it coming back to Gerald and more so even than his "dying words" firming Gerald's resolve as he put one foot in front of the other, skirting the fringe of trees at the road's edge and listening into the gathering dark for any sound to tell him there was something headed their way.

As the night settled in, the moon's pregnant crescent appeared behind the trees and the stars came out one by one. They looked less like great flaming balls of gas than the frays of string left over from a missing button. The image stuck in his mind such that by the time they reached where the 12's two lanes ducked under the overpass supporting the 400's four, it had begun to seem to Gerald that maybe the universe itself was coming undone.

They'd crawled up its far embankment and were peering over the metal guard rail. The highway's four lanes were all jammed as far as the eye could see, an endless clog of vehicles, all of them abandoned and pointed north and as lifeless as a collection of Matchbox cars scattered over a boy's bedroom floor after a week of rainy days.

Shoot, Clayton said when he'd stood up beside Gerald, who was tracing with mounting dread along the span of cars and trucks and there seeming to be no end to their reach. I—

But what he'd meant to say next was lost within the shroud of his gape, his mouth hanging open and his eyes growing wider in disbelief, the spectacular calamity before them quieting all but the ragged huff of his panted breaths.

They came onto the road, shimmying between two school buses. Forswearing the earlier caution that had kept them on the fringes, they walked along the yellow dashes in the centre of the northbound lane, soaking in the immensity of it all and neither of them saying a word.

Most of the vehicles were buses, the majority of the school variety and others of the kind used by city transit, their digital screens dead and bearing no clear sign as to their origins. A meagre few were Greyhounds and amongst them was a spattering of cars and trucks, most of which were older models. There weren't any of the self-driving varieties at all and that came as a bit of a surprise since Gerald had been hearing for years about how they'd come to dominate the road. Their absence was maybe a clue as to what had happened but how that might have fit into the grander scheme was anyone's guess. Littered between the vehicles: empty water bottles and candy wrappers, chip bags and the odd suitcase or duffel rent open and disgorging crumpled pants and shirts, and all of the assorted debris one might expect from a plight of refugees fleeing the safety of their homes and later their cars, taking with them, at last, only what they could carry. A seemingly never-ending transit of detritus so profound in its panorama that the more they moved within its scope the less it spoke to them of a mass migration and the more it forced upon them a thousand or more isolated dramas.

Here a soiled diaper discarded on the hood of a sedan, its flaps open to reveal a splattering of offal hardened and flaking, nothing about it to divine whether the mother was loving and gentle as she tended to the child's needs or harried and frantic, battered by the bustle of passersby and the turbulence of her infant's scream. There the thin and delicate frame of a ten-speed racing bike with a wobbled front wheel lying crumpled before the open driver's-side door of a rust-battered Volvo station wagon. The car's front windshield was smashed as if with a golf club and that spoke of a violent altercation, though who's to say the scene didn't end with an act of contrition, effusive apologies and the abiding remorse of one stranger tending to another stranger's wound? A lesser act of mercy amongst strangers, perhaps, in a stippling of cigarette butts beneath the yawning tailgate of a Ford pick-up truck. Or was it the site of a couple's last stand, an argument devolving into an angry storm of recriminations, someone dragging her away and someone else him, and never again the twain should meet? Gerald couldn't say and there were fewer conclusions still to be made on the matter of the burnt-out husk of a Jeep on the highway's shoulder or the anomalous sight of a thirty-foot yacht hitched to an abandoned trailer with its sails set aloft and snapping ecstatic against a stiffening breeze or the myriad of other artefacts, the all of them bearing witness to little but the unremitting inscrutability of humankind.

There were puddles of what looked like puke impeding every second or third step and other, darker stains that looked like dried-up blood, most congealed with chunks of some indeterminate organic matter so that on second look they didn't seem much like blood at all. Gerald wove onwards through these until at last he came to within view of a sign on the side of the road, a solar-powered beacon of sorts, flashing a message in orange pixels: *Destruction Ahead Expect Dismay*. At first, Gerald took it to be somebody's idea of a joke, a not-so-subtle manipulation of the old standard, *Construction Ahead Expect Delays* — a bit of gallows humour to pass the time while waiting on some undisclosed and long-past day for the promise of help that might never come. But as he drew closer, he wasn't entirely sure it was that. Venturing into its bleating light, he paused, scouring ahead and finding the highway's interminable dismay stretching to the limits of his view, wondering if maybe the sign wasn't meant to be some kind of a warning.

Clayton had fallen behind. He could hear him hastening to catch up, his walking stick knocking along to his irregular shuffle.

Looky what I found, he said as Gerald turned back.

Clayton was pointing at himself, showing off the brand-new shirt for which he'd exchanged his prison jumper. It was of a breed that might have been called "Hawaiian" — it was garish enough for that. But in place of the requisite palm trees there was a less tangible design, splashes of colour in a vertical flow like someone had emptied several fifty-gallon drums of neon paint into a water-fall. It was three sizes too big, and owing to that and the baggy jean shorts Clayton had found to go along with it, and the ever-present rabbit-eared hat and stubble of straw-like whiskers on his chin, he'd never looked more like a scarecrow than he did right then.

Pretty sweet, huh? he said. It's silk.

It suits you, Gerald lied.

Sure beats that old prison jumper.

It's nice.

There's a whole suitcase full of 'em back there. I could get you one.

He was already turning around.

That's okay.

You sure? he asked turning back. Ain't never worn a more comfortable shirt.

His expression had taken on a delicate pleading, as if Gerald wearing the shirt would have meant the world to him.

All right, Gerald relented.

Yeah?

No harm in trying one on, I suppose.

You won't be sorry. You'll see. It's like wearing a shirt made out of a cool summer's breeze!

G erald had taken to rooting through glove boxes and side compartments and under front seats. What he was looking for was a map and he'd already gone through a dozen cars. All he'd found of worth so far was a couple of lighters — no small thing — and a Car Buddy multi-tool. The latter had a small LED light and he'd been using it to expedite his search but had still come up empty.

Clayton had brought back to him a pair of green cargo shorts and a shirt identical in design to his own except that in place of a neon waterfall it did in fact have on it a grove of palm trees, their trunks all blurring together so that it looked like the artist had poured turpentine over the rendering of a tropical beach. It was comfortable enough all right and Gerald left it unbuttoned so as to further allow whatever breeze there was to cool the sweat glistening in the coarse curls plastered to his chest, a welcome balm against the night's stifling heat.

He took the northbound lane, weaving back and forth among the vehicles, and directed Clayton to do the same in the southbound. The scarecrow had barely managed six cars, tirelessly amused as he was by the innumerable trinkets he'd found, appraising each with the care of a diamond cutter and if they passed his muster collecting them in a scavenged backpack. He'd come upon a pair of scissors somewhere and carried these to where Gerald was rummaging through a storage box in the back of a battered old Silverado. It held little except a collection of empty oil jugs and others that had once contained windshield wiper fluid and engine coolant, the all of them floating in three inches of water along with a four-foot span of elastic cord, the kind used for bungees.

Can I borrow that light of yours? Clayton asked as Gerald fed the cord through his belt loops to keep his shorts from slipping.

He passed the Car Buddy down and was just tying off the cord when he heard the faint murmur of an engine. Scanning ahead down the road he could see two spots of light on the southbound lane's shoulder, too close together for it to be a car or a truck, could have been a quad or a side-by-side. It was maybe a kilometre away and drawing nearer. Crouching low, he climbed over the truck's side and dropped to the ground. Clayton was standing at the truck's side mirror, using the penlight and scissors to trim the straggles of his beard.

God, he said not looking back, I look like a damn hillbilly.

Shhh, Gerald hushed him. There's someone coming!

Clayton froze mid-snip and both of them listened. The engine murmur was getting louder.

We got to get off the road, Gerald whispered.

Just give me one second.

Clayton took two more quick snips and stood a moment eyeballing himself in the mirror with brazen satisfaction.

Now!

Gerald had crept to the edge of the truck's bed. He peered around its side, getting set to make a run for the steep slope beyond the shoulder. He was stalled in this by a sharp *yip yip!*

What in the hell was that?

Clayton was crouched beside Gerald, zipping his knapsack.

Sounds like a dog. Give me the flashlight.

Clayton handed it over and Gerald lanced its beam towards the shoulder. It was a dog, all right, of the toy variety. No more really than a bristling ball of white fur, with two black eyes peering above a conical snout. It snarled once and barked twice again. Gerald fished his knife from his sock, not thinking of the dog — he'd hardly need it for that — but of its owner, if it had one.

He took one crouched step closer and a voice rose in a harsh whisper, Mia, get back here!

The dog turned tail, slinking away.

Gerald followed after it with the flashlight beam and struck upon a face suspended above the guard rail. The face belonged to a man who was old, into his seventies at least. He had a bushy beard of white curls stained with the yellow taint of nicotine and was wearing a toque in defiance of the night's heat. It had once been blue but was now greyed with grime and bore the outline of a maple leaf.

Pssst! he said, though both Gerald and Clayton were looking straight at him.

Before they could say anything, Mia yipped another staccato burst and the old man turned around, flailing his hand at her in a dismissive wave.

I'm getting to it! he snapped. Then turning back to the road: I just thought you should know, them soldiers catch you looting, it'll be your ass.

Soldiers? This from Clayton.

You hear them coming, don't ya?

The grind of the approaching engine was hard to ignore.

Those are soldiers? Clayton asked.

Half the damn army's down the road a stretch. They'd shoot you as soon as say boo, they catch you looting.

Oh, we weren't looting, Clayton protested.

What do you call what you got in the pack?

Ain't nothing but a few clothes, a pair of scissors, a bunch of junk.

I seen a man shot for less.

For less than a bunch of junk?

The light hadn't wavered from the old man's face and in its dim glow there was no mistaking the incredulity writ large in his eyes, darting from Clayton to Gerald and then back to Clayton again. And when their dumbfounded yawps didn't reveal much except that he must have been dealing with a couple of simpletons, he said, You two boys been living under a rock or something?

No we's— Clayton started only to be cut off by Gerald grabbing his arm. He wasn't so much worried about what he might say as the sudden shower of bright shining off the windshields at their back and the engine's rumble drawing ever nigh.

We really need to get off the road, he said.

The old man was gaping at him much as he might have if his dog had suddenly started speaking Chinese.

That's what I've been trying to tell you!

They hunkered on the downslope, lying prone on their chests, Mia bundled in the old man's ski parka with his hand clamped tight over her snout, and all of them listening with stifled breaths as the engine's grumble faded towards the south.

They'll be coming back this side, the old man said when it had. We can wait them out in the tunnel.

He led them along the foot of the embankment until they'd reached a narrow strip of asphalt dotted with a white line down the middle, one side bearing the outline of a bicycle and the other a pedestrian. This led them into a tunnel under the highway, eight feet high, as dark as a bottomless pit and soured with the odour of piss. Mia growled at its threshold and her owner picked her up again, bundling her within the seam of his jacket.

Hush now, he cautioned when she growled again as he stepped into the tunnel.

She's giving fair warning to the bear, he said by way of explanation.

Gerald and Clayton were following him in, the former probing ahead with the Car Buddy's light.

Bear? Clayton asked, nervous.

Run into him one time we was passing through. He'd stolen someone's garbage pail and was rooting through it right about where we are now. I was inclined to let him go about his business but Mia, well she had other ideas. She let out a growl and set off after it. I just barely managed to grab her by the tail, hold her back. She was none too happy, let me tellya. And the bear was none too happy neither. He'd rolled onto his feet. He let out a huff, stomped at the ground. I was sure he was about to charge.

What'dya do?

Not much I could. I apologized for the intrusion. Backed away as slow and quiet as I could. Of course, Mia was yapping and growling the whole damn time, the little idiot. She's been looking for him ever since. I guess they got some unfinished business.

They'd come about halfway through before the old man stopped. He cocked one ear listening and then sat down with his back against the wall, Mia cuddling into his lap. Clayton and Gerald sat down beside him, sliding their backs along the tunnel's wall, its cement as flat and cold as a prison cell's.

You can turn that light off now, the old man said.

Gerald complied and they sat in the dark, listening for a while and hearing nothing but a cricket's chirp echoing about the walls.

Gerald, you fought a bear one time, Clayton finally said. Ain't that right?

And when Gerald didn't answer he added, All he had was a knife. And he killed it too, with but one stab.

You say your friend's name is Gerald? the old man asked with more than a passing interest.

Yeah, and I'm Clayton.

And where was it you say he killed that bear?

I don't know. In the woods somewhere. Hey Gerald, tell him where it was that you killed that bear.

Clayton was nudging him with his elbow like maybe Gerald had simply fallen asleep and wasn't then locked in a losing battle to keep his hand from lashing out, smacking Clayton upside the head. His arm had stiffened so Clayton might as well have been knocking against a tree and he seemed to get the point from that. He kept quiet for a few moments and then:

So what's with all them buses and cars anyway?

What do you mean? the old man asked.

Why— I mean, where'd they all come from?

Down south.

Things must have got pretty bad down there.

You could say that.

We under attack?

Attack?

By the Americans.

The Americans? Where'd you hear that?

I don't know. Around. Are we under attack or not?

Not that I heard.

So what's with all the cars?

They're on a cause of the pickerel plant.

The pickerel plant?

It done went up. Radiated the whole damn city.

What city?

Toronto, what'dya think?

The pickerel— You mean Pickerin'?

Is that what it's called?

If you're talking about the Pickering nuclear power plant, it is.

I guess that's the one.

And you're saying it went up?

That's what one of the soldiers told me anyway.

The same one killed someone over less than junk?

No, that was a young fellow. This one was older.

And what'd he say?

Only what I told you. He wasn't much in the mood for talking. Can't say as I blame him. It was a real shit-show there for a while. I guess it probably still is, somewhere.

And when was this?

When the plant went up.

Yeah?

Oh, four, five weeks ago now. You never heard about it? You really must have been living under a rock not to hear about that.

No, we—

Clayton had the good sense to stop there. Then after a moment:

You hear anything about Marmora?

What's that?

It's a town. Where I come from.

Never heard of it.

It's just outside of Peterborough. You heard of Peterborough?

Course I heard of Peterborough.

It's only an hour drive from Pickering.

Then I expect it's been evacuated too.

Clayton was quiet a moment, must have been thinking on that.

Is that why the power went out? he said after a few breaths.

What?

On account of the plant going up?

No, the power'd been out for days by then.

And you ain't never heard wh—

Clayton felt Gerald's hand clamp on his leg and if that wasn't enough to shut him up, the faint groan of an engine surely was. It rose as a sudden swell, like a gust of wind carrying a hint of thunder, fading just as quickly as it had arisen and then rumbling forth again.

They waited until the engine had passed overhead and then they emerged from the tunnel, Mia leading the way, Gerald following after her, and Clayton and the old man behind him. After the tunnel's cloying heat the open air felt coolish, though it couldn't have been much less than thirty degrees.

You live around here? Clayton asked as he stretched his neck against a cramp.

The old man eyed him with a wary look.

Not far, he said.

You got any food?

The old man averted his gaze, looking at the dog by his feet, and then bending and picking her up, cradling her to his chest.

Food's pretty scarce these days.

What about a map? This from Gerald.

A map? Of what?

Ontario.

No, I ain't got a map. Where you looking to be?

Capreol.

Capreol? That where you from?

You know it?

Heard tell. Then shooting Gerald a quick glance: And you said your name was Gerald?

Not me—

But your friend did.

You must have misheard.

Gerald was looking at him with a hardened glare and the old man didn't seem inclined to press the point.

Capreol, he said after a moment. That's just north of Sudbury, ain't it?

Gerald nodded.

Quickest way would've been to take the highway. But you don't want to do that.

Thinking for a moment, chewing on his lip.

You could take the tracks.

The train tracks?

They'll lead you right there, last I heard. Mind you, it'd be a fair slog through the bush to get to them.

I never much minded a slog through the bush.

In the dim light Gerald could just make out the old man nodding his head.

No, he said, I wouldn't expect *you* would.

The sudden flutter came out of the trees with the bluster of a moose's stampede, peppering them with a shower of broken twigs and startling Clayton into a gallop like he thought he was about to be trampled. He'd only made it a few steps before he saw that it was a grouse, itself startled by their trespass and now in frantic flight for the safety of some higher perch. It was fattened from its summer forage and hardly seemed like it should be able to fly at all. But somehow it made it onto the branch of a fledgling elm tree, a meagre seven or eight feet off the ground, not ten paces from where Clayton stood gazing after it with laboured breaths.

The ground at their feet was pebbled with stones overgrown with moss, a dried-up creek bed that for the past half hour had been leading them roughly northeast, or so said the compass that had come with the Car Buddy. The dawn had broken about the same time as they'd found the creek. Its light wasn't yet strong enough to render the sky anything but a froth of milky white, but it was plenty bright for Gerald to locate a stone about the size and shape of a flattened mandarin orange amongst the rubble.

Cinching it between his thumb and forefinger he stalked past Clayton, who had since become wise to Gerald's game and had taken to staring back at the bird with a hungry lust tinged with the ecstasy of revenge.

Don't get too close now, he whispered when Gerald had come to within ten feet of the elm tree. You'll startle it.

Gerald ignored him. Grouse weren't overly bright and once they'd found the safety of a higher perch, you could practically come close enough to grab them before they took flight again. He paused only when he'd come to within five feet of the bird, cocking his arm back and exhaling slow and steady as he might have done if he'd been holding a rifle instead of a rock, letting fly with the same easy stroke he'd have used skipping a stone.

The rock struck the bird in the breast, knocking it from its perch even as it made a flustered attempt at flight, its one wing broken and useless and its other lashing about in frantic palpitations driving it downwards harder still. It had barely hit the ground, flopping about and squeaking like a rat caught in a trap, when Gerald was upon it. He grabbed it by the neck and wrung the life out of it with a quick jerk of his wrist.

Afterwards they collected a half dozen stones apiece, pocketing five and each keeping one in their hand at the ever-ready. Gerald had also picked up a stick and as they forded along the creek bed they both used theirs to knock against passing tree trunks. In this way they startled four more birds from the undergrowth. Three of these also came to roost on a low hanging branch and he let Clayton have a first go at each of them. He missed with every throw and Gerald killed two of them the same way as he had the other. After Clayton missed again with the next, Gerald found a flat boulder about the height of a picnic table and set the three birds he'd killed on that. While he began the onerous task of plucking them without the benefit of a pot of boiling water he watched Clayton throw six stones at the last bird. It had come to roost on a branch in a beech tree not six feet off the ground and none of Clayton's throws came close enough to give it any reason to depart.

Use your stick, Gerald offered while Clayton stuffed his pockets with a few more rocks.

What?

Your stick. Walk up to it and knock it on the head.

It'll just fly away.

Not if you make like you don't see it. They ain't overly bright. If it thinks you can't see it, it'll let you walk right up.

Clayton grimaced his disbelief but turned back to the bird nonetheless. He approached it with delicate footsteps, his eyes averted to the ground, Gerald all the while watching after him, thinking about how he said he'd planned to set off into the wilds after he'd killed his stepfather and here him not even having enough sense to know how to hunt a grouse.

When Clayton had come to within a few paces of the beech tree, he glanced back at Gerald, seeking reassurance. Gerald waved him on and he took one more step, his foot *crackl*ing over a fallen branch and the bird taking sudden flight. Clayton cursed, Shit!, and thrust after it with a vain swipe, striking his stick on the branch upon which it had sat, and that serving only to break off its end. The four-inch piece flew, pinwheeling, after the grouse, Gerald watching in disbelief as it hit one of the bird's wings, knocking it off kilter and sending it reeling into the trunk of an oak tree.

Clayton stumbled after it, chasing it in frenzied mimicry of its palsied flop over the ground, Gerald even then giving the bird ten-to-one odds that it would somehow end up coming out on top.

They found the tracks two days later with the sun fading towards evening, its shine broken into parallel shimmers along either rail, leading on a straight path through the forest.

The mosquitoes that had plagued them most of the morning had relented to the day's simmer though the deerflies never had. A horde of them buzzed in dive-bomber fashion about their heads and crawled into the drape of their shirts, Clayton flailing at them in mounting hysteria and then surging forward, limping as fast as his wounded leg would carry him down the tracks, as if he could outrun their menace. Gerald knew better and sufficed to swat at them as he ambled in pursuit.

You ever seen so many deerflies? Clayton asked when he'd caught up with him.

Just wait till we get to Capreol.

They's bad in Capreol?

I once seen 'em carry off a dog who made the mistake of falling asleep on the porch, Gerald said. It was something his grandfather had often joked about. Last I saw of the dog was it disappearing over the treeline. They's bad all right.

Blueberries grew in wide swathes along the embankment and there were other berries too, sun-shrivelled raspberries and blackberries the size and shape of thimbles. They descended from the tracks at leisurely intervals, eating to their heart's content and then starting off again in their weary trod. Clayton had filled his water bottle with the fruit and took gulps from this as he struggled along behind, Gerald stopping every few paces to let him catch up.

How's your leg holding out? he asked when he'd come into the shade of a rock cut. A trickle of rust-tinged water drained out of a crack in the granite's wall and Gerald pressed his lips to it, slurping at the liquid tasting of dirt and leaving a coppery dryness in his mouth.

Feels like the dressing's full of broken glass.

Clayton filled his bottle from the trickle and then shook it up with the berries. Its orange tint turned to blue and he gulped half of it down in one swoop and then filled the bottle again.

How far you figure it's to Capreol? he asked as he recapped the bottle.

A fair ways yet. Three hundred kilometres, maybe more.

I ain't never going to make it on this leg.

Gerald didn't have much to say to that. He looked down the tracks to keep from seeing the despair in Clayton's eyes.

Why don't you rest awhile, he said after a moment. I'll see if I can't find some more of that staunchweed.

He wasn't more than a few hundred yards into the forest atop the rock cut when he caught sight of a flick of white.

Looking up and seeing the tail end of a doe bounding off to the left with its jackrabbit hop, zigzagging across a meadow and forsaking the cover of trees as if its aim was something other than mere flight. Habit had Gerald scanning to the right, sighting at once another deer poised at the edge of the meadow. Its coat was darker than the first and it was smaller. An adolescent. It was frozen, statuesque, and staring straight at him, Gerald holding his breath and hearing Evers's voice as clear as day.

Why'd it just stand there like that? It's almost like it wanted me to shoot it.

He'd been five when he'd said it. They'd spent the morning creeping through the woods on the far side of The Ridge, not ten minutes north of their house. Evers was carrying the bow Gerald had made him and Gerald was unarmed except for the knife sheathed at his belt, for they weren't after deer that day, weren't after anything in particular except maybe a chance for Evers to make his first kill, a chipmunk or maybe a squirrel. The rustle of leaves at their feet had startled a doe from its graze. Evers had brought the bow to bear, drawing back the arrow notched in its string, but before he could release, Gerald had set his hand on the boy's shoulder, stilling him and pointing to the other deer, not more than twenty paces hence. Evers had swung around, sighting on it and inhaling one long slow breath, as his father had taught him. Just before he was to release, Gerald had grabbed at the arrow, staying the shot. The deer had bounded away and Evers had looked up at him, frowning in petulant dismay.

What are you doing? he scowled. I had it in my sights.

Oh, I know, Gerald consoled. But that bow ain't strong enough to kill a deer. Probably just have wounded it and that wouldn't have been fair to the deer.

But if I'd wounded it, Evers countered, you could've chased it down. You done it before, ain't ya?

How'd you know about that? For he'd never once mentioned it to the boy.

Mom told me all about it.

She did, did she?

Said you lit after it one time when you was hiking on the other side of the lake. She said she thought you'd abandoned her in the woods, you were gone so long. Said she was some mad—

Mad, hell. She was fixing to skin me alive.

An hour or some later she heard you whistling. When she finally tracked you down, you were carrying the deer over your shoulder.

I was carrying the deer over my shoulder? That what she said?

Uh huh.

Well, your mother does tend to exaggerate.

While they were walking home Evers had asked him about the second deer.

Why'd it just stand there like that? It's almost like it wanted me to shoot it.

No, it weren't that. It just thought you'd go after his mother. I'da guess that's why she was making such a ruckus while she run away.

You'da guess?

I don't know for sure. I ain't read it in no book or nothing. Just something I've noticed over the years.

The boy had thought on that.

Just like that grouse we saw the one time, he'd said after a moment.

Gerald had nodded, knowing exactly what he'd meant.

One morning, that same spring, they'd been walking up the trail to the lake and it had swooped past them, clipping Gerald on the arm, and then diving onto the path not five feet ahead, thrashing about like it had a broken wing. Evers had chased after it, just like Clayton had, except it wasn't really wounded, it was just playing at being hurt. The proof of that Gerald found in a sudden flurry of wings from the bush: a mother grouse and several of her chicks taking flight. As soon as they were safely out of sight, the other had made a miraculous recovery and flown off too, a few scant inches from Evers's grasping hands.

It's just the way of things, Gerald had concluded. Ain't no mystery to it. In nature, parents'll often sacrifice themselves to save their young. That's the way it should be. Hell, I'd do the same for you.

The boy was looking up at him like maybe he didn't quite believe what he'd said but when he spoke Gerald knew he had something else on his mind.

I hope it never comes to that, he said and Gerald had laughed.

You and me both.

A sudden shame now at the memory, flushing heat at his cheeks, thinking of how he wasn't there when Evers had needed him most, twice over now. The first after he'd shot Ellis Wilkes for the sin of killing Millie, and him and the boy had fled with reckless abandon into the northern wilds. Regardless of the story he'd told that Jordan Asche fellow during his incarceration, the nine months he'd spent on the run from the law had cemented in his mind as a form of mania — a monomaniacal flight from all reason and hope save for the promise of one more meal, one last sunset. A fragile paucity of minor triumphs that couldn't have led to anything other than insurmountable defeat, the full scope of which had haunted every one of the nights he'd spent locked in his cell at Central North, cursing himself from dusk to dawn for his vainglorious pursuit of the impossible.

The second, five years later, stuck in a prison cell as the world teetered on the brink of what, he couldn't exactly say, except it was plenty bad — maybe even The End — and his son out there to face it all alone.

His hand reached, as if by instinct, for the photo strung around his neck. Looking down at the picture and seeing Evers on the birthday rock, so fierce and wild. Hearing then someone calling out his name. A frantic dispatch that seemed to have sprung from his own addled thoughts, calling him towards home.

He heard a thin rustle and when he looked up again he caught the young deer's tail end darting into cover of the woods and he grit his teeth, his legs bent like springs, as if he meant to chase it down like the one he had before.

Gerald!

It was clearer this time and coming quite distinctly from behind him. When he turned around, Clayton was waving to him from the edge of the scrub.

I got us a lift! he hollered.

A what? Gerald yelled back.

A ride. Come on, man, they ain't going to wait all day!

By the time Gerald came back onto the top of the rock cut, Clayton was limping down its far slope towards the tracks. Gerald trailed after him, approaching the rock cut's edge with stilted caution, craning his head ever so slightly forward and looking down at the tracks.

A white pick-up truck was parked just below, the kind with retractable train wheels so it could drive right onto the rails. It had *CN* decaled in red on its front door and in the driver's seat there was a man leaning his arm out the window. He was in his forties and had an auburn beard almost as full as Gerald's and was wearing a camouflage hunting suit and a green wide-brimmed hat, could have been a Tilley. At the back of the truck was another man, younger than the first and with a neatly trimmed blond beard. He was wearing the same outfit except for a ball cap, also with a camo design, and was standing at the open tailgate, offering Clayton his hand. Clayton took that and let himself be pulled up onto the truck's bed. On its floor there was a large beaver alongside four ducks but it was towards the rifle in the younger man's other hand that Gerald's attention had become fixed. It looked to be a .303 and had a scope and a stock of some dark wood, maybe walnut.

After he'd helped Clayton into the back, the man looked up at Gerald looking down, appraising what must have appeared to him to be some sort of crazed surfer bum, such was what the dire squint that had come into his eyes told Gerald anyway. He'd since shifted the rifle into his arms, cradling it not unlike a soldier standing at ease, keeping his finger near the trigger, on guard against the possibility of a threat hitherto unrevealed.

Any reservations Gerald had about the man's intentions were put to rest by the time the truck had resumed its travels.

As it picked up speed, Gerald settled onto one of the wheel hubs in the open truck bed beside the dead ducks. He quickly surmised that the man was halfway blind and squinted as a matter of course like he was fighting a constant battle to keep whatever he was looking at in focus.

He lounged in a casual slouch against the cab, with the rifle propped beside, and the moment the truck was underway he took a pack of smokes from the breast pocket of his shirt. Lighting a cigarette, he offered the pack to Clayton, who took one with the eager fumble of an addict, and then to Gerald, who waved him off.

So where you two coming from? the man asked with his first exhale.

Up, uh, Midland way, Clayton answered. We was, uh, working there.

After lighting his cigarette, he'd laid down on the floor with his head propped up on the beaver and puffed away with the idle delight of someone spending a leisurely day at the beach.

You heard about the train all the way up in Midland? the man asked.

The train? Clayton asked right back. What train?

You ain't heard about the train?

No. We's just walking the tracks, trying to get back home.

And where's that?

Clayton opened his mouth and Gerald gave him a subtle nudge with his foot and an even more subtle shake of his head.

Uh, Clayton said stuttering. N-North Bay. It was the only place he could think of. I got family up there.

If you're going to North Bay then you're on the wrong tracks.

These tracks don't go to North Bay?

Not unless you're taking the scenic route.

Shoot. We must have taken a wrong turn.

You don't want to go to North Bay anyhow.

And why's that?

You heard about the Pickering plant?

Of course we heard about the Pickering plant. Have to be living under a rock not to hear about that. What's that got to do with North Bay?

Army diverted all traffic up Highway 11. After what happened on the 400.

That was a real shit-show, huh?

That's one word for it.

The man shook his head at the thought, smoking for a time in solemn contemplation.

Across from Gerald the forest broke into a lowland swamp. The tops of trees — spruce mostly — poked through the water's murk around the cross-thatched dome of a beaver lodge. As they passed it by there was a sudden flapping of wings and the man snapped to attention, bringing the rifle to bear at his shoulder, squinting through its scope then relaxing, seeing it was only a heron. It laboured towards the sky as heron always do, with its contradictory mix of anxious perturbulance and casual grace, the two reconciling somewhere between the swift thrust of its wings and the gangly dangle to its legs.

No, the man said, watching the heron swoop over the treeline and out of sight. I'd say you're about better off anywhere other than North Bay right now.

Exceptin' maybe Toronto.

The man looking up with a crinkled smile, finding some sort of consolation there.

I'd guess you're right about that.

They puffed on their cigarettes for a while and when he was exhaling his last, Clayton asked, You were saying something about a train?

It was me and Brett who found it, the man answered, pride swelling his voice. Brett, that's my brother. Say hello, Brett.

The driver gave a cursory wave through the cab's window and the man continued.

Found it, oh about three weeks ago now, when we was hunting. Had a neighbour worked for the CN. Told him about it. Larry, that's my neighbour's name, he's the one who got it running and drove it up to the crossroads where it's parked now. This is his truck. He lets us use it any time we want. Heck of a guy. We elected him quartermaster. Anything you need, you just ask him. I'll introduce you when we get there.

And when'll that be?

Fifteen, twenty minutes. Not long. Wait till you see it. I never could have imagined such a thing was even impossible.

How's that?

Offering a devilish grin.

I wouldn't want to spoil the surprise. You'll see.

Clayton took a last drag of his cigarette and ground it out on the floor.

You got a doctor there? he asked with eager eyes.

· No, the army took all the doctors. But we scrounged up a couple of nurses. Even built a hospital for them.

I'd sure like someone to take a look at my leg.

I was going to ask about that.

I think maybe it's getting infected.

Clayton had sat up and was unwinding the creep vines, removing the bark cast. The camomile leaves had become plastered to the wound and, wincing, he peeled them away. His calf was swollen to almost double its size and yellow puss was oozing from the ragged gash, the flesh a fiery red fading into a deep purple towards the knee.

It's infected all right, the man said.

Burns like the devil.

You get bit by a dog or something?

No— Clayton cast Gerald a skittish look that could have only meant trouble. A bear.

A bear?

A big old grizzly. Come upon me when I was sleeping. He glanced back at Gerald, who was glaring at him with mounting hostility though that hardly quieted his mouth. I guess it was looking for a midnight snack. Tried to take a chunk out of me.

This was up in Midland?

Just outside.

Ain't no grizzlies Midland way, far as I know.

Then I— I guess it must have been a black. I— I don't know. It was pretty dark. All I know is I was woke up by something biting into my leg, dragging me into the bush. Next thing, G— uh,

J-Jason here was up on top of it, plunging his knife into its eye. Killed it too with just the one stab.

He killed it with a knife, you say?

The man was squinting over at Gerald again, his pupils pulsating in rapid dilations, trying to get a fix on the other as if Gerald had given in to the sudden urge to jump up and lunge out of the truck, though the only thing moving about him at all was his jaw muscles, contracting in ligatures as taut as an elastic band about to snap.

Clayton too was staring at Gerald, his mouth hanging open, as if he was trying to think what he could say to get himself out of the mess he might have just made for them. But the man didn't seem to have drawn any undue conclusions between the stranger sitting on the wheel hub and the story his friend was telling. He clicked his teeth, shaking his head, and looked back at Clayton's leg. The wound was bad enough that it wasn't hard to imagine that a bear had done it. His hand was then reaching into his pocket and drawing out the pack of smokes.

He lit one and held the pack out to Clayton. Clayton took another and inserted it in his mouth, craning forward to let the other light it and peeking back at Gerald, finding some comfort in how the other was leaning back with his arms folded and his eyelids shut.

Sounds like you two've had one helluva time, the man said, easing his back up against the cab, the cigarette drooping out of the corner of his mouth, a pencil sketch of smoke rising from its ember and narrowing his eyes to slits.

Clayton drew heavy on his cigarette.

You sure as hell don't have to tell me.

G erald had almost fallen asleep to the truck's gentle *clackety-clack*.

He was shocked into wakefulness by the loud blast from a horn. The sun was glaring at him full-faced when he opened his eyes and he brought up his arm to shield them from its bright.

As the truck slowed to a gliding stop, a woman's voice rose in virulent chastisement.

Brett Townsend, it scolded, you almost made me pee my pants!

The forest had relented into a field of scrub and low-lying bushes, a lone trunk standing above them, its branches spindly and charred so that Gerald knew a fire had once raged here sometime in the not-too-distant past. Maybe twenty paces from the tracks, knee-deep in a thicket of blueberries, stood a woman wearing tan slacks and a matching turtleneck. The grey mesh of a bug hat mostly concealed her face but the frail croak to her voice and the way she stood half-stooped over with her hands contemptuously pinioned on either hip hinted at her advanced years. Beside her crouched a young girl, no older than four, dressed in a pair of pink shorts and a pink frilly shirt embroidered with a unicorn. Her hands and mouth were stained blue and a dribble of the same was running down her chin. She was staring over at the truck with something akin to genuine alarm.

Better you pee your pants, Brett said, than being food for the wolves.

Wolves?

There was a pack sighting on you through the trees when we pulled up. Five or six at least. Every one of them looking hungrier than the last.

The woman's face blanched and she spun on a hard pivot, Gerald following her alarm to the treeline, two hundred yards hence, and seeing nothing but the sun prickling at the ragged spires of the evergreens.

Lucky we came by, Brett was saying as the woman turned back. You'd have been food for the wolves for sure.

The woman was shaking her head, onto his game.

Don't you got anything better to do than scare the living daylights out of an old woman? she said. I ought to put you over my knee.

Don't you tease me now, Ella, Brett joked.

Gerald couldn't see the old woman's expression but he imagined it was somewhere between utter contempt and shameful delight. The girl beside her was bent over, stuffing her mouth with blueberries, and that at least gave the woman a reason to look away.

Slow down, Bridgette, she urged, you're going to give yourself the runs.

The truck lurched slightly forward, Brett shifting it into gear.

You need a lift back? he called over.

We just got here. The old woman had knelt and was getting set to return to her own forage. If you're heading back this way in a half hour or so . . .

I'll see you then, Brett said, adding as he applied the gas: Mind them wolves now, you hear.

T he truck slowed again as it rounded a bend.

There she is! the younger man called out.

He'd turned to face the front and Clayton clambered up beside him hopping on his one good foot as if he was worried that with the dressing off, his leg would no longer be able to support his weight. He leaned against the cab, soaking in the view and whistling his amaze through the gap in his front teeth.

You got to see this, he said cocking his head at a half turn towards Gerald though Gerald had a pretty good view of it from where he sat.

The tracks continued in their westward arc for a few hundred paces hence. Where they straightened out there was a freight car, the first in a ceaseless train spanning the distance towards the horizon. On the left, which was the direction Gerald was facing, there was another field much like the one they'd just passed, though its blueberry bramble had since been remade into a garbage dump. Within its ten or so acres, mounds of refuse rose in staggered pyramids, most of them fashioned out of brightly coloured plastics, bottles and sundry containers, the tallest maybe eight feet high, and covered with blue or orange tarps to secure them against the wind. There was a wall of brand-new tires stacked in six-foot pillars and another wall of cardboard boxes bearing the name *Maytag* stacked two by two on top of each other and ten boxes deep, and yet another wall of smaller boxes alternately stencilled *Sony* and with the black Apple logo. A cluster of brand-new mountain bikes, all of them with white frames and spelling out *CCM* in blue letters, were propped in rows against a multitude of chrome barbecues. Beside those there was a pile of what looked to be surfboards wrapped in cellophane, another of what appeared to be ornate stone fountains, and other heaps of assorted goods too numerous to absorb in such a few short moments. It looked like the backlot of a Walmart on delivery day, such was the impression that it made on Gerald, and at first he thought that was what Clayton must have meant.

Except Clayton was looking the other way.

As the truck slowed to a stop Gerald swivelled his head towards the east to see what had marvelled Clayton so. The forest there had been clear-cut, leaving only a dozen or so blue spruce at intervals standing in solitary vigil over what looked to be a refugee camp for derelict RVs and buses, about a hundred of which were spread out over the twenty or thirty acres of cleared land, all of it teeming with the industry of its thousand or so inhabitants. There were about twice as many tents scattered among the vehicles, most of a design and colour — sky blue — that suggested they'd come out of the same box. Towards the rear, at the receding and greatly diminished treeline, someone was building what appeared to be a gazebo, one man standing in its newly erected trusses and another man on the ground, passing him a board from a stack of lumber. He could hear the stuttered knock of a hammer as the man nailed the board to the gazebo's roof, elevated above the general sort of restless murmur one could expect from so many people living in such close proximity. Mingled with their din: the caustic blare of hard rock from a speaker beside a man suntanning on the roof of his motorhome, the bark of dogs tied to staked lines and the playful snarl of the ones left free, the latter fighting in swirling packs like whirlpools of fur and teeth, their revelry muted by the buzz of chainsaws from somewhere out of view and the low grumble of quads and side-by-sides winding through the ever-shifting maze of people.

On the far northern side of the encampment there was what looked to be a pond, fifty yards deep and almost as wide. As the truck pulled to a stop at the first of the railcars blocking its way, Gerald could see that it wasn't a pond at all, it was a field of solar panels much like the one they had outside of Capreol, though this one was only about a tenth its size. And what had looked like solitary blue spruce, he now recognised as solar generators too, the kind designed to look like thirty-foot Christmas trees, just one of which, he'd heard, was capable of powering an entire household — a feat that spoke as much to humankind's ingenuity as the teeming industry of the refugee camp itself.

It was all too much to take in at a single glance (or a dozen) and Gerald sat in stunned wonder as the younger man hopped over the truck's side and strode towards its rear. He was just popping the tailgate open when a boy, maybe five, appeared from within the drape of an orange and blue tie-dyed curtain hanging over the open door at the back of the freight car five feet from the truck's front bumper. He had close-cropped brown hair and was naked save for a pair of swim shorts and a diving mask and was holding a jar of peanut butter cradled to his chest, a metal spoon clutched in his other hand. He hadn't been standing there for more than a second before he turned back to the freight container, calling out, Daddy's home!

The man looked up, beaming at his son.

Hey Bud, he called to him, what you got there?

The boy stepped to the edge of the freight car's stoop, stuck the spoon in the jar of peanut butter and held it up, as happy as a kid at Christmas.

It's peanut butter!

Peanut butter?

They opened a whole car of it. Enough for everyone. Sophie even got one.

That right? Is it the crunchy or the smooth?

Crunchy.

Oh, I like the crunchy. They find any saltines?

What's a saltee?

It's a cracker.

The boy thought hard on that for a moment, then turned back and shouted into the open door.

Mom, they find any saltees?

After a moment he turned back.

Mom said they didn't find any saltees.

That's a shame. Nothing goes better with peanut butter than saltines.

The boy didn't have anything to say to that and pried the spoon loose from the jar. It was covered with a thick dollop of the spread and the boy stuck it in his mouth, sucking at it as he might have at a lollipop.

Clayton had since hopped onto the open tailgate and the man was offering him his hand, helping him down. Brett had joined them and while he grabbed a duck in either hand, he passed a clipped glance over at Gerald, who was now standing, stretching out his back and trying not to read anything undue — recognition, perhaps — in the way the man shied away from meeting his eyes.

I'm going to get these to Lottie, Brett said to his brother. I'll be back for the beaver.

Gerald watched him struggling over the rail bed's loose gravel, thinking that if the man didn't look back, that'd mean he hadn't recognized Gerald after all.

Wendy, Brett said in greeting as he passed by the foot of the ladder leading into his brother's freight car.

There was a woman now standing at the open door. She was in her early thirties, slightly younger than Brett's brother and pretty and thin except for the unnaturally crimson hue to her cheeks — a rash of some sort — and the pregnancy bump pressing out against her summer dress's floral design. Beside her, a toddler wearing nothing but a saggy diaper was straining under the weight of the peanut butter jar in her hand, a mess of the brown goop plastered over her face and hands.

Can you ask Lottie if she has a recipe for duck that goes with peanut butter? Wendy called after her brother-in-law with a smile that seemed a little too earnest.

Brett turned towards her, raising a duck and pointing a recriminating finger.

Don't you even think of giving her any ideas, he said a little too stern, though there was already a smile cracking the corners of his frown as he craned his head a touch more, casting one last ominous glance back at Gerald before hurrying off, out of sight.

T he hospital was on the far north side of the camp.

The younger brother had produced a wheelbarrow and pushed Clayton in that. As they walked along the mud-rutted path beside the tracks, more a wagon trail than a proper road, he greeted everyone they met with a broad smile and nod. Most answered him with a quiet deference — nods of their own and shy smiles — and a few called out in passing, Devon! In this way Gerald and Clayton came to know his name and also that he'd assumed a position of some prominence amongst his fellow refugees, as likely because of his unwavering affability as because he was one of the camp's founders.

All the freight cars they passed had also been converted into domiciles. Laundry lines were strung between most of them and extension cords snaked through drilled holes in their steel frames. Emanating from each were all the sounds one might expect in any busy household: the insistent cry of babies, the sprightly banter from a children's cartoon and the *rat-a-tat-tat* of videogame gunfire, the hushed patter of voices gossiping over coffee, the oddly out-of-place domesticity of a vacuum cleaner's buzz. There was hardly anything at all in the constituency of its parts to suggest calamity but as Gerald trailed behind Clayton and Devon the whole of it spoke to a catastrophe well beyond any attempt at a sober reckoning.

There's Larry now, Devon said as they approached a white freight car, the first of a dozen in a row, the gentle hum of their fans telling Gerald they were refrigerated.

The simmer of grilling meat infused with hickory smoke drew Gerald's attention to a thin and pale man, sixty or so, wearing a black ball cap with *CN* embroidered in red on its front and flipping steaks on a charcoal barbecue at the foot of the ladder leading into the refrigerator car. A woman, about the same age, was sitting on a garden bench a few feet past under the shade of a patio umbrella zip-tied to the bench's back. She was wearing a simple tan dress and keeping one eye on the page of the hardcover book in her lap and the other on a toddler in a one-piece and bucket hat who was trying to wrestle a knotted rope away from a growling pug.

Hey Larry, Devon called out and when the woman looked up from her book, smiling as warm as if she was greeting a favourite grandchild, he added, Afternoon, Chris.

She went back to reading her book and Larry turned squinting towards them.

Looks like you might have brought some weather with you, he said.

Devon glanced back the way they'd come. Sure enough a vanguard of black clouds was amassing just above the treeline on either side of the tracks and the stiffening breeze brought with it the inchoate smell of rain.

At least it ain't the only thing I brung, he answered.

He'd set the wheelbarrow down and was reaching for the duck he'd slung over the wheelbarrow's handles.

Ain't she a beauty, Larry said as he passed it over.

Well, you said you were getting sick of eating steak.

You got that right. We opened another carful this morning.

More Leadbetter's?

Yeah. Having a sale on them. Buy one, get one hundred for free. You need any?

I already got six defrosted in my fridge.

What about your friends? Then looking from Clayton to Gerald: You hungry?

I'm about half-starved, Clayton said.

Well boy have I got the cure for that.

He forked one of the steaks onto a cardboard plate and added to that a cob of corn still in its husk from the stack piled on the grill behind the meat.

Sorry, we don't have any butter for the corn, he said as he passed it over.

But that was the last thing on Clayton's mind. He'd picked up the steak in his bare hands and was already three bites in before Larry handed another plate to Gerald.

They the mesquite again? Devon asked, seemingly to pass the time.

No, the hickory.

Oh, I like the hickory.

Larry was shaking his head, mirthful, watching the two men devour the steaks.

God, they really are half-starved.

They should be. They walked in from Midland.

Midland? They heard about the train all the way down there?

They say they were just walking the tracks. This one's Jason, and he's— I never did get your name.

Clayton, he answered, stuffing the last of the steak in his mouth and tearing at the cob's husk. Clayton Crisp.

Larry had forked another steak from the grill and was dropping it on the plate in Clayton's lap.

God they's good, Clayton said.

Plenty more where that came from.

Larry gave Gerald another too and even before Gerald had taken his first bite he was thinking about the four still on the grill.

Plenty of corn too. Then turning to Devon: I could fill the wheelbarrow up for you.

I got a dozen still.

What about coleslaw?

When'd you get coleslaw.

Opened a car a couple of hours ago.

Is it the creamy or the Dixie?

Dixie?

The one with the bigger chunks? And sometimes carrots?

That's the one.

I only like the creamy.

What about Texas toast?

What's that?

It's garlic toast wrapped in tinfoil. You cook it on the barbecue.

You find any spaghetti sauce?

Not yet.

Nothing better with garlic toast than spaghetti.

Ain't that the truth.

You'll tell me if any comes in?

You'll be the first to know.

L arry had given each another steak and cob of corn for the
way.

Gerald had finished the former and was starting on the latter
as they passed two water trucks parked on the far side of the
path leading along the tracks. The first was dispensing water to a
lineup of people carrying jugs and the second had a firefighter's
hose leading into a building fashioned out of chinked logs and
labelled with a sign that read *Showers*. Beyond these there was
a row of porta-potties — a dozen in all — and those more than
anything lent the place a festival-like atmosphere. Thinking
that recalled to Gerald how he'd thought the same thing when
he'd first come into the prison's field after being freed from his
cell, and look how that had turned out. Each subsequent step
increased his dread at even pace with the certainty that there had
to be a catch here somewhere. With Brett's ominous glance so
fresh in his mind, he got to thinking that maybe the only catch
was simply that there was no place at the settlement for him.

Clayton had said something, Gerald didn't catch what, and
Devon was answering, We got a saying around here, Just ask
and the train shall provide. Those solar panels were in one car
and them solar spruce in another. And you see where they's
building that gazebo?

He pointed towards the rear of the camp.

It came out of a car too. There was fifty of them, which seemed
kind of useless at the time and then someone got the idea that if
you put a few of them together they'd be perfect as a bandstand.
We're going to have a concert come Saturday. Already got a half
dozen acts signed up.

Shoot, I'd like to see that, Clayton enthused.

Well you're going to, come Saturday.

I can't believe you did this in a few short weeks.

Just people helping people, that's all it is.

They'd come to a T in the path. One way continued on along the tracks past the solar pond and the other turned right, leading past a row of RVs on its way to a green canvas tent with a large red cross painted on its peaked roof. The tracks beyond the T split into two lines as well, one running parallel to the other. The outer one was all freight cars and the inner one just four black cylinders, petroleum most likely. Two soldiers tethering a German shepherd on a lead were walking their way and several others were stationed on top of the containers, standing watch at intervals.

Seeing them, Clayton clenched his knapsack tight to his chest, no doubt thinking about what the old man with the dog had warned what a soldier was likely to do with someone caught looting.

What's with the soldiers? he whispered as Devon turned the wheelbarrow towards the hospital tent.

They showed up a couple of weeks ago, said they'd come to protect the fuel.

Protect it? Protect it from who?

They didn't say.

A fella we ran into said half the army was down the road a stretch.

They set up in Parry Sound. They got a refugee camp there for all them people fleeing Toronto. Most of them were pretty sick with the radiation, far as I heard.

You seen it?

Devon shook his head.

No, but I've met plenty of people who have. More than enough to know I'd never want to.

They trundled on, none of them talking until Devon had pushed the wheelbarrow up to the two closed flaps at the front of the hospital tent.

Here we are, he said, raising the wheelbarrow's handles to allow Clayton to wriggle out.

You're okay taking it from here? he said, turning to Gerald.

Gerald nodded and Clayton, wiping his hands on his shirt, reached out, grabbing him by the arm to support himself.

If you need anything else, Devon said as he spun the wheelbarrow around, you know where to find me.

Just inside the flaps, cordoned off with a sheet of green canvas, was a waiting room big enough to house ten folding chairs, all of them empty, and a small desk painted a metallic grey, in the chair behind which sat a woman in green scrubs. She looked about the same age as Clayton — barely out of her teens — her youth further evidenced by a pimple she'd picked to a scab at the corner of her mouth. Otherwise her skin had a milky white complexion, unblemished except for a smattering of caramel-coloured freckles on either cheek. Her long chestnut hair was woven into a thick braid and when they came in she was picking through the loose fray of it for split ends, snipping the ones she found with a pair of surgical scissors.

Setting the scissors aside, she looked up at them with a mild diffidence but even that was enough for Clayton to forsake any and all pretence of infirmity. He surged away from Gerald, swiping the rabbit-eared hat from his head and running his hand through the greasy mat of his hair in a vain effort to smooth its tangle.

The nurse shrunk a little in her seat as he approached, grimacing at him, no doubt the same as she would have if a guy like Clayton Crisp had the audacity to ask her to the high school prom.

Clayton didn't seem to register her disdain, or if he did he was used to that kind of reaction from the opposite sex such that it had long ceased to bother him.

Devon said you'd take a look at my leg, he said.

Gerald watched as the nurse craned forward ever so slightly and her frown deepened, no doubt as much a result of catching sight of the wound as by the fecundity of the body odour emanating from Clayton. She wiped her nose as if with a sudden urge to sneeze as she settled back in her chair, taking up a pen from the desk and brushing off a few snipped hairs from the piece of paper on the clipboard in front of her.

Your name? she asked.

Clayton. Clayton Crisp. That's Crisp with a C.

She wrote it down, the very act seeming to restore to her a professionalism suitable to her vocation, for when she looked back up her expression had resumed the diffidence with which she'd greeted their entrance.

And you were bit? she asked.

That right. By a b— Cutting himself off short and then leaning in closer, lowering his voice a tad. I was a bit by a dog. A big old German shepherd.

And when was this?

Three nights ago.

And have you treated the wound since?

He did. Motioning towards Gerald. Used what he called staunchweed.

The nurse looked up from her scribble, appraising the man standing just inside the flaps. She seemed to find him as lacking as the man standing before her.

Staunchweed, she said, with a dismissive upward lilt to her voice as she wrote it down.

Then:

Are you allergic to anything?

Ate a batch of mussels one time and my face swelled up like a balloon.

But no medications?

Oh, no.

Writing that down too and then standing with the clipboard, turning towards the flaps in the back of the tent and motioning for Clayton to follow.

The moment they were gone, Gerald slipped out the front door.

The sun had disappeared beyond the bank of charcoal clouds billowing in from the south and there was a warm breeze blowing in from the same, carrying with it the now distinct smell of rain on asphalt. An elderly couple walking a black Lab on a leash passed by and this was followed by a young couple swinging a three-year-old boy by the arms between them and an elderly Black man with a towel slung over his shoulder, naked save for flip-flops, purple trunks and a matching swim cap. All of them nodded to Gerald, who returned the gesture even as his gaze roved over the camp, not looking for anything in particular until it had settled on a group of four men standing at the tracks where the road divided in two, knowing then that was what he'd been searching for all along.

Brett was foremost among the men and he was pointing towards the hospital. He wasn't looking at Gerald but two of the other men were, each casting specious glances his way and then turning back to the fourth man. He was dressed all in blue and elsewise nodding with the formal countenance of a cop as Brett spoke in urgent bursts. Gerald couldn't hear what he was saying and had no way to confirm that they were even talking about him but given the solemnity instilled in the bob of the cop's head it might just as well have been, *Way I heard, he's a stone-cold killer, as likely to shoot you in the head as give you the time of day.*

The cop nodding again and setting his hand on Brett's shoulder, maybe answering, *If it is him you're lucky to still be alive, that's for sure. And one thing else is for sure, he isn't likely to come quiet. We got to be smart about this.*

The three men listening with rapt nods of their own so it wasn't hard to imagine the cop feeding them instructions on how to best go about apprehending such a violent man as Savage Gerry, the first of which would be to go fetch their rifles, maybe round up a few other people.

We'll meet back at the bandstand in, oh, five minutes.

The men were already turning away when the cop said something else, his hands moving in a downward suppressing motion so it could very well have been, *And whatever you do, keep it on the down-low, you hear?*

Brett and the other two men stalked away along the row of freight cars, picking up speed with every step. A young boy ran past them, heading the other way. All of a sudden he tripped, falling right in front of the cop. The officer responded by helping the boy up, dusting off his shirt before sending him on his way with a friendly pat on the head, and with the lawman momentarily distracted, Gerald ducked back into the waiting room.

He stood just inside the flaps, breathing hard and his eyes darting about, finding the desk empty and then striding on a straight line for the flaps leading into the back. He hadn't made it halfway there before they opened and the pretty young nurse appeared from within, her expression startling at the man surging towards her, everything about him seeming to suggest he was about to attack her. Gerald catching the look of fright and stopping short, swallowing hard and catching her off guard with the joviality of his tone.

I was just going to check on my friend, is that okay?

Nurse Maddox is still with him, she answered, putting the desk unmistakably between herself and Gerald. It'll just be a few minutes. You can see him then.

T he nurse disappeared back through the flaps shortly after, maybe spooked by Gerald's restless jitter.

He'd tried sitting in one of the chairs, acting all casual, but hadn't managed that for more than a few seconds. An increasingly dire scenario was playing out in his thoughts and that had driven him back to his feet. Standing at the flaps and peeking out through a crack, not seeing anything to prove him right but thinking nevertheless, *It'll be any moment now.*

Tracking in his angst the likely progress of the posse he was certain was then amassing at the bandstand, six or seven men all with rifles and the cop with his sidearm, the latter charting the plan with a stick in the dirt.

We'll station two men around back, in case he tries to escape. Another here — drawing an X on one side of the tent — and one man here. The rest of us will go in the front. I'll take the lead.

Standing back up then, taking out his gun and checking the cartridge, not to make sure it's loaded — he already knows it is — but because it lends the necessary imperative to what he has to say next.

This is a dangerous man, a real psycho. He killed three men in cold blood already, two of them peace officers. If we don't do this right, we could be looking at a hostage situation, so if you see a shot, you take it. That understood?

All the men nodding with solemn expressions suitable to their task.

All right then, let's go!

Gerald so certain about his impending doom that he turned towards the rear of the camp, looking for any sign to tell him he was right. The bandstand was hidden behind the haphazard maze of RVs and tents and he couldn't tell if they were marching away from that or not. Otherwise he saw no evidence to either confirm or deny his suspicions and yet that only gave him further cause for worry.

You can see him now.

Gerald jerked his head towards the nurse.

She was standing behind the desk, her hands on the back of the chair, her fingers drumming a nervous patter on its wooden frame, looking ever so much like someone who'd been briefed on the situation and was sent back in to maintain the illusion that everything was still on the up and up.

Could be they were waiting to grab him the moment he stepped through the flaps, or maybe they'd just start shooting.

Telling himself, *If they really were back there, they'd have never sent the girl. They'd have just shot you through the flaps.*

That not seeming too likely either.

If they missed or the bullets tore right through him, there was nothing but a thin layer of canvas to stop them from hitting someone in the camp. The cop would've thought of that.

No, they'd be lying in wait for you outside. Hell, they probably already are.

Nodding to himself even though the whole thing was seeming more far-fetched with every passing breath, all there was to tell him it wasn't just his imagination running wild being the race of his heart and the sudden impulse to lunge through the tent flaps, come what may.

You want to see him or not?

The nurse was looking at him like she could read his thoughts and Gerald gave her a pinched smile as he moved on quickening legs towards the back of the waiting room. He burst through the flaps into a much larger space. The front half of it had been sectioned off into cubicles made out of the same green canvas as the tent, three to a side. Beyond these there was an open area lined with beds resembling army cots. All the ones he could see were empty and the spaces between cluttered with a wide array of medical equipment, a defibrillator and saline bags on poles, heart rate monitors and a refrigerator. It was the back wall of the tent he was most interested in though and he stalked past the examination cubicles, trying to divine if there was another way out.

He could hear a phlegmatic cough from the first of the cubicles, eclipsed by the reassuring croak of an old woman's voice.

You're doing great, honey. Get it all up. You'll feel better when you do.

From the cubicle across the hallway there rose then the voice of another woman carrying a much sterner demeanour.

I don't care when the last time was you had a shower, you're not to get out of that bed until I say so and that's an order.

She'd hardly finished when the last curtain on the left opened and a woman backed out from within. She was wearing a stethoscope and a doctor's lab coat and had a thick wash of starch-white hair pulled back into a ponytail. That and the folds of deeply tanned skin wrinkling her face into a desertscape placed her age anywhere between sixty and seventy-five, though there was something decidedly more youthful about her than that. Her eyes maybe, the brilliant bluish-green of a tropical sea undiminished by the passage of time, and also the spring to her step as she intercepted Gerald on his way past.

You must be Jason, she smiled. And then she did look her age, her teeth yellowed and streaked with brown, and the unmistakable musk of a body in decay about her.

Uh, Gerald said, confused for a minute and then remembering. Yes. Jason, that's me.

Your friend's been asking for you.

Looking downwards at him, for she was a tall woman, approaching six feet. The gentle, almost shy, curl of her lips and the strand of hair in a casual drape about her cheeks again lent her the impression of a much younger woman. She set her hand on Gerald's arm and opened her mouth as if to say something when a violent fit of coughing erupted from across the hall.

Nurse! the old woman's voice called out. Nurse!

Excuse me.

Gerald watched after the nurse until she'd stepped into the other cubicle and then turned towards the rear of the tent, telling himself he wouldn't get a better chance than this.

That you out there, uh, Jason?

Taking one more step and then cursing under his breath, turning on a hard pivot and pitching through the tent flaps on the last cubicle.

There you are, Clayton said, grinning wide. I thought maybe you'd took off on me again.

He was lying on a stretcher, with the head rest raised. His leg was dressed with gauze wrapped from his knee to his ankle and there was about him the sharp odour of antiseptics.

I was just outside. Checking on the line for the showers.

Boy, I sure could use one too. I can barely stand the smell of my *own* stink. But Nurse Maddox said I had to stay in bed.

That's good advice.

She also said you might'n maybe have saved my leg with that staunchweed, only she called it yarrow.

It was just lucky I found some, is all.

Lucky, hell. I'd been dead twice over if it weren't for you.

Clayton was staring at him again with that unbridled adulation and it made Gerald feel as uncomfortable as it did the first time, doubly so for what he was planning to do.

He averted his eyes.

I ought to get going, he said. Clean myself up a bit.

He was turning towards the curtain when Clayton spoke again.

I'm going to be holed up here for a couple of days, he said. Nurse Maddox said, if you want, there'd be a spare bed for you too.

I might just take her up on that.

Parting the curtain, he moved on stealthy steps towards the back wall, seeing a seam in the canvas that might just have been his way out.

Can I help you with something?

The young nurse was standing beside the first of the cots, hidden from view by the back wall of the last cubicle across from Clayton's. She was holding a plastic bottle in her hand like the ones bleach came in and was about to pour it into a metal bowl, maybe sterilizing some instruments. She was glaring at Gerald as if she suspected he was up to no good.

Gerald took a hard left, sidling towards her as if on the sly, all nonchalant, no different than he would have approaching a nurse in a real hospital looking for directions to the bathroom.

Say, he asked in an urgent whisper, is there a back way out of here?

T he wind had picked up some.

  As Gerald tore through the woods couched along the eastern side of the settlement he could hear it thrashing about the treetops and in the ominous creak of Jack pines, the frantic rustle of poplar leaves whispering to him what seemed a dire warning and harrying him onwards as heedless as to what they had to say as he was to the wind's bluster, sheltered from the force of its gale not so much by the trees as the forest proper, as if the latter weren't merely an accumulation of the former but an entity unto itself — a living, breathing thing all of its own, the trees themselves as irrelevant as the sprouts of hair upon the chin of a beast that had swallowed him whole.

  It wasn't but a couple minutes later that the forest broke at the edge of a lake. He came to its shore, gasping, his legs feeling like they'd turned to rubber, a sad state of affairs for a man who'd once taken pride in his stamina above all else. He stood there a moment staring out at the water, trying to catch his breath.

It wasn't a big lake, maybe a half kilometre across at its widest and twice as long. Grey swells rippled away from the shore in mimicry of the ones bludgeoning the sky. The swells further out were capped with curls of white, and the sun was a pale disc refracted within its turmoil as if it wasn't cast from above but from below, a distant beacon straining up from some underworld realm, calling out to him in warning or distress, there was no way to tell.

He stood there staring at it until between one swell and the next it disappeared, swept under by the waves as if it had been drowned. There was almost immediately then a clap of thunder, so loud it might as well have been two mountains colliding as weather fronts. It was rumbling itself out when he heard the barking of dogs. They arose as a sprinkle of rain would on far-off leaves and merged into such a sudden and urgent threat that the thought startled into his head, *They're coming for ya!*

Shocked into flight and running with the desperation of a fox with the hounds on its tail, though hardly with the same grace, crashing blindly through the trees buffeting the lake, not so much a forest now as a loose conglomeration of impediments put in his way to trip him up.

Hearing the dogs barking, closer yet, and dashing into a bog of cattails crowding the shore. He sank up to his waist before he made his third step and waded on until he was up to his chest then crouched down low until the murky water was lapping over his chin. He heard another clipped bark followed by a growl and scanned back the way he'd come.

There were two golden retrievers fifty paces away. They'd found a black garbage bag someone had tossed into the woods. It had been torn open and the one dog was licking at a bubble of plastic like the packaging that vacuum-sealed steaks came in, barking and growling at the other whenever it came too close. He heard then the grumble of an engine and a man's voice calling out, Buster, get away from there!

Through the cattails all he could see of the man was that he had a swollen gut pressing against a black-and-red button-down shirt and was wearing a yellow ball cap. He was sliding out of the driver's seat of a side-by-side, one of those with a roof so that it looked like a golf cart with oversized wheels, and chiding after the dog, What I tell you about eating garbage? Go on, shoo!

He swatted at it with a hand that didn't come within five feet of it but the dog acted like it had been kicked, whimpering and turning tail, fleeing in a widening arc away from the man, the other dog watching it with lolling tongue so that it looked like it was laughing at its friend. The man, Gerald could now see, was wearing work gloves. He bent at the garbage bag, plucking the wrappers from the ground and stuffing them back through the hole in its plastic, picking the bag up delicately then between both hands, all the while muttering to the dogs or maybe just to himself, Goddamn pigs. It would have taken them more effort to haul the bag out here than bring it to the dumpster. Ignorant sons of bitches!

He'd brought the bag to the side-by-side and was heaving it onto the garbage already piled high in the trailer hitched behind, Gerald watching the man slide back into the driver's seat and turn the vehicle around, feeling more the fool by the second.

You're no better than Clayton scared by that grouse.

He'd extricated himself from the muck and was following a deer path leading him around the lake's western shore. The thought of Clayton produced in him a sudden shame, for leaving him as he had and for also lying to him, making him think he was coming back. Seeing the familiar gloss of unbridled admiration in his eyes and hearing his voice echoing from some distant recess, *I'd have been dead twice over if it weren't for you.* Imagining what would have happened to him in the moments following his own cowardly escape.

That cop coming into the waiting room, his gun at the ready, sighting on the empty space, waving a hand back through the door flaps, motioning for someone on the other side. Brett coming in with his rifle, the others already scattering about the perimeter a moment too late to see their quarry slipping out the rear, the nurse when he'd asked pointing at it wordlessly — relieved, it seemed to Gerald, that he was looking for a way out — not towards the back of the tent but to the far side, between two of the cots where there was a slit cut in the canvas sealed with Velcro, handwritten letters in black marker running vertical on either side reading EMERGENCY and EXIT.

The nurse then stepping through the flaps and Gerald seeing her startled docility in the way she faced the cop and her gaping back at him like a deer sighting on a hunter, certain that if it didn't move it wouldn't be seen. The cop stalking towards her with the wary resolve of a wolf, whispering, Where is he?

The nurse starting, I— then stopping, fairly certain she knew who he meant and yet not so certain that it didn't give her pause to consider.

Who?

Gerald Nichols.

The cop impatient, blurting it out, perhaps a little too loud, loud enough anyway that if his quarry was still hiding in the back he'd be able to hear it. The name meaning nothing to the nurse and the cop seeing that, adding, The man who just came in here. Looked like a crazed surfer bum.

The nurse startled into docility again.

Is he here or not?

He—

What?

He went out the back.

When?

A minute ago?

Her voice upraised at the end, for that uncertainty had returned, making her question herself, her relief at getting rid of the man, thinking now she'd done something wrong not reporting someone so blatantly suspicious right away.

The cop cursing under his breath as he turned back to Brett but before he could say a word beyond a muttered, Shit, the nurse interrupting him, eager to make amends.

But his friend is still here.

That giving the cop pause to consider and Brett asking, What do you want us to do there, chief?

The cop answering, Well I reckon you better fetch the dogs.

Except he wouldn't have said "I reckon" like some small-town sheriff in one of those old westerns Gerald and his grandfather used to watch and whom, the older he got, the more his grandfather had begun to sound just like. Gramps most certainly would have used "reckon" though it would come out "reckin" in his adoptive Southern twang. But the cop he'd seen earlier would have more than likely used "I guess" or "I suppose" or some suitable substitution deprived of any and all colloquial seasoning but still making his point clear enough.

The sound of their pursuit startling you as the wind lashed against the trees, except it wasn't them coming after you, it was just someone cleaning up the woods.

That doing little to counter the feeling that he was being chased. Likely he was already outside any sense of jurisdiction the cop would have contrived for himself, the limits of which would have begun and ended with the camp that had sprung up around the train and wouldn't, surely, have extended this far into the bush, especially since Gerald hadn't harmed the cop or his family, nor anyone within the entirety of his purview.

These musings failing to account for much but, in the very least, bringing him back to where he'd started from.

It weren't fright made you run, he told himself. *It was shame. The shame of leaving the scarecrow behind, or rather, the shame of having to face him again after they'd led you back into the camp.*

They'd likely put you in one of them empty freight cars until they've figured out what to do with you.

Seeing its door opening and the fading light chasing at its dark, finding Clayton sitting against its rear wall, squinting against its bright as they manhandled Gerald inside, hearing the clank of the door shutting as terminally as the clank of the one in his jail cell, every damn night he'd spent at Central North.

Except . . .

The word forming in his mind without any instigation from him, as if his subconscious somehow knew better and Gerald flummoxing after it, trying to make any sense as to why that word would have suddenly sprouted in his mind.

Except . . .

Turning the word over on his tongue and that leading quite naturally to the thought:

Except you weren't thinking about Clayton when you'd heard the dogs, you were thinking about . . . Evers.

Remembering that first gust of wind thrashing through the trees, like something had burst, unleashing a gale with the force of a dam breaking. Looking up at the ominous sway and hearing the creak of Jack pines and the frantic whisper of poplar leaves, recalling the last time he'd done so. It was six days before him and Evers had been caught by Charlie Wilkes, whose own purview would have extended to the ends of the earth if that's what it took to bring the man who'd murdered two of his sons to justice.

They'd had a few close calls the previous year, the odd helicopter on the horizon, the drift of smoke that could have been a hunting party as likely as someone hunting them, once the distant yelp of dogs, the latter keeping them on the move for four days until a hard rain had finally washed away any semblance of their scent. It was the day after that they'd lit their first fire, to dry their clothes and to heat the last can of beans squirreled away in Gerald's backpack, saving it for a special occasion and their escape from the dogs seeming plenty special enough.

While the beans simmered on the fire Evers had suddenly asked, Why'd they have to go and kill mom?

It seemed to have bubbled out of nowhere though it was plain in the way he'd been fretting with a stick, stoking it in the fire, that he'd been brooding on it for some time.

It was a-an accident, Gerald answered, the tremble in his voice making it seem not altogether the truth. They were shooting at me. They didn't know they'd hit your mom.

Why were they shooting at you?

Gerald thinking of the bear trap springing around Ellis Wilkes's leg even as he said, It was just a mis— a misunderstanding.

If it was just a misunderstanding, then why'd you go and shoot those men?

Gerald didn't have an answer for that. Every time he'd tried to make sense of it, all reason was lost to the memory of Ellis Wilkes floundering on the ground as Gerald came around the back of the pick-up truck, Ellis's older brother, Wade, lying dead on the ground and the bear trap's sharply toothed grin clamped around Ellis's ankle, looking doubly malevolent in the crimson glow from the truck's taillights. Ellis had his cell phone pressed to his ear and as Gerald levelled his grandfather's old Smith & Wesson at his head he'd whimpered, Daddy, he's going to kill me.

Gerald flinching at the memory of what came next and looking back to his son. The boy was staring at him with a facsimile of the expression Ellis had worn that day and Gerald averted his eyes. Evers must have got the point and had gone back to fretting with his stick for a moment. Then:

What'll they do if they catch us?

Gerald was levering the can of beans out of the fire with two sticks and waited until it was safe on the ground to answer.

They'll put me in jail.

For how long?

Forever, I'd guess.

And what'll they do to me?

I'd imagine they'd put you in a foster home.

The boy considering that with downcast eyes, prodding the fire with the stick and catching a flame on its end, holding it up and staring at it with plaintive deliberation.

That ain't never going to happen, he said and punctuated his resolve by blowing the flame out.

The dying ember cast his face in a reddish hue and the ribbon of smoke trailing from its end split it in two. A bitter and steely-eyed veil had then lowered over the boy's face like a shroud and that had filled Gerald with dread, for all that Evers had lost and more so for the child he feared he'd never see again.

I t would be the fireflies that brought the boy he'd known back to him, if only for a moment.

They'd wintered in a cave on the other side of Ishpatina Ridge, the highest point in the province and also the tipping point for the entire continent, the waters beyond all flowing into Hudson Bay. Ishpatina was a six-hour hike from the nearest road and the cave a half a day's walk north of that. Their shelter wasn't much more than a gaping dome in the base of a hundred-foot ridge, its ceiling some thirty feet at its peak, its floor a wreck of crumbled granite leading upwards and tapering into a small recess towards the rear. They'd enclosed that with a frame cobbled from birch saplings and tarped with cedar boughs and deer hide. They made their beds out of the same and when they'd lit a fire it was right cozy, even in the dead of winter. For the seven months they'd stayed there, the cave had begun to seem almost like a home and even come the melt they'd rarely strayed more than a half a day's walk from it.

One evening, early in the spring, they were returning from checking their traps and had come to the backside of the ridge from where the cave was. The ground there rose on a steep slope towards a cliff face some eighty feet at its summit and was populated mostly by poplar trees though there were a few maples amongst a sparse sprinkling of birch. Through some mechanism foreign to him the ground beneath them was almost entirely uncluttered by underbrush and fallen branches, while on the front side the forest floor was a tangled web of toppled trunks and tumbled boulders, raspberry brambles and poison ivy growing in thick swathes among them. Because of the latter, they always used the back way to get into their cave. That meant scaling the eighty-foot ridge and then climbing down through a crack in the cave's ceiling that formed a natural sort of chimney. It really wasn't much of a bother. Both the ridge and the chimney seemed almost exclusively designed for the purpose of climbing, the former with plenty of handholds and ledges upon which to rest and the latter with a staggered series of outcroppings which formed a natural staircase to what Gerald began referring to as their own personal penthouse suite at the top of the world.

It had become Gerald's custom to climb an ash tree perched at the edge of the summit in the evening, Evers joining him less and less as the months progressed, the same as Gerald himself had rarely accompanied his grandfather to The Ridge in his teenage years. He would sit with his legs dangling beneath a high branch, watching the sun setting over a world he no longer belonged to and feeling more and more what his grandfather must have felt, revelling in the victory of having made it to the end of yet another day. And as he approached the cliff it was with the thought foremost in his mind that if they were quick about it they'd get there just in time to catch what was promising to be a doozy.

It was late in April, or maybe early in May, but already so hot that every breath seemed a trial unto itself — the kind of heat that sapped the energy right out of your marrow. It seemed he had barely the strength left to pull himself the first few feet off the ground, much less the next eighty. When he turned back to see what was keeping Evers, his son was standing with his back to him at the crest of the slope. The forest beyond was already shading towards dark and within its gloaming there arose a sudden flicker amongst the trees. A moment later a second flicker and then a third and a fourth, the flickers thereafter appearing at such a rate so as to be beyond enumeration but hardly comparison. The easiest was with the number of stars in the night sky except their languid drift didn't so much resemble stars as it did the waft of fluff from a field of dandelions rent aloft by a sudden gust and then set ablaze. But any real accounting for the sight in words could hardly express the wonder that had suddenly overcome Gerald, seeing the air enlivened so.

You ever seen so many fireflies?

Evers was looking back at him with craned head. His own amaze was straining through the bitter resolve and it had seemed, in that moment, that the fireflies had brought the boy he'd once been back from the dead. Gerald opened his mouth to answer, I sure haven't, but found his mouth was too dry to utter more than a crackled, No.

They both went back to watching the insects' flicker, dwindling at even pace with the darkening sky. The last dozen or so winked out all at once and in the next instant they heard the thrash of treetops above and the distant rumble of thunder.

There's a storm brewing, Gerald had said, casting a furtive glance skyward. We best be getting inside.

They'd made it about halfway up the rock face when the rain started, a few drops as fine as needle points giving them fair warning before a sudden torrent. It was coming from the south. That should have afforded them a measure of relief but the wind was whipping around the ridge with all the force of a hurricane. The rain pelted them in lateral sheets and they were getting it from both sides and sometimes from below. Every which way they turned their heads there it was: rain like iron drops dashing into their eyes and nothing they could do about it now but stay where they were and try to hang on. Gerald had made it to a ledge, eighteen inches wide and canted at a moderate twenty-degree angle. There was a horn of granite that came out of the main rock and he was holding on to this and looking up for his son, who was only five feet above him and all but lost within the swirling sheets of rain.

The ten feet past the halfway ledge was the trickiest part. Evers would have been lucky if he had two inches square of firm ground on which to stand and had somehow managed to get a hold of the spindled roots dangling down from the ash tree perched at the edge of the summit.

Evers! Gerald called out above the gale. Come down! It ain't safe up there. Evers!

No sooner had he spoken than he heard an explosive snap that brought to mind bridge cables giving way during an earthquake. Cast against the sky's turbulent black, there was a shadow of something blacker still. It looked like a giant hand reaching out of the sky, about to pluck them from their perch and then there was a lumberous *swoosh* as the ash tree plummeted past. One of its roots lashed out, striking Gerald in the neck. It felt for a moment as if it might have taken his head clean off, such was the shock of pain it wrought. But he could still see, so it couldn't have, and he was even then looking up, searching out Evers and glimpsing a dark shape with pinwheeling arms hurtling past. His hand darted out, grabbing for something — anything — and snatching his son miraculously by the bob of his ponytail.

Evers's face coming back into his mind now, peering up at him with stark terror as Gerald dragged him onto the ledge. In the years since, he'd had plenty of time to reflect on that night and in his mind it had always become paired with the day Millie had taken that first birthday picture. On that morning he'd never felt more terrified than he had cradling his son after he'd saved him from a plunge of barely four feet and there was Evers plunging from a height ten times that. Yet it wasn't fear he'd felt clutching at his son, the boy's body heaving in great braying sobs against his chest. In that moment he'd felt — there was no denying it — suddenly invincible.

Three days later the bear would prove him anything but.

As he now ducked low beneath the branches of a tamarack tree, feeling their yellowed needles flittering down his back and sticking to the sweat of his skin, the real truth of that evening imparted itself with a gravity that had his legs almost buckling at the knees.

You might as well have let him drop for all the good you've done him since.

T hunder had been rumbling after him ever since he'd left Clayton back at the camp. But it wasn't until the deer path had led Gerald to a mud-rutted quad trail on the south side of the lake that a four-pronged fork of lightning quartered the darkly frothing sky. At the trail's end he could see the orange of a school bus blocking his way. That told him he'd come full circle around the lake and he stood there for a moment feeling more lost than ever now that he knew exactly where he was.

Hey you!

Gerald spun towards the water, seeing a man standing in an aluminum fishing boat, twenty feet from shore. He was holding a rod with its line trailing into the water behind him and wearing a faded orange life jacket over jeans and a black sweater. It didn't take more than a second glance for Gerald to know there was something off about him, it being in the low-thirties with lightning flaring on the horizon, and him dressed as he was and standing in an aluminum boat with the waves dashing its hull, making it jostle and bob so it looked like at any moment the man would be pitched over the side.

Hey yourself, he answered.

Whooer you?

The boat was drifting closer and Gerald could now see the man's face was oddly elongated, like someone had squeezed his head in a vice. A ragged gash cut his forehead almost in half as if his fractured skull had pierced the skin while they'd done it and his mouth was agape, a trail of drool spanned from its droop and draining onto his lifejacket, which is to say he posed about as much of a threat to Gerald as a piece of driftwood washed up on the shore.

Gerald, Gerald called back to him as if it was the most natural thing in the world, saying his own name. Whooer you?

The man all of the sudden grinned wide and looked over his right shoulder, dusting his knuckles against his life vest as if knowing his name was a feat of great distinction.

Trent, he said. Whadya doing?

I was thinking of maybe going for a swim.

A swim?

It came out pinched and he shook his head with the alarm of a dog shaking a bee off its ear. Holding his hand out, he then pointed at Gerald with a chastising finger.

No swimming allowed!

I must have missed the sign.

The man's gape returned for a moment and then he held his hand up again, this time pointing towards the sky and waving his finger like some scientist in a moment of divine inspiration.

Leeches, he said.

There's leeches in the water?

Leeches, the man repeated. Eeew.

Thunder rumbled and the man's eyes grew wide, but it wasn't the thunder he was worried about.

Uh, oh, he said. Darlee's mad.

The words were barely out of his mouth when a woman's voice was calling out from behind Gerald: Trent!

Darlee was stalking up the quad path — a woman in her mid- to late forties with a mess of brown curls and wearing a pair of green capri pants and a flimsy yellow T-shirt through which the warp of an orange sports bra was just visible. She had on pink flip-flops and her one foot was muddied to the ankle, which spoke as much to the integrity of the path as it did to her mood, about the same as a mother's who'd just caught her son trying to flush his sister's favourite doll down the toilet. But the woman couldn't have been Trent's mother since they looked to be about the same age. She must have been his sister, or perhaps his support worker.

What the hell do you think you're doing? she yelled as she came to the shore.

Fishing, Trent answered, holding up his rod as if there was still some doubt to his enterprise.

And what did I tell you when I laid down for a nap?

Trent frowned, trying to think of what she might have meant.

No fishing, he finally said.

That's right, no fishing.

Too dangerous.

You're lucky you didn't get struck by lightning.

I'm lucky.

That's one word for it. Now quit your foolishness and bring that boat in to shore.

Trent looked at his feet and then back up again.

Where're the oars? Darlee asked.

Trent pointed towards the stern.

Back there.

You lost the oars?

They broke.

Broke my ass. You dropped them and now they're floating in the middle of the lake.

Yeah! he exclaimed, his voice swelling with an undeniable pride like such had been his life's work.

It hadn't seemed that the woman had noticed Gerald at all but she now acknowledged him with a plainly exasperated sideways smile in his direction, happy to have someone there to bear witness to her trial.

He could tell she'd been pretty in her younger years but the sag to her cheeks and the lines spiderwebbed from the corners of her eyes spoke more to the life she'd lived as a woman than to the girl she might once have been. And yet he could still see traces of that girl in the way she smiled, full-faced this time with eyes gently imploring — a coquettish come-hither look, like she, or at least her younger self, was used to getting her way with men.

You mind giving me a hand?

As Gerald dragged the boat up onto the bank — leaning forward at a steep pitch with its rope slung over one shoulder, his feet slipping, unable to find purchase in the shallow's murk, his muscles taut against the strain and Trent perched in the rear seat, holding on to the gunnels as if for dear life — he caught parcelled glimpses of the woman watching him. It was hard not to intuit a subtle lustfulness in her gaze. Millie had often looked at him the same way when she'd first come to live with him at the farm, or rather after she'd never left the night she'd followed him home from the Legion.

Gerald had always been startled by the intensity of Millie's gaze as he went about his day-to-day, whether chopping wood or fixing an eavestrough that had come loose in a storm. And she was never more delirious in her zeal than when they were in bed after they'd both come and she lay beside him, plucking at the meagre hairs on his chest or running her fingers over the trenches turning his stomach to rock-hard dunes, the first time she'd done so giggling as she said, God there's not an inch of fat on you, is there?

An odd state of affairs for a man who'd never been with a woman until he was twenty-one that his first would show enough interest in him for a dozen. And here another woman was looking at him with a trace, albeit slight, of the same lustfulness though he was practically a skeleton now, and about the same shade of white.

He'd taken off only his shoes, sparing himself the look of startled concern that no doubt would have confronted him had he taken off his shirt and she'd seen the thatch of claw marks on his back and the groove of scar tissue indenting his left shoulder from where the bear had taken a bite out of him. While he slipped back into his sneakers the woman helped Trent from the boat and then reached back in, retrieving his rod.

I'm Darlene, by the way, she said, walking towards Gerald with Trent in eager pursuit.

She was reaching out her hand and Gerald offered his. The skin on her palm was moist and cool and reminded him of the pizza dough Millie had sometimes left overnight to set in the fridge.

He's Gerald, Trent said before Gerald could answer. Gerald!

That didn't even raise a tic in her appreciative smile.

Pleased to meet you, Gerald.

Lightning forked and thunder crashed and she threw a nervous glance skywards. She seemed to have forgotten she was holding his hand or was reluctant to release it. Either way, when she turned back she realized her oversight. She jerked her hand from his, smiling shyly and looking at her feet, glancing up at him again without raising her head.

I don't know what I would have done if you hadn't come along.

Weren't no bother, Gerald answered. I was planning on going for a swim anyhow.

The woman nodded.

You staying at the camp? she then asked.

Just arrived today.

Well I sure am glad you did.

Happy to help.

Another clap of thunder.

I ought to be going, Gerald said. He was already turning towards the bush.

Least I can do is offer you a cup a tea, Darlene said.

Maybe another time.

But Trent wasn't taking no for an answer. He'd pushed himself past Darlene and was wrapping Gerald's arm within the crook of his own.

This way, he said, pulling him down the quad path towards the settlement.

Trent, Darlene protested, you know you're not allowed to go grabbing people!

Trent released his hold and his body suddenly went stiff, his arms shaking like they were fixing to fly right off. He let out a cry like a cat with its tail caught in a door and jammed a balled fist into his mouth. He only had three teeth that Gerald could see, the two front ones on the top and one incisor on the bottom. All of them were stained brown and sprouted at odd angles and as he bit down hard on his knuckles it seemed to Gerald one or all of them were about to snap off.

Oh cut it out, Darlene scolded, not overly concerned by the display. Then turning back to Gerald, seeing the alarm on his face: He always does this when he doesn't get his way. Glancing back at Trent then: The man's busy. He'll visit another day.

But Trent would not be abated. A dribble of blood was sprouting over his knuckle.

It's okay, Gerald said. I'm thinking maybe a cup of tea wouldn't be such a bad idea after all.

The quad tracks brought them back to the camp, only a few paces from where Gerald had left it.

It wasn't dark yet but it was getting there. Lights shone through the windows of all the RVs in sight. The blue spruce were lit up too with strands of multicoloured Christmas lights and there were solar-powered torches stuck in the ground delineating the paths criss-crossing the camp.

The first pricks of rain were needling at the bald spot at the back of Gerald's head as Trent pulled him in a near-frantic pace past the hospital tent, Gerald craning his neck backwards and again feeling a hot flush of shame, wondering if Clayton was still in there or if the cop really had locked him up. Trent was then dragging him right, guiding him along a narrow causeway between the outer row of RVs and school buses converted into domiciles and the city of mostly identical blue tents crowding the interior. Deep in the heart of the camp now, he felt little of the wonder he had when he'd first seen it from the back of the truck. It no longer looked so much like a festival than what it truly was: a refugee camp filled with an anomalous blend of suburbanites playing at vacation and a host of down-and-outers clinging to the last few crumbs that had fallen their way.

Most of the RVs and motorhomes were seemingly bursting at the seams with a variety of household goods spilling onto whatever meagre yard they'd been able to claim as their own and now tarped off against the rain. The tents too seemed to be overflowing, but with garbage. Bags of it were dumped in haphazard piles between the rows, and discarded chip bags and steak wrappers, sheets of cellophane and other such detritus flitted about in sudden gusts or were plastered against the blue canvas, held there at the wind's mercy.

Plenty of dogs were about — some nosing at the refuse and others tied to metal stakes and a few seeking refuge in the cubbies beneath the trailers — but most of the people had fled inside. There were only a few still about, all of them making last-minute preparations in advance of the storm — an old couple tying an orange tarp over their tent and a burly, bearded man using the same to cover up his quad, a young girl hefting a folding dollhouse as big as a suitcase towards the metal retractable steps of her parents' thirty-five-foot trailer, her mother at the door urging, Hurry up, it's startin' to rain!

They were nearing the far side of the camp and still Trent was pulling him onwards. Darlene, a few paces ahead, had come to the line of RVs separating the field from the swamp on its eastern side.

We're just down here, she called out above the wind's bluster, pointing to the right, towards the tracks. She turned around to hurry off but stopped mid-stride, apparently seeing something happening a little further on. When Trent had pulled Gerald astride, he had no such reservations and was tugging at the other's arm with renewed vigour, Gerald pulling back, slackening his pace, as alarmed as Darlene by what he saw.

There was a young man with dirty-blond, shoulder-length dreadlocks standing in the middle of the path, twenty paces hence. He was naked save for a pair of grey boxer briefs and was carving a crude square into his chest's ghost-white skin with what appeared to be an exacto knife, but it was neither that nor the look of crazed abandon in the young man's eyes that had stopped Gerald short. It was the cop standing with his back to them not ten feet away. He was the same one Gerald had seen before. He had one arm raised and was pointing his sidearm at the dreadlocked man.

You want a piece of me? The man was peeling the square of flesh from his chest. Ripping it free in a welter of blood, he held the quivering chunk of skin out to the cop. I got a piece of me right here!

That he was a Euphoral addict in withdrawal there could be no doubt. One of the early signs was self-injury. Gerald'd had to clean up after enough of them at the prison to know that. There was a crowd of maybe a dozen people who'd come out to see the show and at least one of them must have known what was likely to happen next.

You better thoot him there copper, he was shouting in a lisping drawl, you know what'th good for you!

Shut up! This from a younger man also dressed in a police uniform. He had his knee on the back of a woman who was on the ground. She had dreadlocks and pale skin, same as the man, and the officer was fumbling for the handcuffs on his belt. The heckler must have been needling him for some time and he was clearly at wits' end.

Thith your firtht day on the job there, offither? the heckler continued unabated.

I said shut the fuck up!

Mutht be. Otherwithe you'd know there ain't nothing you can do exthept thoot 'em.

The cop was looking like maybe he'd have rather shot the heckler, but that was the least of his concerns just then. The woman's body heaved in a sudden and violent convulsion beneath his knee. It looked like she'd been jolted with twenty thousand volts and Gerald knew it was a sure sign that she'd hit stage two in her withdrawal. That usually only lasted a few seconds and was followed almost immediately by a maniacal rage of almost unfathomable proportions. Stage three might last for only a few minutes and never more than an hour before the addict went into cardiac arrest and it was in this interval that they became truly dangerous. Already she was foaming at the mouth and her eyes had rolled back into their sockets. She looked like one of those Japanese fuck-bots set to rodeo bronc and the cop drove his knee deeper into her back, all thoughts of getting the handcuffs on her lost to the spasmodic thrashing of her arms and legs.

Her boyfriend was shaking uncontrollably too. His arms were shimmying at his sides and the exacto knife was dashing into his leg, slicing at the flesh, ribbons of blood spattering out of his wounds.

He's crazy, Trent said to no one in particular. He was shaking his head and pointing his finger, wagging it accusingly at the man. You're crazy!

Fingernails raked over Gerald's arm as Trent's hand sprung loose. Darlene was dragging him on a hard left, through a gap between the tents, sidestepping a bag of garbage and Trent stumbling over the same, looking back at Gerald as if he might be in danger of getting lost. Gerald started after them and was turned back by a hateful shriek. It was the woman. She was lunging at the younger cop, who was somehow now on his back, struggling to wrest his sidearm from its holster. But the woman was already on top of him, wailing her fury as she flailed towards him, straddling him, her head pitching forward, her teeth chomping down, latching onto his cheek. The cop was screaming now, his own hands flailing, clawing at her hair, trying to wrench her free.

Bang! Bang!

The older cop fired twice.

Both shots struck the dreadlocked man in the chest, knocking him onto his back. He hadn't even hit the ground when the cop was swivelling towards his partner, taking aim at the girl and pulling the trigger. Another *Bang!*, this one swallowed into a clap of thunder, an incongruous shock of lightning flaring after, electrifying the sky and rendering a single, solitary instant as clear as in any photograph: the woman slumped over the younger cop, her chin nuzzled into his neck as a lover's might be — the older cop with his gun still poised in his outstretched hand, his head slightly downcast, his eyes averted, as if he couldn't face what he'd just done — faces in the crowd captured with expressions of shock and awe, dismay and fright — a young woman with a light-dazzled chimera of orange hair dishevelled by the wind, its strands cast upwards in a mad fray and her hand clamped to her mouth, her legs turning tail and frozen in mid-flight until, in the next instant, the lightning itself had fled and she was again swallowed into the dark.

The younger cop was pushing the woman off and sitting up. A chunk had been torn clean out of his cheek and lent him a ghastly air as the older cop strode towards him, holstering his weapon and proffering the other his hand, pulling him to his feet. He was saying something but his words were lost to the wind and so it was the heckler who'd have the final say.

I toldya you thould have jutht thot 'em! he yelled.

The younger cop, his hand clamped to his cheek and his eyes

pits of unfettered hate, took a step in his direction. His free hand was on the butt of his gun and the older cop was grabbing him by the arm, saying something else Gerald couldn't hear, most likely, *He's not worth it*, or some derivation of the same. The younger cop seemed to get the message and his hand shortly eased off his weapon.

Gerald scanned backwards, looking for Darlene and Trent and finding no sign of them between the tents. Searching then in a widening arc past the crowd. It was dispersing as the sky unleashed a torrent of rain, the all of them bent over and scurrying for cover, jostling past, and Gerald hearing someone calling out,

Gerald Nicholth!

There was a skinny little runt hustling towards him. Lightning flashed, a sheet of sheer brilliance that lent the man's face the appearance of a grisly mask. It looked to have been shorn clean off and if that wasn't enough to tell Gerald who it was, the door knocker bobbing up and down where his nose should have been most surely was.

It'th me, he said when he'd reached him, adding then, Zip, though he needn't have.

Gerald opened his mouth, but he had no words to express the apprehension he felt, witnessing what he just had and seeing this man now smiling like the night couldn't have ended any better.

Jutht like back on the range, huh? he said. They'll never fuckin' learn.

His eyes were widening as if he expected Gerald to say something but he was spared the need to do this by the approach of the two police officers. The younger had a folded handkerchief pressed to his cheek and was glaring at Zip as the older, still clutching him by the arm, dragged him on as wide a perimeter as the narrow causeway allowed. Five steps down the path leading towards the hospital, the older cop shot a short sharp glance back at Gerald and it left little doubt in Gerald's mind that he was serving him notice that he'd be coming for him next.

Zip was staring after them, shaking his head and clucking his tongue against his gums. Gerald scanned away, searching down the rows of RVs and seeing Darlene leaning out the front door of a thirty-foot Airstream, the last trailer before the tracks.

I geth the thow'th over, Zip said. You feel like a beer?

When Gerald turned back Zip was looking at him with a keen sort of malevolence starkly out of place for a man who'd just offered him a refreshment.

We got a trailer up by the woodth. Got it real cheap, you know what I mean. Fully thtocked too. I know Popth'd love to thee ya.

The mention of Pops sent a shudder down Gerald's spine. If he was here along with Zip it meant there'd be other Sons about too. Could have been they were the ones the soldiers were tasked with guarding the fuel against or maybe they had their eyes set on the reserves of food or maybe they really were just evil mother-fuckers like Jules had said and had something far more diabolical in mind. The latter idea was added thrust by the memory of the hell they'd unleashed on the good people of Penetanguishene, a thought barely found purchase before Darlene was calling out Gerald's name. When he turned towards her, she was standing at the edge of the Airstream's awning, unwilling it seemed to breach the curtain of water spewing from its metal overhang.

Zip was then chucking him on the shoulder again.

Gotcha, he said, winking as he did, the earlier malevolence replaced by a lopsided grin. Another time then.

He started off at a leisurely pace as if the wind whipping needle points of rain at his back was nothing but a light summer's breeze. A sheet of lightning illuminated the fluttering backhanded wave he offered in his passing and the jaunty country lilt of his voice trailing out of the ensuing darkness took on an ominous tone in the rumble of thunder shortly thereafter.

I'll be theeing you around, Gerald, he said. You take care now, you hear.

In the few short moments it took to reach Darlene's trailer, each passing step seemed to amplify the threat Gerald had inferred in Zip's parting words. By the time he was ducking his head under the veil of water flowing in pearled rivulets from the Airstream's awning it had amounted to a biological imperative urging him again towards flight.

Darlene was standing at the foot of the retractable steps. The rain had soaked the frizz of her hair and it clung in sodden tendrils down her cheeks and over her eyes. She'd since changed into a pair of grey track pants and a grey T-shirt bearing a faded green leprechaun clutching a pint of beer below a sign reading *Murphy's Pub*. She was holding out a pink towel, sun-bleached and frayed at the edges. As Gerald took it, saying thanks, he couldn't help but detect an entreaty in the way her eyes, disconsolate, seemed to be pleading with him. It was wholly out of sync with the welcoming embrace of her smile and the disparity between the two recalled to Gerald what Zip had once said about half the world going crazy and everyone else trying to pretend it was business as usual. She seemed to have a foot in both camps but was sliding towards the former.

I'll get you some dry clothes, she offered while he wiped the wet from his beard and from his hair.

Don't trouble yourself on my account.

It's no trouble at all.

She forced a strained smile that suggested it would be more trouble to refuse and the matter was settled for good by the intrusion of a high-pitched whiny voice sounding in shrill alarm.

Trent, it said, put some pants on!

Trent had just stepped into view in the doorway behind Darlene. He was wrestling to get a blue fleece sweater over his head and was naked from the chest down. His penis hung limp as a length of rope between his legs, about four inches long, and his balls were dangling in their veined and hairy sack an inch or two below.

God, Trent, Darlene scolded turning around, nobody wants to see that.

I'm stuck.

It was all Trent could manage to say and Darlene grabbed him by the arm, spinning him around.

Put on some pants before you give Linda a heart attack. Go on, git!

Trent yelped as if he'd been pinched and that seemed as good a sign as any that it was safe for Gerald to look up again.

I told him to stop doing that, the high-pitched whine was saying as Darlene stuck her head back out the door.

The desperate entreaty had returned and it struck Gerald that maybe it wasn't watching the two Euphies gunned down that had conflicted her so, it was simply the natural by-product of her current circumstances. Could have been it was the new normal for the entire world.

Come on in, she was saying, don't be shy now.

Stepping up and in he saw the Airstream wasn't really a trailer but a motorhome, the interior of which looked like someone's idea of the future, forty years ago. The once-shiny chrome of its appliances and cupboard doors was misted over with a thin film and the white of its linoleum floor was scoured with the imprint of a thousand dirty footprints, its edges peeling against the walls and several cracks in its veneer plastered over with packing tape. There was a small kitchenette on the right — a stove, a microwave oven, a fridge and sink — and across from that a table wedged between two orange cushioned benches, both with expansive cracks like fault lines parting their vinyl. On the left was a small living room with a matching orange sofa that looked like it folded out into a bed. Cupboards and storage cabinets lined every vertical surface except for a few feet above the table and the sofa where there were windows, both with their blinds drawn.

It was the woman sitting on the sofa who must have raised the whiny voice.

She had the face of a pouty child but Gerald guessed she was in her mid- to late fifties, a true reckoning of her age enshrouded by the Downsy droop to her face. In her lap there rested a child's colouring book. Gerald couldn't tell much about it except that it was an inch thick and on the open page someone — likely the woman herself — had worn out a purple crayon on the picture of a Christmas tree surrounded by presents.

When she caught sight of Gerald looking at her, she harrumphed and raised the book to hide her face. The cover had the words *The Night Before Christmas* above a picture of Santa Claus about to drop down the chimney of a snow-frosted house and while Darlene retrieved a kettle from the stove, the woman snuck spurious glances out from behind its screen.

Don't be rude now, Linda, Darlene chided as she filled the kettle at the sink, say hello to our guest. His name is Gerald.

Linda slapped the colouring book down on her lap and glared at Gerald like she'd rather do anything but. When she spoke it was with the exaggerated petulance of a child forced out of her play so a parent could introduce her to some aging relation she'd likely never see again.

Hello, Gerald, she said. My name is Linda. How are you today?

I'm doing fine, Gerald answered. How are you?

To that she responded with another harrumph, raising the book over her face and holding it there this time with the unwavering determination of an ostrich burying its head in the sand.

You can change in the bathroom, Darlene said with a backwards jerk of her head. It's the first door on your right.

At a glance, the bathroom didn't look like much more than a shower stall encased in calcified stainless steel, and a tiny one at that. When he came in, the light activated by itself and there he was staring at himself in a mirror. He looked lost and forlorn, the same way he'd looked in Evers's birthday picture, year one, except his age was showing in the gauntness to his cheeks and the cracks around his eyes and the erosion of his hairline washing deep coves on either side of a thinning peninsula.

As he undressed he kept his back to the mirror so he didn't have to face the scar tissue carving a groove into his shoulder, fighting against his dread by telling himself maybe he'd look back on this as one of his happiest days, too. Reoccurring thoughts of Zip bidding him to take care now, you hear, gave him every reason to suspect otherwise and he was spared further thoughts of that by a gentle rap on the door.

I got your clothes, Darlene said.

He opened the door, keeping his scarred left side hidden and smiling obligingly as she passed him a neatly folded pair of blue swim trunks and a black T-shirt.

You find the toilet all right? she asked.

Toilet?

He glanced backwards trying to figure out how he might have missed it.

It's a fold-out. You just press on that section there. She pointed to the far wall before setting her hand on his arm. We've been using the port-a-johns. No use filling up the tank if we don't have to. But a night like this isn't fit for a dog to piss in the yard.

I'm okay for now.

She nodded, smiling at him again.

I'll take your wet clothes.

Oh.

He bent to get them off the floor and when he straightened up she was staring at the photograph of Evers still strung around his neck. Water had leaked in from where he'd cut through the laminate. There was a stain the colour of coffee bubbling its bottom edge but the image was clear enough and seemed to have a malignant effect on Darlene. Her smile sagged and a pallor came into her cheeks. She looked like she'd seen in it someone she knew, perhaps her own son whom she hadn't seen for years, and the surprise of suddenly being reminded of him was too much for her to bear.

I'll put them in the wash, she said, averting her eyes and reaching out blindly for his clothes.

When he came out of the bathroom a few moments later, she was pouring hot water into four mugs on the counter.

I put the stuff in your pockets on the table.

Trent was sitting on one of the benches, holding the stick-knife Gerald had made.

What's this?

It's a knife, Trent, I already told you that.

Trent's face scrunched as if she'd done no such thing.

A knife? he asked, incredulous. No it's not. It's a stick!

Darlene was setting a mug embossed with frolicking dolphins in front of him. She took the knife and placed it on the far side of the table next to the two lighters and the Car Buddy, all that Gerald could call his own. When she looked back at Trent he was raising the mug to his lips, looking as if he was going to gulp it all down in one go.

Stop! she yelled. It's still hot. Let it cool down.

Trent set it back down again, saying, Blow on it.

That's right. Blow on it. Then turning to Gerald: We don't have any milk. She proffered him a look of strained deprecation, like it was her own failing and not mere circumstance. But I've got plenty of sugar. They opened a carload of it a few days ago.

That'll be fine.

He drank his tea sitting on the table's padded bench across from Trent. The rain's patter on the roof sounded more like hail, and gusts of wind rattled the window beside him, battering an imperfect staccato of errant beats in perfect synchronicity with the addled fret of his increasingly restless mind. The window's inside screen was pocked with holes sealed with bits of peeling Scotch tape and he couldn't see much through it but still cast furtive glances in its direction between sips of the raspberry-flavoured beverage, wondering what The Sons might be brewing up out there in the dark.

Darlene was cooking four steaks on a countertop grill and into the oven she'd put a foil-wrapped loaf that Gerald suspected must have been Texas toast. The allure of simmering meat and garlic butter was quickly overpowered by a fog of smoke, Darlene lighting one cigarette from the cherry of the last and puffing on them like she was trying to make a living at it. They were the same brand as the ones Devon had been smoking so they must have opened a carload of them too.

So you just arrived today? she asked, taking a break from prodding at the meat with a fork.

I did.

From where?

Uh, Midland?

How they making out down there?

Food's pretty scarce.

Well that's at least one thing we don't have to worry about. They say there's enough food on the train to last us all winter.

That so?

She was piling two steaks on a plate and adding to that half a loaf of the Texas toast and three heaping spoonfuls of coleslaw.

I hate to think about what all those people in tents are going to do when it starts snowing.

Shaking her head then and grimacing, really not wanting to think about that. Her expression brightening then:

It was lucky I still had this old beast, she said as she set the plate in front of Gerald. Don't know what we would have done without her.

He was feeling lightheaded and slightly nauseous from the smoke and the humidity. He didn't think he could eat even half of what she'd made for him but picked up his knife and fork nonetheless.

The knife was of the steak variety with a stainless-steel serrated edge that made the meat, when he cut it, seem like it was made of warm butter. As he ate, he sliced off increasingly larger pieces, his hunger growing with every bite. Trent was holding his own steak in his bare hands as he gnawed it, and Darlene had gone off to where Linda was sitting on the couch in front of a TV tray to cut up hers. When she was done, she lit another cigarette and stood leaning against the counter, looking at Gerald almost meditatively, seemingly entranced by the simple act of watching a man devouring a meal she'd just cooked for him.

No one spoke until Trent was forking the last mouthful of coleslaw into his mouth.

Good, he said.

You can say that again, Gerald agreed.

For a moment it looked like Trent would, but instead he said to no one in particular, He's my friend.

We know, Trent, Linda said, frowning as if what he'd said was meant as a personal affront. God. You're always talking about it. We know he's your friend. He's my friend too. God!

Gerald was standing with his plate, about to carry it to the sink, but Darlene intercepted him before he'd managed more than a step.

I'll take that.

Smiling then at him, warm and deferential.

I'm tired, Trent said, yawning, and she turned to him.

You should be. It's been a busy day.

Worms, he said as he stood.

Don't worry, I'll wake you up in plenty of time to catch worms.

Worms, he said again. Eeew!

W hile she folded down the table and pulled the benches together to form a bed, Gerald excused himself on the pretence of having to take a leak.

You can use the bathroom, she said as he started for the door.

It's okay. A little rain never killed no one.

But really what he wanted to do was take a look outside, see if he could discern any sign that The Sons might be hatching something. The door got away from him as he opened it, slamming hard against the side of the motorhome. The wind was lashing rain on a horizontal against his back as he forced the door closed, thinking, *They'd have to be crazy if they're planning something on a night like this,* but that doing nothing at all to ease his dread as he walked to the swamp side of the awning.

It provided little shelter from the swirling rain. His shirt was pretty much soaked through by the time he was done and the damp fabric clung to the outline of his ribs and the sharp nubs poking from the lean of his chest. It was cooler now and at least it provided him with some relief from the sticky heat.

The lights went out as he approached the Airstream's door. He was just reaching for its latch when it opened a crack, the wind snatching it from Darlene's grip and Gerald lunging forward, grabbing it with both hands to keep it from slamming again. He was just closing it behind him when Darlene put her hand on his arm, whispering in his ear, We'll go up front.

The Airstream's cab had a domed ceiling high enough for Gerald to stand up in. Someone — maybe Darlene herself — had painted it black and then speckled it with a Milky Way's worth of glowing white dots made to look like stars. Gerald was admiring the view as Darlene shut the door behind them, squeezing past, putting her hands on his shoulders as if to steady herself and Gerald flinching when a finger foundered into the groove of scarred-over tissue where he'd been bitten by the bear. She didn't seem to have noticed anything odd about it and plopped down in the driver's side of two swivelling chairs, both of which looked to have been carved out of a single giant egg.

Letting out an exhausted Phew!, she sat for a moment, sprawling her legs before her and closing her eyes, letting her hands hang limp off the chair's armrest. She held the pose for barely a second and then snapped back to life, swivelling the chair left as her hands groped towards the storage compartment in the door.

Gerald had since sat down in the passenger seat. It was more comfortable than it looked and when he leaned back it reclined along with him. A footrest extended from beneath it like on his grandfather's La-Z-Boy, providing him, it seemed, with a window seat at the very edge of the universe. There was a clicking sound followed by a flicker and then he smelt the faint tang of weed. He sat up, swivelling towards Darlene. She had a small pink metal pipe pressed to her lips and was sucking the lighter's flame through its bowl. She took a long slow draft and released the smoke in a billowing stream, Gerald basking in its musky allure, watching it mingling in eddies under the starred dome and then sweeping through an open crack in the window as Darlene worked its crank.

You puff? she asked, holding the pipe out to Gerald.

I might have one.

He took it, put it to his lips and leaned forward, letting her light it and taking a good long drag himself before passing it back. Darlene took another and then offered it again. Gerald shook his head — he ought to stay at least halfway alert — and she tucked the pipe into a small metal tea box that he could see was mostly filled up by a Ziploc bag, no doubt her supply. She stuffed this back into the side compartment and tucked her feet up under her legs. In the way she looked questioningly at Gerald she seemed about to ask something but it was too dark to tell for certain and she spoke to him not a word.

They sat there for some time, listening to the storm's rage. It was muted somewhat and came to them mostly as whispers and the clatter of branches broken off in the gale and battering at the windshield, which was already plastered with leaves and pine needles whelmed in the currents of tributaries streaking on a fast-flowing horizontal so that they looked like tiny canoes caught in a flash flood. Gerald followed them with the lackadaisical delight he might have had watching a stick trundle down a creek when he was kid. The needles shimmied in dizzying circles and were washed into a nettle at the edge of the glass. There was an anomalous bleating — sounded like goats — calling in far-faint distress. As the needles were plucked upwards and sent reeling into the night, the bleating began to sound like screams, as if the canoes were full of people wailing as they were sucked into a tornado. Their cries were shortly overshadowed by a splintering crash — a tree toppling. It sounded like it was coming down straight on top of them and Darlene sat bolt upright. Her hand darted out and grabbed Gerald on the leg, the both of them frozen stock still, listening then for any sign of the damage it may have wrought, hearing only the wind's bluster and the goats crying out in renewed despair.

God, Darlene said, releasing her hold and tucking her feet back under her legs again, it feels like the whole world is coming apart.

Gerald had thought much the same thing, couldn't have been more than a few days ago.

But it wasn't the wind made him think so, it was . . .

Fighting through the hazy dim of his weed-softened mind, struggling to remember where he'd had cause to think that.

It was the stars. Like the frayed ends of string left over from a missing button. That's what it was.

Recalling then the sky's twinkling bright as him and Clayton had come onto the 400. Remembering all those abandoned vehicles, the dread he'd felt then now oozing from his belly — a thick and hot tar that seemed to be coursing through his veins, melting his bones, remaking him into some gelatinous thing about to pool into a puddle on the floor. Leaning back, he stared up at the starscape riddling the ceiling, gazing as if into infinite depths, thinking not of Clayton now but of Millie, of how one night when she was pregnant with Evers and it had been too hot to sleep they'd gone up to The Ridge. He'd brought a blanket and stretched that over a patch of dewy moss preserved from the sun's scorch by the viewing rock's shade, lying down on that and Millie cuddling against him, slipping her hand under his shirt and plucking idly at the triangle of downy hair that spouted from his chest as he stared up at the night sky, feeling in that moment that they were the last two people on earth and he couldn't have been happier for it.

And so it was that Millie was foremost on his mind as he felt himself floating amongst the stars, a lone astronaut cast adrift, letting their idle twinkle guide him towards sleep.

H e awoke into a clamorous dark.

The rattle of window glass, the batter of eaves loosed from their moorings, and a violent tinkling of wind chimes, someone all the while shaking him as if the place was set to come down on top of them.

Gerald! Millie was crying out.

There was a fury in her voice to match the wind's bluster and the sharp rebuff of her nails digging into his flesh shocked him bolt upright. She was sitting up too, a comforter groped around her legs like potting soil, her body as thin and tremulous as a newly sprung fern. A voice, his own, was crying out as if from a corner of the room, *You're dreaming!* He knew it to be true yet he was powerless to awake or to extricate himself from the pantomime playing out between himself and Millie.

What? he asked, without feeling his lips so much as move. What is it?

I heard something.

What?

It sounded like . . . someone screaming.

The hell it did.

It was coming from the barn.

You're imagining things. It's only the storm. Lying back down, rolling over and drawing the covers over his head. Go back to sleep.

But Millie wouldn't be mollified and shook him again.

I'm telling you—

Her nails were gouging his arm like an eagle's talons holding on to prey and that disabused Gerald of any notion he had of going back to sleep.

All right, all right, he said casting the covers aside and setting his feet on the floor. The hardwood trembled from the gale as if maybe the house really was coming apart. Pushing himself upwards onto legs clumsied by sleep, he tottered away from the bed, his hand outstretched like a blind man's cane, reaching out and feeling for the window's pane, his fingers touching the glass and stilling its rattle. Leaning into it, he scanned over the yard's dark, searching out the barn's monolith of darker yet.

You see something?

He shook his head.

No.

The word was barely past his lips when there flared a sudden spark as fleeting as a firefly's flint. Another flash a few feet further on and then another: a light winking between gaps in the barn's slatted wood.

Son of a bitch, he said.

What?

Tracing ahead with clenched teeth, searching out the barn's door. After a moment it was haloed by a sudden bright like a lantern coming around the bend in a mine shaft.

Ellis is after your crop again, isn't he?

Gerald not answering but the flustered creak of floorboards as he crossed the room provided a response clear enough. Flinging open the closet door, his hands groped under a pile of sweaters on the top shelf and grasped at the butt of his grandfather's old Smith & Wesson.

I told you not to put that bear trap out there!

There was a bitter recrimination in her tone and when he turned back to the bed with the gun upraised in his hand, there was a bitter recrimination in her eyes too.

It'll be all right.

What are you going to do?

I'm just going to have a talk with them.

If Ellis stepped in that old bear trap, I doubt he's going to feel much like talking.

That's why I got the gun.

He smiled, trying to ease her worry, but her lips were curled into a tight frown and he turned towards the door, his free hand groping for its knob. And then he was walking down the stairs, a sudden and jarring shift that again planted the fleeting idea in his head that he was dreaming, the urgency in the thought immediately quelled by the faint whimper of their Staffordshire terrier, Daisy. She was hiding under the couch as she often did during a storm. When he'd reached the bottom, the whimpering stopped and then he could hear the rake of her claws as she scrambled out from underneath the sofa, scampering across the hardwood floor. She found him at the front door as he pried back its sash to steal a look out and he felt the cold and wet of her nose dabbing at his bare leg.

Nudging her away with his hand and peering through the bevelled glass with the Smith & Wesson upraised, seeing nothing beyond the outline of his truck parked at the foot of the porch.

Craning his head then, searching for the dark shape of the barn. Above it a river of clouds flowed black and turbulent against the creaking frenzy of the metal rooster spinning atop the barn's roof and he turned his gaze towards the road, seeing nothing of value there either. Snapping open the revolver's chamber, checking that it was loaded, seeing it was and clamping it shut. Reaching then for the door's knob, taking a deep breath and hearing the creak of stairs from behind.

Gerald, Millie urged, wait!

Twisting the knob nevertheless and pushing at the door, the wind pushing back. Fighting against the gale and squeezing through the gap. The wind was like a hard current of water, drawing against his bare chest and at the curls of his beard so he could feel them lashing against his throat. The hair on his head was standing on end and his fingers were fighting to maintain a hold against the door's slam. Easing it shut and turning to the yard, scanning past his truck and the barn and finding only the sway of trees, the black river of clouds running in violent swells overtop. Feeling like God's own fool, standing there naked save for a pair of boxer briefs and holding the Smith & Wesson as if he meant to play gunslinger, never more unsure in his life of what he meant to do next.

On the awning over the porch hung the wind chimes he'd made for Millie's last birthday. Five twelve-inch spans of aluminum pipe tied to fishing line and jangling against a hexagonal disc he'd cut from a maple log on its way to the fire. Listening past their frenzied tinkle and searching about the yard, windblown grit in the air dashing at his face and squinting his eyes, telling himself whoever it was must have been long gone.

The bear trap coming into his mind then, thinking, *If Ellis had really stepped in it . . .*

And that thought turning him towards the road, tracing the channel between the cedars that marked the driveway and catching sight on his periphery of a speck of bright darting between their boughs. A flashlight swinging at a brisk pace. Someone running down the potholed gravel.

Thinking, *The bear trap is forty pounds and the only way to release it is with a special wrench, like a double-jointed tire iron. Fat chance anyone would find that and even if they did they sure as hell wouldn't be running down the road. It'd be lucky if they were ever able to run again.*

And that thought leading him right back to the barn door at the moment a sudden flash erupted, no brighter than someone lighting a cigarette. There was a hollow *pop!* and then the sear of flesh, like a hot poker thrust into his arm. That still not enough to wake him even as it jarred him out of all sense of time, what happened next skipping about in fits and starts, time returning to its usual flow only when he was lying on the floor inside his front door, panting heavy and feeling the sticky heat of blood running in rivulets down his arm. His voice was rebounding in his thoughts, *You've been shot!* A silent scream followed by the faint, almost imperceptible, shattering of glass though it would have been a slim chance in hell that he'd have thought that between when the bullet passed through his arm and when it struck the window beside the door.

Gerald! Millie cried out again.

Not so much panic in her voice anymore as confusion. And pain.

His head turning left and seeing Millie lying sprawled on her back. A well in her chest like water oozing through a hole in river ice, her head turning towards him, her chin lolling in a slow decline, coming to a rest against her shoulder, her mouth slightly ajar and her eyes become static globes, bereft of life but hardly accusation. Feeling in that moment that he'd never really been certain he'd loved her until then, that love now become a terrible thing with her lying maybe dead on the floor, and nobody's fault but his own.

Scrambling to his knees and bending over her, screaming, Millie? Millie!

His own voice was all of a sudden overcome by another whispering in his ear. The panic in it was as sharp as a siren and bleating with the same frenetic undulation.

Gerald, it said. Gerald. Gerald, wake up!

When he opened his eyes, Darlene's face was pressed inches from his. Her hand was on his shoulder, shaking him into consciousness, and there was a look of fear in her eyes. His first thought was that he'd been screaming out in his sleep, but it wasn't that.

There's some people outside, she whispered. They're calling for you.

And then he could hear it fighting through the gale's batter — a familiar lisping voice shouting out his name with the urgency of a master calling his dog home.

Gerald! Zip was yelling. Come on out, Gerald. I know you can hear me. Don't make uth come in there now!

A brief pause and then a shattering of glass, the skittering thud of rock skipping across the floor, the dull thump of it hitting the wall.

That wuth your latht warning, Gerald.

Catapulting himself out of his chair, skirting through the cab's door, coming into the Airstream's living room. The drapes on the window beside the cab's outer wall were blowing inwards almost horizontal and he hunkered low, approaching the window, not sure he really wanted to see what was out there. Broken glass crunched beneath his sneakered feet and there was a funnel of wind blowing through the hole, through which he could see Zip standing on the path just beyond the Airstream's awning. The rain had stopped and the moon had come out just short of a quarter full. In its sparse light, Gerald could make out that Zip was holding an assault rifle of a military grade and there was another man standing beside him, a hulking behemoth approaching seven feet tall, naked save for a pair of jeans cut off just above the knee, muscles like they were breeding on him. His skin was unnaturally grey, as if it had been smeared with ash, and his head was shaved and crowned with a red stripe. He was wielding a hunting knife in each hand, both almost big enough to be called machetes, and it didn't take a second look for Gerald to know it was one of the grim riders he'd seen at the prison.

Who are they?

This from Darlene. She was still standing in the cab, wrapped in shadow, afraid to come any closer.

How to explain?

He couldn't.

Just some old friends, he lied, and Darlene rebuked him with the firm declaration of a parent catching her son doing the same.

Well they sure don't look like old friends to me!

Facing another door, all those years ago, men who maybe wanted to kill him on the other side too, he'd heard Evers calling down to him from the stairs.

Dad, what's going on?

He was standing on the top step, rubbing sleep from his eyes. He was wearing a T-shirt loosely hung over his boney lank and had a curtain of hair almost as long as Millie's draped over that. Gerald couldn't see his face and couldn't tell of his expression but he imagined it must be the mirror image of his mother's when she'd called after him, only moments before. He hadn't looked back at her then but saw her reflection in the boy now and felt treble the terrible pang his love had wrought, for the boy's love for her was even greater than his own.

Evers had taken a cautious step down.

Dad? he asked, halting his descent and stooping over, prying at the dark as if he'd seen something on the floor but couldn't yet tell what it was.

Gerald's mouth opening and words forming in its aperture though he had no idea what they'd amount to until he was yelling, Stay there! Don't you come down here!

The boy heedless. Taking another step and then another, Gerald helpless but to watch as the grim awakening stalled the boy's descent. Daisy had wandered to Millie and was licking at her wound as she often did when one of her family had cut themselves and he was helpless to do anything about that either. All of a sudden the dog's head snapped towards the door and she let out a low growl an instant before a shock of bright blanched the room. Millie then revealed before them: the dim cast to her eyes, the bloom of blood on her chest, the palm of her hand upturned on the floor as if beseeching alms for the dead.

The boy screaming, Mom!, and the light from the driveway fleeing like it had never been. Daisy barking mad at the door and Gerald spinning to the window beside it. A hole in the glass at about chest level, shards arrayed around it, like a child's drawing of the sun. And beyond: the crimson glow of taillights at the back of a pick-up truck, two men framed ghastly within. One was leaning back against the open tailgate — Ellis Wilkes! — and the other — his older brother, Wade — was bending to lift one of Ellis's legs, its ankle caught within the bear trap's sharply toothed grin.

A rage overcoming Gerald then as he'd never felt before, his foot like it was spring-loaded kicking at the door, its frame shattering. He'd come out onto the porch gun a-blazing, sighting first on the man in the pick-up's driver's seat, shooting at him three times and him pitching sideways so Gerald knew his aim had been true, turning the gun then on Wade at the tailgate. Wade was already pivoting towards him, a sidearm in his hand, pointing it at Gerald as he came to the porch steps. Gerald pulled the revolver's trigger twice, hitting Wade once in the shoulder, the second in the neck. The other fired wild, the shot sparking off the cab's roof, and then Wade dropped like his legs had turned to water, Ellis flailing too, lurching off the tailgate, hitting the ground and clawing himself away from the truck.

The bear trap on his leg was like an anchor dragging behind so he'd barely made it more than a few feet by the time Gerald was stepping into the taillight's crimson glow. By then Ellis was lying on his back with a cell phone pressed to his ear, gaping up with mortal fright as Gerald lowered his gun, aiming it dead centre of his forehead.

W hat's going on?

    This from Trent, sitting up on the table-bed.

Glancing back at him with the same horror as Gerald had towards Evers, those years ago. He'd been running from the memory of what came after ever since, and more so from the man he'd become in the nine months following that. Seeing now that becoming that man again was maybe his — and Darlene's and Trent's and Linda's — only hope of making it out of this night alive. Searching out the image of Millie dead on the floor, trying to conjure again that rage. Hearing Evers screaming, Mom!, and Ellis's pitiful whimper.

Daddy, he's going to shoot me.

Gerald felt a twinge of something at last and pushed the door open. The wind wrenched it from his grasp, slamming it with a resounding *bang!* Taking the first step down the stairs like the ground was all thin ice ahead.

He'th got a knife, Zip was saying as he came out from under the awning. Watch yourthelf!

Zip was pantomiming a mawkish display of dire concern

starkly at odds with the triangle of metal affixed to the stick in Gerald's lowered right hand, scurrying away as if he meant to seek cover behind the two men sitting in lawn chairs at the path's edge. Gerald recognized both of them right away. The one on the left was the cadaverous man who'd been guarding the barbecued pig on the night of the prison break and the one on the right was none other than Mathew Del Papa. Junior was holding a cigar to his mouth, flits of its ember trailing off its cherry like a comet's tail blowing in the wind, and Senior was resting on the stock of a machine gun propped in his lap. He nodded to Gerald like he always did whenever they'd passed each other in the unit's common area — a sign of grudging or mutual respect — and Gerald played along by nodding back.

Zip had since dispensed with his pantomime and was walking towards him, his rifle pointed at Gerald's knee caps and his finger itching on the trigger but it wasn't upon him that Gerald's attention had settled. It was the grim rider. He could now see that the man had what appeared to be sharpened bones pierced through each of his pectoral muscles. They looked to Gerald like human ribs. Trickles of blood resembling a red river winding through a desert leaked from the wounds on either side of them.

I don't think you've met my friend, Zip was saying and Gerald looked back at him. He wuth hoping you'd drop by. When you never thowed, figured we might ath well pay you a vithit. Then looking back at the grim rider. Well ain't you gonna thay hi, Ed.

Ed gave a grunt which served him just as well as any hello and then Zip was speaking again.

Ed don't talk much. But take it from me, he wuth real keen on meeting you after I told him how you'd killed that bear, what wuth it, with your bare handth?

He was looking at Gerald like he expected him to contest the point and Gerald gave his head a subtle shake, not so much because what he'd said was a lie but because he knew right then that this had nothing at all to do with Ed and everything to do with Zip. He must have been harbouring a grudge against him all those years at Central North, for the way he'd looked at him one time or maybe for the way he hadn't another. Why he'd chosen to execute his revenge now, it was hard to say. Could have been merely a matter of convenience but looking over the men in the lawn chairs, both armed with machine guns, and the cadaverous man wearing a flak jacket spanned with a line of grenades, got him to thinking that maybe he was to be the opening act — a teaser — in advance of the main attraction.

Whatever that might have been, he doubted he'd ever live to see it.

And I believe it, I do, I do, Zip continued as if he believed no such thing. Ed here, mind you, he had hith doubth, tho I thaid, well there'th only one way to find out.

The grim rider had grown impatient with Zip's preamble and was already striding forward. Zip stepped out of the way just in time to keep from getting trampled and then it was only Gerald and the grim rider, coming at him with the lowered head and upraised eyes of a bull about to go into a full-on charge. His arms were cocked in front of him, the knives as fearsome as any pair of claws, and he was glaring at Gerald with about the same menace as had the bear he'd killed, those five years ago, though this man was as big as a grizzly and the bear he'd killed was a much smaller black.

When he'd first seen *that* bear, it had been raised on its hinds, towering over Evers, sprawled on his ass not five feet in front of it. Hearing Evers's scream and the bear's growl, he'd come hurtling out of the bush, snatching his hunting knife from its sheath and leaping over his son, hitting the bear with such force that it had staggered back. He'd grabbed a hold of it around the neck with his one free arm, and drove the blade into the bear's eye even as its claws raked across his back and its teeth tore into his shoulder.

There wasn't a day gone by in the five years he'd spent at Central North that he hadn't cursed himself for his hubris. It was a word that his grandfather had often used when prognosticating about the presumed fate of humankind. He'd used it so often that Gerald had finally looked it up in the dictionary on the shelf in their living room.

This is what it had said:

Hubris n. *Wanton arrogance.*

And it had certainly seemed like the worst kind of arrogance going after the bear like he had. Blacks were notoriously skittish and hardly ever attacked anyone. All it likely would have taken was a yell to have scared it off but there he was, feeling invincible all over again. He'd been paying the price for it ever since but never in his wildest imaginings would it have occurred to him that his hubris would have brought him to this, facing off against a man as big as a grizzly and just as fierce, coming at Gerald like he was standing between him and his cub.

Holding his ground, Gerald cautioned himself, *Don't you be going off all half-cocked again. You only got one chance at this. You got to be smart about it!*

Tightening his grip on the haft of his stick, like he was actually thinking of using it, his eyes open wide, letting the fear shine through, taking a step back then as if he meant to flee, Trent then shouting, Stop! No fighting allowed!

He was emerging from beneath the Airstream's awning, wagging his finger. A trail of drool spanned from his chin to the collar of a sleeveless white undershirt and he was paying that as much mind as he was Darlene tugging at his arm, pulling him back. Gerald staring after them like he couldn't bear to face his own doom, all the while keeping sight of the grim rider in his peripheral. The rider took the bait, lashing out with the blade in his right hand and Gerald only then sprung to life, lunging forward, dodging the strike even as he loosed the steak knife he'd secreted in his left hand, gripping it blade-down and driving its point into the man's side at the height of his navel, burying it up to its hilt and carving a straight line four inches deep across his belly.

The grim rider was already lashing out with his other hand as Gerald spun around behind him, his head snapping back, trying to avoid the blade veering down, and failing that by less than a hair. The sharp edge of it nicked the corner of Gerald's mouth and he twisted into a roll, coming out of that in a crouching squat five feet behind the other. Watching the grim rider tottering, turning to face him on unsteady feet, taking one step forward and then dropping to his knees, the knives slipping from his grasp and his hands groping for his belly, trying to stop his guts from spilling out through the gash. Gaping upwards at Gerald in muted confusion and Gerald upon him again, slashing downwards with the stick-blade, burying half of it in the grim rider's left eye socket and snapping the rest off with a quick jerk of his hand.

The grim rider lolled sideways and Gerald bent low, snatching up one of his machete-knives and spinning back towards Zip and Pops and the cadaverous man, licking at the blood on his lip as if he was eager for a taste of more. The latter two were now on their feet and Zip was raising his gun, levelling it at Gerald's chest. Gerald took a long and solitary breath, maybe his last. But as he exhaled, Pops was setting Senior on the gun's barrel, pushing it back down in silent reprieve even as Junior raised a flare gun over his head.

A red ball of phosphorus leapt from its spout, lofting skywards. Gerald — and Trent and Darlene too — watched it with craning heads: a trail of burning red whisked up by the wind and streaking across the dark with the celerity of a shooting star. Trent and Darlene stared after it as it fell behind the treeline on the far side of the tracks and Gerald's gaze alone settled back on the three Sons.

Zip was standing in their fore. He was holding his rifle propped against his thigh and he'd since pulled a black bandana tight to the white of his eyes, concealing the wreck of his face but doing nothing at all to dampen the menace in his voice.

You're gonna wanna . . . run.

C layton had nodded off sometime before dark.

He was roused by the hospital tent's crossbeams rattling in the wind and the violent patter of rain pelting the roof, or it could have been his wound, itching like it was teaming with ants. He sat up scratching at his leg, raking the fingernails of both his hands on either side of the dressing as an urgent murmur of voices arose from the waiting room. He couldn't tell what they were saying until he heard the rustle of the tent flaps leading into the examination rooms and all he heard of what followed was the older nurse asking, She bit you? Now why'd you let her go and do that?

Her tone carried the teasing reproof of a grandmother chastising a grandson for his latest misadventure and that seemed to have cowed whoever had been bit. All was quiet again except for the storm and the old man coughing from across the hall. This was broken a short time later by the pretty young nurse sticking her head in through the flaps of Clayton's stall.

Oh, she said, you're awake.

Hard to sleep with all the racket.

Not much I can do about that. How's your leg?

Itching like hell.

That's a good sign. It means it's healing. Try not to scratch it.

It could sure use some more of that ointment.

I'll put some on it when I change the dressing.

I'd appreciate that.

If there's anything else—

She was already pulling her head back out.

I was wondering about my friend?

Your friend?

The one I came in with.

Oh, she said, he left.

Left? Left where?

He didn't say.

Did he say when he was coming back?

He didn't say much of anything. He asked if there was a back way out and I pointed him to the emergency exit.

Clayton thought on that.

You say he went out the back?

He seemed to be in a hurry about it too.

Is that right? Huh.

She shrugged as if it was the least of her worries.

Is there anything else?

Yeah, you got anything to read around here?

Read?

You know, like a book.

A book? She was looking at him like she'd never heard tell of such a thing.

Sure, why not? Don't you read?

I read all the time. Just not . . . books. I thought only old people ever read books anymore.

Ah hell, ain't nothing better than sitting down with a good book.

She'd looked at him cockeyed.

You don't strike me as the type.

What type is that?

The type that reads.

My dad was a big reader, he said, which was the truth. He died when I was a baby. All he left was a shelf full of books. Mom said he'd read every one of them and so I read 'em too, figured we could at least share that. I guess it kinda put me in the habit.

I'll see what I can do.

The flat tone of her voice told him she wasn't planning on troubling herself too much over it but a few minutes later she returned carrying a rumpled paperback.

Nurse Maddox had one, she said, holding it up. The back says it's a mystery.

They's my favourite.

In truth he preferred true crime but it earned him a sprightly smile as she set it on the bed and that was well worth the lie.

It wasn't much as mysteries went, a simple paint-by-numbers written by some old lady who didn't seem to have ever met a criminal and yet was hailed on the back as one of this century's greatest crime writers. He'd got to muttering, Bullshit, every time one of her ex-cons did or said something that no one he'd met at Central North would have ever been caught dead saying or doing. When he was almost halfway through the nurse popped her head through the flap again, this time asking with a look of genuine concern, You okay?

Fine, he answered. I'm right as rain.

How's the book?

It's a good'un.

I'm glad to hear.

The old man set to coughing again, his virulent hack degenerating into a gasping wheeze, and the old woman called out, Nurse! Nurse!

Duty calls, the nurse said, offering him an apologetic smile as if she'd like nothing better than to stand around chit-chatting.

Maybe she's warming to you after all, he thought and that giving him a measure of hope, albeit slight, as he returned to the book, doing his best to keep his muttered, Bullshit!s, to himself as he read on. When he'd got to within four chapters of the end he made a nickel bet that it was the partner who'd killed the cop who'd been shot in the first chapter, though he'd have been plenty disappointed if that's the way it turned out, preferring mysteries, true crime or otherwise, to keep him guessing to the last page and always hoping for the bad guy to somehow turn out to be not so bad after all. And the partner was plenty bad, unlike any cop he'd ever met, but he had to admit, if grudgingly so, bearing at least a passing resemblance to more than a few of the inmates at Central North, most of whom couldn't seem to think more than a second or two into the future, living in an ever-present, at mercy to their every whim, and who could turn violent at the slightest provocation, the same as the partner in the book.

At present he was fucking the dead cop's wife in the bed she'd shared with her husband and that giving him plenty of motive to have killed his partner but absolutely no apparent reason whatsoever to explain why he'd wrap his hands around her neck, as he was doing at present, tightening his grip and squeezing the life out of her.

A shot rang out—

Or so it said on the page at the exact moment the lights winked off.

Submerged in the dark and cursing, Son of a bitch, staring up at the bulb on the ceiling as if it might provide some clue as to

213

what had happened. Despite the book's shortcomings, he'd been drawn into its web of deceit and casual violence and was eager to get back to it.

The old woman was again calling out, Nurse! Nurse!

It wasn't but a second before the pretty young nurse was calling back: It's probably just the breaker. I'll go take a look.

Lying back on his bed, the dark so pervasive he needn't have shut his eyes though he did as he often would when ruminating on something he'd read, thinking about what had just happened and trying to figure out what might happen next.

Maybe it was the woman's son who'd shot the cop.

Except he was only five and autistic on top. It seemed a stretch that he'd have had the will to shoot anyone even if it was the man strangling his mother. Someone else maybe. The real killer perhaps. Maybe it was the heavy breather who'd been leaving messages on her phone after her husband had died, a subplot — and not a very convincing one either — which the author had seemingly used solely to add a little extra tension to the early chapters but which Clayton now reasoned might be linked to the main story. A stalker who was in love with a woman such that he'd killed her husband and had now killed her lover too. Or maybe he hadn't killed her husband and had simply been watching her, seeing the partner choking the life out of the object of his desire and stepping in at the last moment to save his one true love. Clayton imagining then the woman gasping on the bed, pinned under her would-be murderer. The stalker rolling him off and the woman choking for breath, sitting up sobbing, her face spattered with blood and the stalker sitting down beside her, taking her in a gentle embrace, soothing her.

It's okay. You're going to be okay.

The woman getting her first good look at him. She'd have seen him before. The creepy neighbour who was always out watering his lawn whenever she left for work or maybe it was that athletic-looking guy at the drugstore at the end of the block who'd paid for her tampons that time she'd forgotten her wallet and was in urgent need.

Either way, he'd brush the hair from her face even as he reached for a tissue from the box beside the bed, using it to wipe the blood in delicate caresses from her cheeks.

We have to call the police, he'd say, the woman startling at the thought, yelling, No!

But why, No!?

Could have been she'd killed her husband in the first place, which is what Clayton had thought by the third chapter, changing his mind twice in the meanwhile and thinking now that he'd been right from the start.

Maybe—

But wherever that thought might have led would have to wait.

He'd just heard a crackled *pop!* It sounded almost electrical in origin, so it could have been the nurse flipping the breaker. But the lights didn't come back on and it was shortly followed by a second. There was no mistaking that one. It was a rifle shot. Listening as its dying echo was engulfed under a virulent *rat-a-tat-tat!*

Someone's shooting off a machine gun!

An explosion then: a sudden and cataclysmic *boom!* accompanied by a flare of light imprinted in the tent's green as a deep shade of purple and ruffling its canvas, rattling the crossbeams and startling Clayton upright on the bed. As it faded, he could hear a distant scream — a woman's high-pitched wail sliced in two giving way to the old woman across the hall yelling, Nurse! Nurse! What's going on? Nurse!

Swinging his feet over the side of the bed, he set his good one on the floor, testing his bad against the hard-packed dirt and then pushing himself upwards. A sharp stab shot up his bandaged leg.

Bracing himself against his next step and wincing through the pain, he hobbled forward, swiping at the flap blocking his way and lurching through.

He could just make out the old woman standing half in and half out of her own cubicle, too afraid to venture any further. Screams resounded now of a frantic pitch that suggested to Clayton that a rabid grizzly had been loosed in the camp and these were punctuated by gunshots like a posse of twelve had surrounded it and were right then shooting it down. But that hardly explained the explosion, or the fiery tinge leaking through the slit in the flaps leading to the waiting room.

What the devil's going on? the old woman asked as Clayton surged past.

He could hear the ragged rasp of her husband calling out, Sable, which he took to be the woman's name. She didn't respond with so much as a twitch in his direction, her eyes following Clayton, his form now cast in an aura of red from the infernal glow seeping in through the door. Parting the slit and stepping into the waiting room, as bright as the inside of a Chinese lantern but lit from without. Shadows roamed the walls, vague and ominous shapes like creatures of some ancient malevolence fleeing a maelstrom against the crackle of fire, the screams and the sporadic bursts of gunfire. The pretty young nurse was crouched behind her desk, peering over its top, flinching every time she heard a shot. Clayton spied her not two steps in and took a quick sideline, skirting to the desk and crouching down beside her.

What the hell's going on? he whispered.

She shook her head in a quick lateral spasm and that was about all she seemed prepared to say on the matter.

You stay here, Clayton said, I'll go take a look-see.

She grabbed at his arm with a desperate clutch as he stood.

I'll only be a moment, he said. I'm just gonna take a peek.

She released his arm with grave reluctance and he stalked towards the entrance, ducking low and walking with a sideways gait as if such might render him invisible. He was two steps from the tent flaps when they flew open. A man flailed through the part, clutching at his jaw, or rather at the empty space where his jaw should have been. All that was left was its top teeth, the fronts jagged and broken and blood weeping in a steady stream between his fingers as he fell to his knees, Clayton lunging out of the way as the man's head leaned forward at a drastic angle, and his body following that, slumping face-first onto the ground. Tendrils of flame lapped at the shirt on his back and the hair at the base of his skull was singed and smouldering. His hand clawed out in front of him, dragging him forward as if two or three inches more might have meant all the difference.

The smell of burnt flesh and hair tickled at Clayton's nose as he circled wide around him, muffling a cough against his arm, and coming to the door. He paused there, all reason telling him he ought to just turn tail and run, grab the girl, set out for anywhere but here.

But he'd come this far and his hand was already reaching out, pulling back the tent flap no more than two fingers' width. All he could see through the slit was an ocean of flame. The bank of tents was set ablaze and a woman was thrashing out from the nearest of these. She was clutching something to her breast — could have been a baby. The tent had melted over both, enveloping them in the shroud of burning blue, and she was screaming such a horror he'd never even imagined possible, with only worse yet to come.

A hulking figure appeared, striding out of the inferno as if the flames couldn't touch him. It was one of the grim riders Clayton had seen at the prison. He was naked save for a tattered pair of jean shorts and had a weapon raised in one hand, as long as a machete though it was made of steel the thickness of a lawn mower's blade. It was serrated along its outside edge and sharpened on its inner and a barbed prong jutted from its tail end. He was swinging it in mid-arc down on the woman and child on fire.

Clayton released the flap before it struck, dodging backwards and tripping over the man on the floor, landing on his rear and scrambling backwards in a fumbling crab walk. There were hands then reaching down — the nurse's — pulling him to his feet, dragging him towards the back. As he turned, the flaps leading into the examination rooms parted and the nurse grabbed him tight, burying her head in his chest, too afraid to face what might happen next. As a figure emerged from the dark, a subtle waft of vanilla scented with lavender brushed against Clayton's nose. It was from her hair. He'd never smelt anything finer and right then he'd have died a happy man if it meant he'd never have to let her go.

But it was only the old woman emerging from the back.

What in the blazes is going on? she asked in a tentative croak.

They were already bustling past, careening blindly through the door, the nurse in the lead, hauling Clayton by the arm, hobbling to keep up.

Lady, he screamed, you got to get the fuck outta here!

B rett had given Émile the bottle four days ago.

He and Larry, the settlement's so-called quartermaster, had opened a carload of Canadian Club forty-ouncers and he'd sought Émile out in his camper van. It was parked in a small recess on the far side of the solar panels, Émile choosing a spot at a careful remove from the camp the same way he'd always lived on the outskirts of any community he was meant to police.

You'll want to keep a lid on that, Émile had advised after Brett told him there were about a thousand more bottles where that came from.

If his thirty years with the Ontario Provincial Police had taught him anything it was that the quickest way from bad to worse was adding liquor to the mix. He'd told Brett as much and Brett had answered, offering him a backhanded wave as he'd walked away, I'll certainly take that under advisement.

He never had, as far as Émile knew, and making his rounds over the next three days, Émile had to settle an increasingly frequent, and virulent, series of disputes. Mostly it was couples who'd had one too many and were keeping the neighbours up with their foolishness, the worst of them a brawl involving five men and a "friendly" game of cards that had spilled out of a thirty-five-foot cabin cruiser hitched behind a pick-up truck. It'd got Émile to considering that maybe it was time to convert one of the empty railcars into a drunk tank — and that, perhaps paradoxically, had got him to thinking about the bottle he himself had in the van, how it'd take at least a couple of extra nips beyond the two he allowed himself before bed if he'd have any hope of falling asleep.

But on this night, sitting in the van's driver's seat, he'd drunk half the bottle and was as wide awake as he'd ever been, his mind addled in restless agitation not so much by the memory of what he'd done — he'd been a cop too long to lose sleep over shooting a couple of Euphies — but by the memory of what he hadn't. And what he hadn't done was kill that son of a bitch Gerald Nichols when he'd had the chance. How many times had he told one of his constables during the trial that if he'd been the one to find him he sure as hell wouldn't have let him make it out of the woods alive? Killing two officers of the law in cold blood, that son of a bitch, all the while letting his wife bleed out on the floor. He didn't even try to call an ambulance, just left her to die like she was no better'n a dog. And every reprobate and low-life in the province treating him like some sort of folk hero for what he'd done. And who had paid the price? Cops, that's who. Eight more shot in the nine months he was on the lam, and then there was that kid who shot his stepfather, said it was the book that journalist from Toronto wrote about Nichols that had given him the idea.

Fucking Savage Gerry!

Just thinking about it was enough to make Émile want to put his hand through the windshield. He'd tried to read it himself, didn't get past the introduction. Barely even read half of that. The gall — the fucking gall! — calling him a modern-day renaissance man on the first page when he wasn't anything but some no-account dope peddler. And then demanding they reopen the case not five pages later. Saying that Charlie Wilkes had falsified evidence, that Gerald Nichols was the real victim.

A victim? How dare he! He was a fucking animal, that's what he was. No better than a rabid dog. And what do you do with rabid dogs? You don't let them walk around spreading their disease. And you sure as hell don't call for their release. You shoot those motherfuckers on sight!

And here you've had the chance twice now—

Wrenching open the van's door and stumbling out, his feet skewing wildly beneath him on the soggy ground, one hand steadying himself on the door's frame and his other reaching for his sidearm. The rain had dwindled to a sprinkle but the wind was still fierce. It snatched the hat from his head, sending it pinwheeling end over end into the dark, sweeping it under a railcar.

Fuck it, Émile cursed, turning down the road leading into the camp.

It was pocked with muck holes filled by the rain and by the time he'd reached the far side his feet were sloshing in his shoes. He suspected Gerald Nichols was in an Airstream parked along the tracks. He'd seen a woman calling to him from there as he'd led Officer Dawson to the hospital after he'd shot those two Euphies.

He's probably raped and killed her by now. Fucking killed her and then raped her, most likely. An animal like that. Drank her fucking blood, you can bank on that!

Yet no matter how he goaded himself he couldn't summon the will to more than stand at the edge of the Airstream's awning, glaring at the door, listening for any sign of distress that, at last, would have compelled him to act.

All he heard though was the wind whistling through the camp and flapping at the tents and further away, a growling snarl. It was coming from behind him. As he turned towards the tracks there was a sudden whimpering *yelp!* that couldn't have come from anything but a coyote.

They're after the bodies!

After he'd left Dawson at the hospital he'd rounded up Brett, a couple of tarps and two spade shovels. They'd put the bodies of each of the Euphies on a tarp and dragged them across the tracks, laying them beside the grave where they'd buried that family who'd stumbled into camp dying from radiation poisoning. The mother had been carrying a baby who was already dead and the father a three-year-old who'd die two hours later. The parents barely lasted the night. Nobody in the settlement, as far as Émile knew, had learned where they'd come from, or even their names, but half the camp had turned out for the ceremony when they'd laid them to rest in a single grave within the shade of a crab-apple tree on the far side of the tracks. It seemed as good a place as any to bury the two Euphies, and him and Brett had made a go at digging the grave even as the rain pelted down around them, giving up only when the hole had filled to their ankles with water.

Maybe we'll be lucky, Brett had jibed with his characteristic jocularity as they hurried for cover, and the wolves'll make off with 'em before we get back.

Émile had smiled then but he wasn't smiling now as he crested the rail bed. The moon's crescent was winking through a ragged striation of furrowed clouds and in its transient glow he could make out the distinct shape of three coyotes, though they were almost big enough to be wolves. Two were chewing at the bodies and the third was skulking on a narrow perimeter, snarling and growling, eager to get his share.

Get away from there, he screamed, you filthy bastards!

Starting down the slope and his feet sliding out from under him in an avalanche of crushed gravel. He landed hard on his rear and pain shot up from his elbows battering against the sharp stones, that only further inflaming his ire.

Lunging back to his feet, his sidearm in his hand, aiming and firing a shot. It sounded like a cannon going off in his hand, making him regret it even as its echo was swept away by the wind, knowing he'd just woken up half the camp and for what? He might as well have been shooting at the stars for all the good it did. The two coyotes had barely glanced up from their feed before going right back to it and the other was staring at him with the curious expression of a dog whose master had just delivered it an unprovoked kick.

Bending low, he swiped a baseball-sized rock from the rail bed and approached them with it cocked back, daring them to make a move. He'd got to within ten paces before all three of them wheeled around at once, scurrying for the trees, and Émile hollering, You better run!

Flinging the stone after them, he snatched up one of the shovels stuck upright between the bodies and the half-dug grave. He chased them to the edge of the trees with its blade upraised as a bludgeon, panting with the heaving chest of a racehorse run too hard, harder than a man who'd already had two heart attacks had any business breathing.

Feeling doubly the alcohol now churning in his stomach, reducing his legs to a pair of flimsy pipe cleaners, phlegm congealing in his throat. He hacked it up, propped over the shovel, the handle sinking into the muddy ground and his hand slaking along its wetted shaft, almost taking him down with it.

How long he'd stood there — buckled over, spitting up and waiting out the urge to puke — he couldn't say. Felt like an hour but it could have been just a few minutes. He was aroused from his stupor by a sudden fluorescence: a reddish hue flushing over the ground with the urgency of a shooting star, his head craning skywards, his eyes gaping in curious disbelief at the flare bristling against the night sky. The wind whisked it out of sight behind the trees and Émile had almost resolved that he ought to maybe look into that when his gaze settled back on the grave.

The moon was rippling within the watery hole. It looked more like someone had buried a bathtub than dug a final resting place and he stood there a moment telling himself he ought to finish what they'd started, knowing that it'd be a miracle if he even got two feet down before it would be the death of him.

Still, he couldn't just leave them like that.

With the same resolve that had gotten him out of bed every morning when he was a peace officer, no matter how bad it had been the night before, he stumbled forward. He'd just pitched the spade into the sodden ground beside the bodies when: *pop!* It sounded like someone shooting off a rifle. Probably just some drunk, boozed up on Canadian Club, no better than him. It was followed by another *pop!* as like the other that it struck Émile it was simply answering the first, two drunks calling out to each other in the night. He stood up, thinking that if he heard a third he'd have to do something about it.

The tracks were raised some six feet off the field. He couldn't see anything of the camp beyond the vague outline of treetops and then all of a sudden he could: a burst of such glaring luminescence that it seemed to him the whole camp must have been set on fire. Dropping the shovel and lurching forward, hearing the stuttered *rat-a-tat-tat* of a machine gun merging into the concussive shock of an explosion out of which emerged a solitary scream shortly joined by a full chorus growing into a symphony of misery and woe orchestrated, he saw as he crested the rail bed, by a man standing on the top of a school bus parked in the centre of the field. A geyser of flame leapt from the nozzle in his hand, gushing in a sweeping circle of fire over the tents and RVs, their occupants spewing forth from doors and stumbling out of flaps only to be consumed by the infernal spray as the man on the bus picked them off with the casual malice of a young boy burning ants through a magnifying lens.

Émile horrorstruck, gaping with catatonic despair at the panorama of suffering playing out before his very eyes, benumbed by the state of his drunk so that the scene registered in his mind as some far-off thing, a nightmare too terrible to be real. People fleeing in all directions against a staccato of gunshots and a heavier pounding, like a jackhammer. Tracking that towards the woods on the far left as the barrage sliced through those in flight towards the treeline, men, women and children alike shredded in its wake like piñatas filled with blood, spying then a worse blight even than that.

A dozen or so men were emerging from the trees. All of them were giants, shaven of head and bare of chest, their skin as pale as ash. They were carrying weapons of a crude and medieval design and wading into the burning lake of fire, lending their blades to the carnage, hacking and slashing like some demonic vanguard of hell's own army unleashed to wreak havoc upon an unsuspecting earth. That sight at last enough to spur him into action. His hand groped for his sidearm, knowing even as he loosed it from its holster and drew himself forward, propping his arms on the tracks and sighting at once on the man with the flamethrower, that he might as well have been holding a squirt gun for all the good it would do him now.

He squeezed off a shot and it went wide, he couldn't tell by how much, only that the man was still standing. His back was to Émile, the flame-geyser dousing the north side of the camp, and

Émile could clearly see the two tanks affixed to his back. Émile took more careful aim this time, adjusting for the wind's bluster and steadying his hands, taking a breath, pulling the trigger on the exhale and then pulling it again and again and again. The last one must have hit the tanks as a bright flash flared — an explosion of such a rare and brilliant white that it scalded Émile's vision same as if he had been staring into the sun. Averting his gaze and shutting his eyes, and that hardly sparing him from the intensity of its bright. A Big Bang's worth of spectral after-flares exploding from beneath the closed flaps of eyelids and a woman screaming:

Stop! You're hurting me! Let me go!

She was cast against the sea of flames and with his vision still blurred from the retinal burn he couldn't see much about her except that she was short and squat and was being harried along the path at the base of the railway bed by a woman tall and lank, clutching at her hand. She was fighting her every step with the tantrum of a child being dragged away from the playground, slapping at the other's hand and venting her bile in vitriolic bursts.

Let me go! I said. I want to go back to bed! Stop it! You're hurting me!

Two men were chasing after them in frantic pursuit — a scrawny little runt hauling at the arm of a lumbering oaf about twice his size. The first was holding a knife with a blade as long as his forearm and Émile only had to blink once to see that it was Gerald Nichols. Gerald was looking up at him, wide-eyed, as surprised by the cop's sudden appearance as Émile was by his, his expression taking a frightful turn as Émile raised the sidearm in his hand, taking a clear bead at his chest. And there was no doubt in his mind that he would have pulled the trigger too, if his finger hadn't been stayed by the sight of the man stumbling to keep up behind.

He'd met Trent a dozen times and on each occasion the gentle giant had walked right up to him, exclaiming with childish glee, I like policemen! You're my friend!

The first time he'd been with Brett and after Trent had wandered off, Brett had commented that he looked just like Frankenstein's monster if he'd been assembled out of a bunch of gangly teenagers, a startling contrast to his demeanour for he was about the smilingest-friendly person Émile had ever met. Shooting Gerald Nichols would mean he was also as good as dead and he'd have just as soon shot himself than cause harm to a soul as innocent as Trent.

As Gerald dragged him past, the oaf was beaming at the flames, squealing his delight and crying out in fervent exultation, Pretty! It's so pretty!

Émile watching him prance on by, all the while thinking, *God, what I wouldn't do to trade places with him.*

D evon was sitting up, blinking against his drowse and more so against the way the world seemed to be spinning off its axis. His daughter, Sophie, was crying a piercing wail and that felt like someone driving a nail deeper into his right temple with every shriek. He'd probably catch hell for that too, waking the baby with his snoring, which is why he'd thought his son must have been shaking him awake.

He always snored after he drank and he'd been drinking plenty last night while he was playing cards with Larry and his friends, using the storm as an excuse to explain why he was out so late when he'd finally stumbled home. Wendy was sore mad then and her mood wouldn't likely have improved since, especially with the baby crying such an anguish that there seemed nothing Devon could do about it except lie down, close his eyes again and draw the sheet up over his head.

Dad! Hands were shaking him again and Bud was yelling into his ear. Dad, you got to get up. Something's happening. Dad! Dad!

He was pulling at the sheet, Devon's hands tugging back at the thin fabric, feeling it slipping from his grasp.

Dad! Wake up!

Devon pushing back at him, muttering, I'm sick. Let me be, and the boy calling out in panicked defeat, Mom, he won't get up!

A faint and distant clattering. It sounded enough like the sudden burst of hail on the roof of the freight car when he'd finally fallen into bed that he didn't pay it much mind. It was answered by a *bang!* that couldn't have been anything but a rifle shot, loud enough that it sounded like someone had fired it off not two feet from his head.

And then his brother was calling out, Where the hell's your dad?

He's passed out drunk.

The matter of fact tone in his son's voice, like he couldn't have expected better from his father, was finally enough to get Devon to cast off the sheets.

I'm up, he said trying to lever himself back to a sit. I'm up, I'm up.

Out of the dark there appeared a patch of flaming orange hovering before him like a piece of tissue paper set ablaze and bobbing on the end of a fishing line, his eyes trying to focus on it and thwarted in their every attempt. Then it was gone, eclipsed by a shadow as big as his older brother. He felt Brett's meaty hands clasping his arm, dragging him roughly to his feet. Brett's breath stank of rotting teeth and the sour taint of rye so Devon knew he'd been drinking too. The overwhelming stench of it was too much for his delicate state and he heaved over, puking onto the floor, his brother tightening the grip on his arm to keep him from falling down.

You picked a helluva time to turn into dad, he scolded, pulling him back upright, Devon grinning at him, trying to regain his favour.

How do you like them peas now! he said.

It was a line that had formed an almost sacred bond between them ever since Devon, then five, had refused to eat his peas at dinner one night. Their father had flown into a rage, though it wasn't his son he was mad at, it was something that had happened at work he'd been brooding, and drinking, over ever since he'd got home. He'd stormed out of his seat, grabbing Devon by the hair with one hand and stuffing a spoonful of peas into his mouth with the other, all the while screaming, How do you like them peas now! Ever after, when one of them had run afoul of their father and felt the sting of his hand or his belt because of it, the other would search out where he'd gone to sulk it off, offering him the same in what had become an all too common refrain. How do you like them peas now! never failing to get a smile, and that, for as long as they'd lived at home, their only salve against their father's wrath until he'd found God and that had finally cured him of the drink for good.

Except Brett wasn't smiling now. He lashed out, smacking Devon hard in the face with the back of his hand.

Sober up, goddamnit! he yelled. And fetch your rifle. Now!

Leaving him then on wobbly feet and storming back towards the freight car's door, the sting of his brother hitting him finally enough to rouse Devon to the fact that something dire was afoot, for he'd never once struck him before.

Lumbering towards the door and his son appearing in his path, handing him his glasses first, waiting until he'd slipped those on and then thrusting the Remington .303 into his hands. He grasped that as a drowning man would a lifesaver and stumbled on, seeing Wendy's face appearing now in the glow cast from the door. She wasn't angry, as he'd expected. She looked . . . And this was the strange thing. She looked plain terrified. Sophie was at her breast, sucking greedily, and in the absence of her screams he could hear others — an almost spectral wailing increasing in pitch and timbre with each passing breath and drawing him on reluctant feet past his wife and child.

What had appeared as a flaming tissue he could now see was the strip of orange in the door curtain's tie dye. The darker shades of blue above and below blotted out the light but not the orange, which pulsated with such effervescence that it seemed like the very world beyond had been set ablaze. Brett was crouched in front of it with his rifle parting the veil, its barrel tight against the container's steel frame and his one eye pressed to its scope, tracking something with a subtle declination and squeezing the trigger, oblivious to Devon reaching out, prying the curtain's other seam and stepping through the breach, seeing at once that the whole world did in fact look like it had been set on fire.

People were fleeing in all directions, some drenched in flames and others, no better off, fleeing into a briar patch of machine gunfire. And worse even yet: what appeared to be creatures of a demonic descent stalking amongst it all, lashing out at the survivors with blades of a dark and malevolent design, the closest in view not twenty paces away. He was carrying a severed head gripped by the hair in one hand and using the other to slash a spiked mace down on a German shepherd tied to a chain and pouncing at him with snarled teeth. Brett let off another shot, catching the creature in the chest, stumbling him back with the dog lunging at his neck, the both of them pitching backwards, disappearing within the rippling sea of tents.

Brett was then yelling, Get down, goddamnit! You'll get yourself killed!

He seemed so far away.

Feeling a hand on his arm, dragging him down. His head was reeling again, from the screams and the smoke and the booze.

Someone was calling out, faint and indistinct, and that drew him out of his haze, looking up and seeing a huddled mass of figures hurrying down the tracks. The man in the lead was the scrawny little fellow they'd picked up that afternoon who Brett had insisted was none other than Gerald Nichols though he'd looked more like a crazy surfer bum than the man Devon had imagined *him* to be.

Maybe you can get him to sign your knife, Brett had jeered, meaning the one he'd bought online, the same make as the one Gerald's grandfather had given him for his sixteenth birthday and which Gerald had carried on his belt into the northern wilds those six years ago. The derisive tone in Brett's voice had further convinced Devon that he must have been teasing him, knowing how much his younger brother had once admired Savage Gerry so.

The man was clutching at the hand of a simpleton whom Devon knew as Trent and there was something about the way he harried him along — against all reason — and something more about the look in his eyes — the same truculent recalcitrance which had imbued his father's on the day he'd been born again — that told him that maybe Brett had been right after all.

Finding an odd sort of comfort in that and also in the tenor of the man's voice, cutting through the mad holler of screams and the mayhem as if maybe there was still some hope yet to be found in all this madness.

Start the train! Gerald was yelling. Start the goddamn train!

The nurse was kneeling at his side, slapping his face, imploring in a whispered scream, Get up! Goddamnit, get up!

Clayton was lying prone on the ground at the foot of a maple tree, not fifteen strides through the woods at a hard run from the hospital's emergency exit. Couldn't have been more than a couple of minutes since they'd fled the hospital but it felt like an eternity with the wind carrying a chorus of screams punctuated by gunfire from the camp, her all the while trying to rouse him, slapping his face, whisper-screaming in his ear and when that didn't work pinching him hard on the arm. Still, it wasn't enough to get him to more than moan and she was waylaid in her efforts by the frantic crackling-pound of footsteps.

Looking up, she saw two shadows careening out from behind the hospital tent, hightailing it into the cover of trees. There was the shadow of a man shortly chasing after them, stopping as soon as he came into view and raising the silhouette of a rifle to his eye. A loud *bang!* then, followed by a whoop of glee.

Hot damn! I got one!

To whom he was calling out it wasn't clear and the moment after he spoke he hurried off in renewed pursuit of the one that got away. The nurse heard the snap of a branch underfoot from somewhere close and then Clayton was moaning again. His eyelids were flickering but they were a ways from opening yet. Clamping her hand over his mouth, she froze as still as a mannequin, too afraid to move or even breathe.

A spiralling *ticka-ticka-ticka-ticka* sounded from behind her, almost like a rattlesnake shaking its tail. The nurse gripping Clayton harder now and her eyes darting into the dark depths, looking for a way out and seeing only the vague outline of trees and the dark spaces between, neither doing her a damn bit of good. Shocked then into the harsh glare of LEDs, alighting from not five feet in front of her. The flashlight, she could see, was affixed to the barrel of a machine gun from which a laser sight beaded dead centre on her forehead. In his other hand its owner was holding a child's spinny toy.

With a flip of his wrist it let out another *ticka-ticka-ticka-ticka*. She lunged sideways, same as if it really had been a rattlesnake, and scurried headlong into another man as solid as a tree. She peered up at him towering over her, leering right back. In the LED's bright she could see a mess of brackish curls — a hillbilly beard — above which night-vision goggles concealed his eyes but hardly his grin, ecstatic and malevolent as the man clamped his hand under her armpit and hoisted her roughly to her feet, crooning, Well boys, looky what we got here!

She's a real sweetheart, all right.

This from the rattle-man even as she was reaching under her scrubs, snatching at the scalpel she'd secreted in the waistband. She lashed out with it, plunging it into her captor's thigh deep enough to hit bone. His hand sprung loose and she darted forward, dodging for the cover of trees. She'd hardly made two steps before he'd recovered and was snatching out at the trailing wisps of her ponytail, catching a handful and jerking her off her feet.

Twisting the hair around his knuckles as tight as a tourniquet, he dragged her back up. Holding her at arm's length, he propped his shotgun against the tree, using his free hand to pry loose the scalpel from his leg as if it was nothing more bothersome than a thorn.

You're gonna live to regret that, he growled, wheeling around and pulling her, kicking and screaming, into the shadows, any and all hope for a possible future reduced to the rattle-man calling after them: Make sure you leave some for us this time!

He'd since turned his attention to Clayton. He was standing over him straddle-legged with his manhood dangling out of his unzipped pants, aiming a steady stream at the gap parting Clayton's front teeth and cajoling, Wakey, wakey.

What the hell are you doing? a third man asked.

Don't seem right killing a man when he's knocked out, the rattle-man answered.

Clayton came to, sputtering up pee and his head thrashing from left to right trying to get out from the spray, his hands flailing in front of him.

There you are.

Come on, hurry up willya. We're missing out on all the fun.

Won't be but a tick.

The stream dwindled into a trickle of spurts shortly replaced by the flashlight's glare, Clayton blinking against it and trying to see past the blur. His head ached like it had been hit with a brick but as his vision cleared he saw that was the least of his concerns. The barrel of an assault rifle was hovering two inches from his nose.

He could hear the distant rattle of gunfire and a woman — *the nurse!* — screaming a bitter agony from closer by, couldn't have been more than a few feet away. Struggling through his daze and the throb of his head, trying to reconcile how he might have come to this and recalling nothing beyond the memory of the nurse burying her head in his chest and the sweet smell of her hair. Clayton clinging to that as he held his breath, cringing against the shot shortly to come.

He was still waiting on that when he exhaled and then the man was calling out:

Hey, Punch, come on over here!

What? The crunch of feet. What is it?

Take a look for yourself.

A face appeared out of the bright, bending towards Clayton. The man had a pair of night-vision goggles propped on his forehead and was appraising him with beady eyes.

He look familiar to you? the rattle-man asked.

I don't know.

Take a good look.

Punch bending closer.

You don't recognize him?

Now that you— Oh, shoot. It's the damn scarecrow!

That's what I'm saying.

Don't that beat all.

What was your name now again? the rattle-man asked, glaring at him.

C-Clayton? Clayton stuttered as if he himself wasn't quite sure.

That's right. Clayton, Clayton Crisp.

Hands then grappling with Clayton's arms, hauling him to his feet, and a familiar face, and an even more familiar nose, pressing forward, only inches from his. It was bulbous and slightly askew, a boxer's nose — which was exactly what it was.

It's me, the man was saying, Marcus Bonny, though Clayton only knew him by another name. Before Marcus had come to Central North he'd earned the nickname One Punch after he'd knocked out two opponents with a single blow on his way to winning Olympic gold, earning a twenty-five-year sentence shortly thereafter for killing a man in a bar fight with the same type of punch.

That's quite a goose egg you got there, scarecrow, the rattle-man was saying.

In the dim beam from the flashlight now pointed at the ground Clayton could easily make out that he recognized him too. He'd never heard him called anything but DB, as much because his name was David Balmond as because he had a tattoo of a diamondback coiled around his neck, its head rearing up onto his chin. Staring into its beady eyes now hardly did anything to ease Clayton's fright, knowing as he did that DB was about as mean as the snake that shared his initials.

Wasn't that the funniest damn thing, DB was saying, as if all of a sudden he'd forgotten Clayton was there. Him running smack dab into that tree branch?

I damn near pissed myself to keep from laughing.

Were you recording?

You know it.

Come on then, let's have a look-see.

Right now?

No time like the present, I always say.

One Punch produced a holophone from his pocket, thumbing its screen and then holding it suspended horizontal between him and DB. He must have still been recording through the goggles propped on his brow for when a holographic image material-ized in the air above the screen, it was of two hands holding the phone, one of them thumbing it in tandem with its real-life counterpart. The image flickered and then two four-inch figures appeared in their stead, holding hands and running at a hard clip. One Punch thumbed the screen again and their movements slowed to a quarter speed even as the focus zoomed in on the back of what was clearly Clayton's head the moment before it struck a low-hanging branch. As his chin thrust suddenly upwards the image zoomed out again to show his legs flying out from under him with such force that he dragged the nurse down after him, the two men renewing their laughter watching that and DB exclaiming:

That's a keeper all right!

The nurse's screams had stopped though Clayton could still hear the ones from the camp punctuated by bursts of gunfire. He was wondering who it was that might have been out there with her, knowing it was too late to do her any good and yet his eyes still wandering to the shotgun propped against the tree. A quick lunge would be all it took to get at it. If he was lucky he'd shoot one of them before either knew what was happening but that'd still leave the other. He was trying to make up his mind which one he'd rather it be, when DB wrapped his arm around his shoulders, jostling him like they were old friends, though he'd never so much as spoken a word to him before.

Jesus. Clayton, Clayton Crisp. Won't Virgil be surprised to see you?

He'll practically cream his pants, I bet, One Punch added.

He always said the scarecrow had the softest lips of anyone he'd ever met.

Like a little girl's, is what he told me.

Well, he would know.

The mere mention of Virgil had Clayton revising his plan. His eyes darted low, fixing on DB's knife clipped to his belt, not an arm's length away, telling himself he'd never get both of them with that but at least if he tried, he'd never have to think about what that evil motherfucker Virgil Boothe had done to him.

Virgil ever tell you how he got caught? DB was saying.

The scarecrow?

That's who we're talking about, ain't it?

He was coming out of the john when his stepfather clocked him with a rolling pin, way I heard.

DB shaking his head, smiling at that.

You got to shoot 'em in the head, he said, laughing.

Ah hell, everyone knows that.

Clayton thinking, *It's now or never*, at the exact moment DB released his hold, striding away, stopping three paces hence, his knife well out of reach.

You hear that? DB asked.

A piercing screech filtered through the lash of wind against the trees and the screams and the gunfire. It was accompanied by a metallic clanking noise which didn't mean much to Clayton but must have meant something to One Punch.

Shit, he said, they're moving the train.

Then craning his head backwards he called out, Duck! Get your ass in gear, they's taking the train!

Cocking his machine gun and DB doing the same, the latter turning backwards and probing about the woods with his flashlight, Clayton looking after him knowing the nurse must have been out there somewhere.

He's gone, DB said.

What?

Duck. He ain't fucking there.

Well where the fuck is he?

Tracking the light back towards the maple tree, skirting past a figure stepping out from behind its trunk and jerking the rifle's barrel back. The man wasn't visible for more than a camera flash and Clayton only caught a glimpse, but a glimpse was more than enough to see who it was. He'd never thought of him by any other name than Gerald Nichols but it was another that immediately sprung to his mind.

Savage Gerry! he thought as if he was seeing him for the first time, watching him pounce with the swift reproach of a mountain lion, batting away the rifle and driving a knife as big as a machete up through DB's gaping jaw, its point coming out the top of his skull, wheeling around then and disappearing back into the dark, gone before DB had even begun to fall.

One Punch had been looking the other way and it was the crumpled thud of DB's body hitting the ground that spun him back. Spying his friend on the ground and Clayton standing over the body, drawing his own conclusions about the blood pouring through the gash under his chin and his eyes narrowing to slits as he jerked his rifle up, levelling it at Clayton's chest.

You son of a bitch!

Clayton doing his best imitation of a deer in headlights. A sudden movement then from behind the tree: a downward swipe at One Punch's hand. It was too dark to see exactly what it was but it must have been the machete-knife slashing through his wrist. His hand dropped like a dead fish and the rifle's barrel scissored upwards, knocked off kilter, One Punch stumbling back, holding his arm up, blood spurting from its severed end, too shocked to glean what had just happened.

He never would.

Gerald was on him again. His next slash caught One Punch just below the chin. He toppled backwards, swallowed into shadow, and Clayton gained an ounce of courage from that, taking a step forward and hollering out, Who's the son of a bitch now!

240

When Gerald returned to the tree a moment later he was carrying One Punch's gun and stuffing a few extra cartridges into the elastic band of his swim shorts. Clayton was nowhere to be seen but he could hear him calling out in a tremulous whisper from somewhere close, Nurse! Nurse!

Slinging the rifle's strap over his shoulder, he bent over DB, prying the gun out of his hands and hearing the frantic crunch of footsteps on leaves growing near. He brought the rifle's flashlight to bear, freezing Clayton, blinking, in its light as he rounded the maple tree. Clayton's arm was curled around the young nurse's waist. Her scrubs were spattered with blood and so was her face and she was clutching at Clayton with the fierce resolve of a rock climber whose feet had just given out beneath her.

Goddamnit, Clayton was beaming, I knew you'd come back!

Gerald had lowered the gun and was bending to DB, foraging through his pockets for spare clips. He found two and stuck those in the elastic band with the rest. The screams from the camp had quieted and the only gunfire he could hear was coming from down towards the tracks, the steady pummelling of machine guns answered at intervals by the sporadic crack of rifle shots. Two blasts from the train's horn sounded, long and mournful, and when he looked back up the nurse had forsaken Clayton for the shotgun propped against the tree. She must have had some experience with that breed of gun and was pumping it with the confidence of a seasoned pro, Clayton all the while staring at her with that familiar look of unbridled adulation. She cast Gerald a shy yet defiant glance — at once thanking the man who'd just saved her and telling him he'd never have to do so again.

This here's— Clayton started then stopped short, looking to the nurse. You know I never did catch your name.

Jenny, she said and Clayton turned back to Gerald as if he wasn't standing only two feet away. His eyes were alight with unmistakable pride, like an awkward teenager introducing his first belle to an older brother who'd always had a way with the girls.

This here's Jenny!

A hail of bullets chased after them as they fled from the woods, the shots sparking in *ping!*s off the train's container cars as they came onto the tracks, Jenny in the lead and Gerald in the rear, Clayton with hands raised, calling out to the two soldiers sighting on them from the top of the nearest container, Don't shoot! Don't shoot!

The soldiers tracked past them with the fluid movement of wolves on the prowl, both releasing controlled volleys just over their heads, Clayton and Gerald ducking low and Jenny spinning with the shotgun on a quick axis, unleashing a blast of her own.

A woman was calling out, Over here!

She was standing at the back end of the second-to-last car, clutching onto the rail of the ladder leading up onto the platform and beckoning them as the car approached at a snail's crawl. Jenny was pumping her gun and firing again even as Clayton grabbed her by the arm, hastening her towards the woman with Gerald skulking along behind, keeping his own gun trained on the woods and his gaze darting on sweeping laterals about the trees.

Bullets ricocheted off the container's corrugated steel hull and Gerald answered them with three short bursts.

Quick now! the woman was screaming as she came alongside. Get inside! You'll be safe in there!

She was maybe in her late fifties, matronly and wearing a mauve leisure suit. Her hair was tucked under a black ball cap with a red CN embroidered on the front, the same one Larry had been wearing when they'd met him the day before. It was his wife, Chris, and in her free hand she was holding a rifle. Clayton was the first to reach her, clambering up the ladder and bubbling, Boy are we ever glad to see you!

Jenny climbed after him but Gerald hurried on past. Just beyond the final car he could see the lights of the CN truck, inching along behind and taking heavy fire from within the solar pond. The muzzle of a sidearm was sticking out its passenger window and the barrel of a rifle was propped on the truck bed's near wall, the both of them bucking and every shot they took answered with a dozen from below, hammering at the truck. The passenger door was getting the worst of it and the man inside no less.

He must have taken about all he was going to. As Gerald reached the end of the train, the passenger door flew open and the old cop lurched out, scrambling down the loose gravel, his gun blazing like some kind of outlaw delighting in his last stand, screaming out, You goddamn bastards!

The left shoulder of his uniform was caked in blood and he took another shot in the leg before he'd made three steps, his feet sprawling out from under him and his body tumbling down the slope. Gerald cut towards him on a steep angle, emptying his own rifle into the solar pond as he stormed towards the man and then tossing his gun, grabbing for the one on his back and emptying that one too.

Gunfire sounded from above and behind, the soldiers joining in the fray. There was a brief whistle and a resounding *boom!* — must have been a rocket-propelled grenade landing in the middle of the panels. A welter of glass rained down upon Gerald as he slung his rifle on his back and bent over the cop. One ear had been shot off and there was blood bubbling through two holes in the blue shirt bulging at his gut.

He was already as good as dead.

He knew it too, or so it seemed to Gerald as he grabbed him by the hands, trying to haul him to his feet, only to have the cop muttering a gurgled and definitive, No! Or could have been he'd have rather died than be saved by a man such as he. Either way he was too weak to mount more than a feeble protest and Gerald pulled him up by the arms, lifting him onto unsteady feet, letting him then droop down over his shoulder. Turning back up the tracks and feeling his knees about to buckle under the weight and that only firming his resolve as he mounted the slope.

The gunfire at his back had gone still under the unrelenting barrage from the soldiers. Halfway up the bank — the gravel crumbling beneath his feet and every step barely giving him an inch — the truck's tailgate banged open and Devon clambered out. Ducking low, he scrambled to the edge of the rise, reaching out his hand, and Gerald grasped at it, using it to pull himself to the top.

Devon eased the cop off Gerald's back and draped the dying man's arm over his shoulder, half carrying half dragging him towards the back of the truck. He'd just set him on the tailgate and was swinging his legs onto the bed when the guttural growl of an engine turned him back towards Gerald. He was bent over, trying to catch his breath. He craned his head in the same direction and he and Devon gaped in hateful awe at the spectre of a grim rider roaring between the rail lines, his bike bouncing over the ties at a dizzying clip, hurtling towards them.

Slamming the tailgate shut, Devon dove overtop, yelling out, Brett, get us the hell out of here!

The truck lurched forward and then Devon was calling out again.

Goddamnit Gerald, get a move on!

The grim rider had just reached the furthest of the four fuel cars, maybe three hundred yards away. His headlight flared in tandem with the four riders behind and it would have been an even bet as to what had shocked Gerald more, seeing five of the grim riders in pursuit or hearing Devon shouting out his name. His feet didn't seem to care either way and were already tripping over themselves in a mad flurry. Devon was leaning over the tailgate. There was a strange look on his face — an odd mix of serenity and jubilation. The only other person who'd ever looked at Gerald like that was his grandfather and only when he thought Gerald wasn't looking. Why a man such as Devon would find comfort in him just being there was beyond all reasoning but it hardly slowed his pace as he pitched himself up and into the truck.

The moment he was on board, Devon was craning his head at the cab, shouting at his brother, Can't you go any faster!

I can only go as fast as the train! Brett yelled back.

Then give them the horn, goddamnit!

The grim riders were just passing the last fuel car, closing fast on the truck and the train, the both creeping along like they were on a sightseeing tour. Devon had the rifle at his shoulder and was taking shots at the lead bike. Gerald had taken a spare clip from his waistband and was jamming it into the gun but couldn't get it to fit. Must have been the wrong kind. He pitched it out of the truck and grabbed one from the other side. There was a sudden *whoosh!* from behind and overhead. He looked up at a trail of sparks — an RPG of some sort — on a direct line for the closest fuel car. It struck the front of the cylinder, exploding in a cataclysmic blast that at once devoured the five grim riders and seemingly the night itself, such was the intensity of the firestorm it unleashed. Gerald was thrown backwards, tripping over the cop's legs and slamming hard onto the floor, banging his right elbow on the wheel hub and feeling a sharp shiver of pain chasing all the way to his jaw. A piercing whine in his ears that seemed to have infected every cell in his body and at any moment might rend him apart, and fire raining down all around, flaming droplets fanned by the wind and bursting against the treetops, others spattering against the truck, dozens of firelets sizzling along its rails and on the bed, Gerald feeling a sear on his arm and sitting up, slapping his hand at the spot of burning oil.

A hand clasping at his ankle had him staring down at the cop. The left side of his face looked to have melted but that was only from the blood where his ear had been shot off. His one sleeve was on fire but he didn't seem to have noticed, clutching at Gerald's ankle and squeezing him hard as if he meant to do him harm. There was grief in the man's eyes and a tear sprouting at the corner of one. The cop was gasping for breath and spittle was foaming into bubbles at his lips.

Keep 'em safe! he was yelling in a desperate plea with what amounted to his dying breath. You keep 'em all safe!

His grip relented and his head sagged to the floor and Gerald turned towards Devon.

He was somehow still on his feet. He was rubbing frantically at the top of his head with one hand and patting out a fire on his shoulder with the other, stamping out those on the floor with both his feet. The treetops around him were a seething furnace of yellow and orange billowing in gusts, Gerald watching as the fire chased along the treeline ahead of the truck and feeling at any moment it would consume them too.

The night broke into a simmering dawn.

The tracks had turned due north and Gerald was facing due south, sitting propped against the back of the truck's cab and watching the stars wink out one by one against the sky's lightening blue until only one remained, though he knew it wasn't really a star at all, it was the planet Venus. It hung just above the horizon and seemed to grow brighter as the others faded in a futile attempt to challenge the sun's dominion over the day, the first rays appearing as a hazy diffusion of deep reds shading to pink seeping through the cloud of smoke blurring all sense of the world's southerly expanse. When the sun finally did manage to shine through it was well above the treetops, emerging as a perfect disc of shimmering orange about the size of a full moon, its bright dimmed enough that Gerald could stare straight into it without feeling the urge to even blink, a welcome balm against the sight of the dead cop lying at his feet.

Devon had covered Émile's face with a green John Deere ball cap but his missing ear was clearly visible and it was impossible for Gerald not to see in him a shade of his grandfather. When Gerald had finally found him three days after he'd gone to check his traps that one last time, crows had pecked his face clean to the bone, Gerald wishing ever after that he'd never had to see him like that.

He must have fallen asleep staring at the sun, for the next thing he knew Devon was jostling him awake.

Pit stop, he said when Gerald opened his eyes, squinting against the morning bright and at Devon's face, mere inches from his, smiling not unlike Clayton had the first time he'd met him.

I left you some clean clothes. He motioned to the truck's side-wall. Figured you could use some.

He'd stood up and was peering down expectantly at Gerald, waiting for him to say something. Gerald's head was still ringing from last night and his mouth was dry as sandpaper and all he could muster was a curt nod.

It seemed to satisfy Devon just fine and he offered a slightly more boisterous nod in return.

You going to help me or not?

This from Brett, who was standing in front of the open tail-gate. His hands were resting on the dead cop's feet and there was a shovel propped beside him.

I'ma comin', Devon answered, turning and bending to the cop and taking up his arms.

The ball cap dropped from the dead man's face as he lifted him up and Devon motioned to set him back down.

What the hell are you doing? Brett asked.

Fetching the hat.

What the hell's he going to do with a hat, buried in the ground?

Devon must have seen the logic in that and walked straddle-legged to the edge of the truck bed with the cop suspended below him.

Gerald could feel a burning spot about halfway up his arm and when he looked down at it, there was a blotch the size of a quarter — red, raw and blistering — singed into the skin where he'd been hit with the burning oil.

A little staunchweed'll clear that right up, he told himself and that was enough to finally get him onto his feet.

The crunch of footsteps on gravel as Devon and Brett carried the body down the tracks gave way to Brett cursing, Goddamnit, I thought you said you had him! And Gerald could hear other noises too — the buzz of deerflies circling his head and further off a baby's cry and a metallic banging, like someone throwing stones against one of the container cars.

Devon had left him a pair of brown cargo shorts and a green T-shirt. It was pretty much the same outfit he'd worn every summer's day from the time he'd come to live with his grandfather. It was also what he'd been wearing the night he'd fled the farm with Evers, a mild enough sort of coincidence that he didn't give it much thought until he was picking up the shorts. Devon had threaded a brown leather belt through its loops and when Gerald unfolded them he saw that he'd threaded that through the loop of a leather sheath holding a hunting knife, the hilt of which struck him at once as familiar. Its metal was bronze in hue and wound with strips of leather, alternating between black and red. When he pulled the knife up an inch, there was imprinted on the steel just below the tang, *Made In Sheffield, England* and so he wasn't at all surprised that when he flipped it over *William Rogers* was imprinted on the other side.

Damned if that ain't the exact same knife your grandfather gave you on your sixteenth birthday. The same knife you'd carried with you every

single day of your life afterwards. Until . . . Until you left it jammed in
that bear's eye and Charlie Wilkes found it three days later.

The last time he'd seen it was in the courtroom in a plastic
Ziploc bag labelled *Exhibit Q*. A strange enough coincidence that
it had him craning over the side of the truck, peering after Devon,
wondering where he might have got it. Him and Brett had set the
cop's body on the ground, a hundred paces hence, and appeared
to be embroiled in some heated argument, maybe about what
they were supposed to do with it next.

The train had stopped amidst a field of granite humps, smaller
ones like foothills on either side piled into miniature mountains,
the largest fifty or so feet tall. A sparse few spruce had taken root
in the crevices lining the black rock but nothing else grew there
except patches of moss, dried to a flaky crisp. The landscape told
him that he was almost home and also that Devon and Brett were
a long way from burying the body just yet.

He left them to their debate and stripped off his blood-
crusted shirt. He dressed in the shorts and T-shirt, then stepped
over the truck's other side dropping to the ground and scanning along the tracks, looking for any sign to tell him how far
he might still have to go. All he could see were more granite
humps and a smattering of people lingering in the train's shade
or crouched over, picking at the blueberry shrubs growing in
groves along the edge of the rail bed.

Darlene was sitting and smoking with restless deliberation
on the platform of the car four down and Trent was bent over
stiff-legged in front of her. He was picking berries one by one
and holding each of them up to her, showing them off, before
popping them into his mouth, as jovial as ever. Devon's two kids
were picking alongside him, the boy dropping his harvest into the
peanut butter jar at his feet and his younger sister reaching into
that to claim her share, their own nonchalance at complete odds

with the desperation wrought on their mother's face. She was standing a few feet behind them, cradling her pregnancy bump in both hands and gazing in abject longing at some indeterminate point on the horizon, her lips moving in silent prayer as if pleading with her God to show her some sign of his mercy.

In front of the container opposite there was a charcoal barbecue, the same one Larry had been grilling steaks on the day before. It was a younger man tending the grill now. He was as wiry as Larry so it could very well have been his son. He couldn't seem to keep still, endlessly fidgeting at the scruff of his beard and prodding at the steaks with a fork, his eyes all the while fixed as if on a tether to the two women walking down the tracks. They were holding the hands of a toddler between them, swinging him upwards, and the boy was laughing and shrieking his delight. One of them was Chris, maybe the man's mom. That would make the other woman his wife and the toddler his son and after what had happened last night it wasn't much of a mystery to Gerald why he'd be looking so nervous watching them walk away, even though they only ventured to the end of the next car before turning back around.

Otherwise, Gerald didn't recognize anyone else of the dozen or so others milling about. All of them were grouped in twos and threes, huddled together or hugging each other, some laughing through tears and others outright sobbing, some just talking, could have been about the weather or any other damn thing as long as it wasn't about what they'd just been through, every last one of them seemingly trying to figure out a way to cope with their own personal grief.

Gerald played along by reaching down and scooping a handful of blueberries from a bush laden with the fruit, as big and juicy as grapes. As he munched on those he mounted the nearest of the granite humps, hopping from that one to the next, a little higher, and then onto the next after that, higher still. He was twenty feet up when he stopped and turned around, scanning again down the tracks and seeing no more than he had before except for one important thing: Clayton's familiar lank bent over a puddle of rainwater just beyond the last of the pickers. He was bare-backed and washing handfuls up over his face and through the soapsuds foaming in his hair. After he'd done that a few times he reached into the puddle and pulled out his shirt. Wringing it, he started down the tracks in his limpity-hobble, his head craning ever so slightly around the cars, searching out, it seemed to Gerald, the white truck just around the bend.

Plucking a marble-sized pebble from the ground, he waited until Clayton had come to its bumper and then launched the stone. He hit the cab's door between the C and the N and startled Clayton such that he ducked for cover with a mad flail of his arms as if someone was shooting at him all over again, no matter that the shot would have had to come from above and behind. He was quick to recover though and even quicker to smile when he spotted Gerald standing above him. He stepped up onto the same hump Gerald had but the jump to the next seemed to be beyond him.

He took the long way around and when he'd finally made it to the top of the rise, Gerald was peeing off the highest peak and into the valley below. A four-lane highway had been cut through the lowlands but all that was visible to Gerald was a span of asphalt twenty or so yards long. On the far side of it there was a fringe of trees bordering a small lake. Beyond that the only thing he could see to the horizon was a gaggle of geese flying north in V-formation against a cloudless sky, honking in their insistent manner as if they were fleeing some urgent threat right on their tail feathers.

Helluva view from up here, Clayton said coming up behind him, staying at careful remove. He'd found a two-pronged stick and was using it to scratch at either side of the dressing on his leg while Gerald finished his business.

Gerald gave a double shake and tucked himself back into his shorts, turning around, brushing his hands on his shirt out of habit and blinking, as much against the sun's glimmer as against the way Clayton was looking at him, sneaking quick peeks out of the sides of his lowered eyes, struck suddenly shy.

They say how long it's going to be? Gerald asked, more to break the awkward quiet than because he cared one way or the other.

Oh, it'll be awhile yet, Clayton answered. Larry said there was a bunch of railcars blocking the tracks just outside of Sudbury. They's gone to see about moving them. Then they got to switch the tracks. Looking up and peering at Gerald with those eager eyes: They's taking us over to North Bay.

That right?

I ain't never been to North Bay. I guess it's as good as anywhere. Jenny seems pretty keen on going there anyway.

At least it ain't Marmora.

Clayton grinned wide.

You said a mouthful there.

A voice called out, Clayton! and he turned around, finding Jenny standing in front of the CN truck.

What I tell you about scratching your leg? she yelled.

What? Clayton called back. I weren't scratchin'.

She frowned at that, both hands now firmly on her hips.

You find any yarrow yet?

I'm getting to it.

Well hurry up. I told you, there's people waiting!

With that she set off back down the tracks with a brisk stride, shaking her head and Clayton shaking his head too, but for an entirely different reason.

I think she must have a little of my mother in her, he said, and from the sparkle in his eyes it seemed he wouldn't have had it any other way.

He made to turn around then stopped.

That's three I owe you, he said.

What? Gerald asked.

I'd have been dead three times now, it weren't for you.

Clayton was looking again at him shy-struck and it occurred to Gerald that what he was really trying to tell him was that he wanted him to stay. Gerald couldn't promise him that and searched past him, looking down at the tracks, trying to think of something he could say on this the last time, he was certain, he'd ever see the scarecrow again.

He spotted Trent helping Linda down the ladder from one of the freight cars. Beside them, Darlene was looking up at him like she had been doing so for a while, waiting for him to notice her. Now that he had, she waved and he offered her an awkward wave of his own. If it hadn't been for Clayton he'd have never come back to the camp and all three of them would be dead right now.

We'll call it even, he said to Clayton.

Ah hell, I ain't going to let you off *that* easy.

Clayton was already turning around and hobbling away, Gerald watching after him and seeing that Darlene was still looking up at him. He couldn't read her expression but it wasn't much of a leap for Gerald to imagine that she was imploring him to stay too.

You ain't likely to find another woman like her anytime soon, he thought, though really he was thinking of Millie and the life she'd given him.

You could make yourself a new life all over again.

Teasing himself with the thought even as his hand wheedled under his shirt, seeking out the photograph of his son.

A piercing shriek then, Linda screaming, Trent, let me go! I told you to let me go!

She was slapping viciously at Trent's arm and he responded by jamming his fist in his mouth, biting down hard. Darlene pitched her smoke and hastened to intervene, yelling, Linda, stop it! Stop it!

Her eyes were off Gerald for only a moment and that was all it took for him to slip over the edge of the ridge, letting gravity take hold, his sneakers flat against the steeply sloping rock face and his hands levered at his sides with their fingertips brushing against the rough-hewn stone, keeping him on an even keel as he glided down towards the road.

T he highway led him west.

The granite field was shortly overcome by a lightly cultivated forest of mostly evergreens that broke, at the city's limits, against a ten-foot-high wall made of some synthetic compound moulded to look like stone and mortar. It stretched a kilometre along the road and was overseen at intervals by a dozen or so security cameras and had three entrances all guarded by wrought-iron gates, the so-called "safe zone" Millie had never grown tired of railing against.

It had once housed an idyllic suburban paradise reserved for government employees and whatever executives the mining companies had seen fit to leave behind. The task of buffering them against the swelling tides pounding Sudbury in wave after wave of human detritus was placed squarely on the shoulders of its own private security force. The remnants of that Gerald could see in the crow- and coyote-ravaged bodies clad in black riot gear sprawled on the ground inside the smashed in first gate, evidence of a last ditch attempt to muster some sort of defence after the dam had finally, and terminally, burst.

That it was The Sons who'd rode the crest of that particular wave, there could be no doubt. Their shady-tree-at-dusk emblem was emblazoned on the wall, underscored by a spray paint scrawl reading And God said that the end of all flesh has come before me for the earth is filled with violence through us.

How that violence had played out was clearly delineated in the burnt-out husks of a half dozen cars and trucks cluttering the road ahead. All of them had been customized with steel plating over their windows and ornamented with spans of razor wire. A few of the larger vehicles had been equipped with snowplough blades–cum–battering rams as had the semi that had finally smashed through the gauntlet. After it had breached the gate it had crashed into what must have once been a sprawling mansion and was now a toppled pile of blackened wood and household appliances. The truck had plummeted through the house's floor and leaned at a drastic angle into its basement. The rear doors of its trailer were open and it was hard not to image a Trojan horse's worth of heavily armed maniacs storming out, wreaking unholy havoc on the occupants of the "safe zone." Multitudes of those littered the streets and driveways, food now for the hosts of crows and vultures cloistered in delirious squabble over the bodies, overseen by a spiralling mass of their brethren darkening the sky into a great and swirling whirlpool of feathered black.

Such devastation that it surely wouldn't have been out of place in *The Road Warrior*. Yet as Gerald stood at the gate, surveying the wreckage, his gaze at last settled on the decomposing body of a French poodle chained up in the nearest yard, so that it was a line from another movie that immediately sprung to mind.

They killed Chief!

It was from one of the old westerns he and his grandfather used to watch. That particular film was different from the other movies they'd watched in that they'd only screened it once, unlike all of the others — good, bad or indifferent — which they'd seen numerous times. It was also a good deal more violent than any of the other films in his great uncle François's collection and also replete with sexual acts of a most deviant kind, this going a good way to explaining why they'd never watched it again, Gerald being only seven at the time and it being unfit entertainment for a boy even twice his age.

Gerald couldn't remember its name and hardly remembered anything about it at all except how it ended. His memory of that began with a Sheriff sitting at his desk scrutinizing the tin star in the palm of his hand with the doleful expression of a man being led to the gallows. A priest was reciting the last rites over him though the Sheriff was paying that about as much heed as the fly traipsing unmolested over his heavily whiskered cheek.

The door then suddenly burst open and a young boy dressed in a leather coat and chaps and wearing a dusty white cowboy hat two sizes too big barged in, hollering, They're coming!

The scene then shifted to the chug of a steam engine approaching a small mining town, circa 1870. Its main street was empty and the only sign of life was the boy's three-legged mongrel dog, Chief, panting at the foot of the steps leading up to the Sheriff's office. At a blast from the train's whistle, he cocked his head in the direction of the tracks as his owner's voice rose in sharp declaration from behind.

Let me go! the boy screamed. Let me go!

The Sheriff had grabbed him around the waist and was carrying him kicking and screaming towards the cell in the back of the room, where he meant to keep the boy safe until the danger had passed. A growl alerted the Sheriff to Chief, biting at his pant leg trying to free his owner as the Sheriff flung the boy onto the cell's bed and slammed the door shut. As he locked it with a key on a large metal ring, Chief was still clinging fast to his pant leg and the boy, now glaring through the bars, goaded, Bite him Chief, bite him good!

At that, the Sheriff drew his sidearm and pointed it at the dog's head, cocking its hammer back with his thumb.

And though no one watching could possibly imagine the Sheriff actually shooting the boy's dog — he was a good man to a fault — the boy yelled, Run Chief, run!

The dog turned tail, darting as fast as his lopsided gait would take him out the door and into the street at the very moment the train pulled into the station, letting loose another whistle-blast. Back in the Sheriff's office the priest was clasping the key's metal ring to his chest with one hand and making the sign of the cross with the other while behind him the boy pounded at the bars of the cell, hollering, Let me out! Let me out!

With a billow of black smoke and the hiss of brakes, the train ground to a halt and a lone man stepped from its front-most passenger car, exuding the casual flare and fine dress of a big-city poker shark about to show those rubes how the game was really played.

Why hello Sheriff, he said with the uncontained delight of someone greeting a long-lost brother rather than his arch nemesis.

The Sheriff was holding out his holster in one hand, letting it drop into the dirt, speaking not a word. All that needed to be said between the two men was contained within this gesture of sur-render, and to savour the moment — his victory over the forces of good — the Villain retrieved a cigar from his inside breast pocket. He bit off its end before inserting it in his mouth and reaching for the match stuck behind his ear. Striking it on his cheek, he took a moment to study the flame, his eyes then narrowing to slits as he searched out the Sheriff, a devious smile parting his lips and the Sheriff gleaning what that meant, his own eyes widening in alarm as the Villain touched flame to tobacco at the exact moment the train's freight car burst open to reveal the Gatling gun inside.

A pounding then, identical to that which Gerald would years later witness at the prison. Bullets shredding the town in a calamity of splintered wood and shattered glass, spewing over townsfolk huddled in far corners, clutching their loved ones, leaving no building unharmed, least of all the Sheriff's office. The priest bore the full brunt of its fury, caught in the hail of bullets like a marionette dancing at the mercy of some spastic puppeteer and flung up against the cell. The key ring was rent loose from his hand and skittered to within arm's reach of the boy cowering under the bed as the assault continued its unrelenting carnage. Lanterns exploded in the general store and in the livery stable, flames racing up the latter's wall and crackling against the hay, horses whinnying and rearing up in their fright, and the bullets raging on, sparing nothing and nobody in their furor except the Sheriff, who was watching with gathering horror as his town was at once torn apart and consumed by flames, and only himself to blame.

The scene then shifted to the ridge above the town, where there watched from atop a pale horse a lone rider, dressed as a perfect duplicate to the boy who'd sounded the alarm. The Gunslinger was smoking a hand-rolled cigarette and observing the spectacle below with an expression that revealed little except that he had a heart as cold as stone.

As the last few shots echoed about the canyon walls, he turned his horse with the lassitude of a cowboy too long on the range and the scene shifted back to the town, panning over its shattered façade laced with blood-drenched bodies draped out of glass-toothed window frames, and then searching out the livery stable doors, engulfed in flames and fallen off their hinges. A horse, enlivened by fright, bolted through them. A single gunshot rang out and it reared up, crashing to the ground with a terminal thud, and the scene shifted back to the Villain.

A wisp of smoke trailed out of the barrel of his gun as he turned to the Sheriff penitent on his knees two feet in front of him.

I reckin you ought to 'ave killed me when you had the chance, Sheriff, the Villain said.

The Sheriff stared up at him with quivering hate, a last act of defiance before the Villain swung his revolver butt-first at his head. But it was not the dull thud of steel on bone that sounded, it was the splintering crunch of the livery stable's roof collapsing, belching a mire of sparks from the inferno within.

Some time had passed, for the building was toppling at the same moment the Gunslinger was riding into town, puffing on his hand-rolled cigarette, oblivious to the devastation, his eyes fastened on the saloon at the end of the block where the Sheriff had been hung, crucified, from the eave over the front door. Blind even to the boy slumped in the dirt, cradling his dead dog. Blood matted Chief's fur and there was a smear of it on the boy's chin.

They killed Chief! he cried.

Looking up and seeing the Gunslinger passing by without a glance, the sorrow etched in the boy's face turned to rage.

Don't you care? he screamed, scrabbling to his feet and yelling after his hero. Don't you care about anything?

Tears were now streaming down the boy's cheeks and on the night he'd watched it with his grandfather Gerald was crying right along with him, great braying sobs like he couldn't have imagined anything worse than a three-legged dog being shot down in the street. The old man watching him from his easy chair, not moving a muscle, letting the boy cry himself out, the way he couldn't when they'd buried his mom not five days previous, her son standing over her grave as stone-faced as any gunslinger.

For years after, whenever Gerald had found something dead, whether it be a squirrel or a racoon run over by a car, or even a dead fish washed up on shore, he'd remember that dog. He'd counter the corresponding pang rising in his chest by looking up in mocking mimicry of the boy in the film and crying out, They killed Chief! In this way he'd taught himself never to cry again.

Staring now over at the poodle, he wished he'd saved a tear, if not for it — left by its owners to die chained up in the yard — then at least for his son, whom he'd treated no better.

Thinking again of the boy in the movie crying out his desperate plea to an uncaring world and that carrying ahead to Evers, doing the same standing in the open front door of their house, his mother dead on the floor behind and his father standing in the driveway before him, his diminutive form at odds with the heft of the army duffel slung over his back, holding his rifle in one hand and his bow in the other, imploring the boy, Get a move on!

Flinching now from the impatient tone of his voice, like the boy was dilly-dallying with his chores and hadn't just found his mother bleeding out through a hole in her chest and then watched his father, in cold blood, kill the three men responsible.

Evers then crying out against an even greater injustice: We can't just leave her here!

And that finally producing a twinge in Gerald's chest, a slight pang as far removed from a tear as a grain of sand was from a mountain, but still it was something. Knowing that he'd left his son to a fate far worse than he'd seen in any movie and looking to the sky again, the swirling masses of carrion feeders telling him that Sudbury wouldn't be any better than the "safe zone." The name of the street where Evers lived in foster care was all he could recall from the address Jordan Asche had inscribed in his copy of *Savage Gerry: Canadian Outlaw*. He only had a vague idea of how to get there and even if he did manage to find the right house, it wasn't likely to do him any good.

If Evers hadn't been able to get out of Sudbury when the shit hit, he'd probably be dead along with everyone else.

Fumbling then for the picture tied around his neck, wrestling it out of his shirt and staring down at Evers, so fierce and wild standing with his bow upraised on the birthday rock, the pang growing in Gerald's chest like a dying ember given new life by a sudden gust of wind. Staring then deeper into the picture than he ever had before, as if it might contain a message hitherto unrevealed, knowing in fact that it did.

Evers's best chance at survival, he told himself, *would have been up at the lake.*

Feeling something else then, he wouldn't have called it hope but at least it was something other than despair. Turning back the way he'd come, he started off at a brisk walk, his pace accelerating with every step so that by the time he'd come to the corner of the wall it was escalating towards an all-out run. Hearing a voice then — his own — screaming out its own desperate plea to an uncaring world.

I'ma coming for you Evers. I'ma coming!

He approached Capreol under the cover of dark, shuffling along the tracks as a ghost might, willing away his
hunger and thirst, his all-abiding exhaustion, seeing nothing and
feeling nothing either except that the tracks were but an illusion
drawing him not towards home but into some ethereal nether-
world, as if he'd died somewhere along the way and he was
now but the spectral manifestation of his former self spurred
onwards by a longing so intractable that he'd be doomed to
walk upon them forevermore.

In this way Gerald came at last to where the rail line crossed
Highway 84, which the locals called Capreol Road, perhaps because
they couldn't reconcile the two lanes of pothole-laced blacktop that
ferried them in and out of town with anyone's reasonable defini-
tion of a highway. But it wasn't the sight of the crossing that at last
forced his weary shuffle to a tentative surrender, it was the sight of
the moon glimmering off the rippled surface of what appeared to
be a small lake on its far side. It had appeared the same to Gerald

years ago, the first time he'd passed the solar field, riding in the pick-up truck beside the old man who the woman at the children's aid in Sudbury had told him was his grandfather.

The world had seemed plenty unreal to him then, too.

He'd felt about the same as he had sitting in his closet mere hours before, listening to his mother being shot down by the police, his hands clamped over his ears and his eyes squeezed shut, muttering to himself, You're just dreaming. Wake up wake up wake up!

The old man beside him proof enough that he never had, for he couldn't really have been Gerald's grandfather since all his grandparents had died before he was born, his mother had always been plenty clear about that. So it must have just been some terrible dream. Looking up through the windshield as the truck bounced over the tracks he could see the noonday sun shimmering off the surface of a small lake, that meaning nothing to him until the road had straightened out and the lake had broken apart like a puzzle thrown into the air. It seemed the pieces were setting to float right off into the sky and he'd been filled with a sudden elation.

You are dreaming!

How could it be otherwise? Lakes don't just break apart like that.

Pinching himself hard on the arm, which is what his mother told him to do when he was having a nightmare, seeing in that same instant it wasn't really a lake at all but a field of solar panels tilted up on metal posts. Thinking it was a lake had just been his imagination playing tricks on him and he'd known then that he *was* in the middle of a nightmare but it was a waking one and there would be no way out of it.

In the intervening years, the solar lake had come to reside in his mind as nothing more remarkable than the Esso station at the corner of Highways 84 and 80, the latter's four lanes leading west into Hanmer — not so much a town as a loose conglomeration of subdivisions gathered around a mall, a couple of fast food outlets, two groceries stores and a Canadian Tire — or the green sign on the side of the road a half klick beyond reading *Capreol 6 km, Wahnapitae 18*. Just another way-marker telling him he was almost home.

It spoke to him now of that simple truth again.

With nothing more substantial between him and it than a few kilometres of potholed blacktop he eschewed the orderly trespass of the railway's ties for the road's crumbling chaotic of asphalt leading him on a widening arc away from the tracks and then looping back, running parallel to them for the last three kilometres into town. Where the road straightened out there were three white crosses raised up on the shoulder to his left — memorials to three teenagers who were walking along the road one night and had been struck by a drunk driver. They'd been killed some forty years earlier but every year since someone had returned to repaint the crosses and string new wreaths over their beams, sometimes adding little gifts — toy cars and stuffed animals, a baseball glove with a ball clasped in its mitt. He could see a hulking form amongst them, large enough to be a bear cub, except it reminded him more of a dog, its two ears raised in static alarm from the top of its head and its two eyes glinting in the moonglow, tracing after him as he walked by.

His hand instinctively went for the hilt of his knife and he angled for the far shoulder, giving it a widening berth. In so doing he saw that it was a dog all right but of the stuffed variety, its largesse immediately reminding Gerald of the ones they gave out at the game booths every year during the fall fair in Hanmer.

Now you're scared of a damned toy!

Shaking his head and that not enough to keep him from smiling, thinking of the monsters he'd faced not twenty hours ago. Treading on, drawn ever forward by the fluorescent speckle of streetlights appearing in the distance, lining the road leading into town. The town itself was effusing a faint glow — the thin and hazy waft of light pressing into the sky's gloom doing nothing at all to diminish its star-fraught splendour and Gerald deriving no small comfort from the idea that Capreol had somehow managed to get its power back on.

It was a feeling that barely lasted a step.

Cast under the first of the lights, overlooking the turn-off for Capreol Lake Road, he could see the boxy outline of a vehicle, its pitch-black shell made even darker still within the fluorescent's bright. It looked like a tank on wheels but he knew it went by the name of Light Armoured Urban Tactical Vehicle, several of which Sudbury had been gifted by the province after the passage of the Northern Ontario Repopulation Act. Gerald had only ever seen one of them up close, some fifteen years previous, during Capreol Days, the annual celebration commemorating the town's birth in 1918. They'd driven it out for display and had let the kids climb in and out of it as if it was some sort of a jungle gym. Evers, then four, had made a big fuss when Millie wouldn't let him join in the fun. In fact, the moment she'd laid eyes on the urban tank she'd turned right around, marching back home with Gerald hurrying along behind, carrying Evers slung over his shoulder, wailing his distemper.

Showing off a thing like that, she'd fumed. It's like they're bragging about how the world's gone to shit. Well count me out. I ain't gonna have no fucking part of that, no fucking way!

Millie hardly ever swore and though she'd never said as much, Gerald took her furor to mean she'd had a less-than-pleasant encounter with one of those urban tanks when she'd lived in the city. The sight of the same now guarding the entrance to Capreol wasn't enough to add more than a stutter to his weary plod, but it did have his eyes darting about the dark expanse of trees on either side of the road.

There's plenty of other ways to get to Stull other than the highway. You could cut back over the tracks, take the dirt road that runs along the Vermilion to Lakeshore. And if it's guarded too, you could swim across the river, stick to the cover of the forest along its far shore, swim back when you come to where the river split, right across from the old farm.

He was looking away from the road only for a moment but that was long enough that he didn't see the crater where the asphalt had crumbled into the ditch. His right foot plunged into it and slid away from him on the loose gravel, toppling him forward, his legs splaying out beneath him and his left knee knocking against the lip of the hole, sending a sharp spike of pain shooting up his leg. Bent over on all fours, trying to push himself back up and barely having the strength left to even lift his head.

There was a red beam lancing out of the dark on the far shoulder and it was shortly joined by another from the near side, the both of them playing at a game of tag on his forehead as two shadowy figures emerged onto the road, not ten paces hence.

Hands up! a muffled voice ordered as they approached. Where I can see them!

Hefting himself up and raising his hands above his head, gasping out a feeble, I surrender. I— I surrender! Feeling the words in every fibre of his being.

The two figures were both clad in black riot gear — body armour, masks and helmets — and shouldering assault rifles. They came to a stop five paces from Gerald and from the rifle on the right there flared the white beam of LEDs. It probed over

Gerald's upraised and trembling arms first and then scanned down over his face, finally settling on the knife at his belt.

He's got a knife, the one said, though he didn't seem overly concerned.

I see it, the other answered.

Nice and easy now. I want you to take the knife out and put it on the ground. And when Gerald paused a moment the man took a step closer: I won't ask you a second time!

Lowering his one hand and fumbling for the sheath, unclipping the clasp and drawing the knife out, setting it on the ground in front of him.

Slide it over here.

Gerald giving it a shove and it barely moving two feet.

The one with the flashlight was circling around behind him. He felt the barrel of the gun pressing into the base of his skull and a hand pulling up the tail of his shirt.

He's clean, the man with the flashlight said, circling back towards the other.

I don't know. He looks like a Euphie to me. And he sure smells like a Euphie, too.

He'd have track marks if he was a Euphie.

Could be he was injecting between his toes. They do that, you know?

He's not a Euphie. You just have to look at his eyes to know that.

The abrasive scour of the light again over his face, and Gerald fighting to keep his lids from shutting, letting them take a good look.

He's just half-starved, the one said after he'd switched off the light. Hey buddy, where you coming from?

Gerald opening his mouth and barely a croak coming out.

Give him some water, will you?

A hand was shortly reaching out, handing him a black metal canteen. Its cap was already unscrewed and he took it up, raising it to his mouth with a trembling hand. Water splashed over his beard but enough got in his mouth to set him to coughing.

Take it easy there, buddy. You're going to drown yourself.

He took another sip, smaller this time, and managed to get that down. He was just draining the canteen when a burst of static erupted in unison from the radios clipped to both men's collars.

Everything all right out there? a decidedly feminine voice inquired.

Another burst of static and one of the figures answered, Just another stray. Clicking off his radio and then reconsidering. You better bring out the quad. I don't think he's going to make it on his own.

Roger that.

The man who was talking was walking away and the other towards Gerald. The latter bent at Gerald's knife, plucking it from the ground and Gerald watching him, thinking that it was the last time he'd see it. But when he reached Gerald, he held it out hilt first and Gerald took it and slid it back into its sheath. Then the man was grabbing him by the arm, helping him to his feet. He could hear the rumble of an engine and presently two headlights swivelled around the urban tank heading in their direction.

The man was patting him on the shoulder. It was only a light tap but Gerald's legs almost buckled under its force, fighting against wobbled knees and buoyed in his efforts by the jovial tone that had crept into the man's voice when he spoke again.

Welcome to Capreol!

The quad was a black side-by-side driven by a woman wearing the same uniform as the others but lacking the helmet and mask so that Gerald could see she had short blonde hair with a single braided strand dangling over her left cheek. Her skin was unnaturally dark for a white person's and pulled so taut it reminded Gerald of a woman at Central North by the name of Struthers who'd been a champion bodybuilder before she turned guard.

The driver had given him a brown paper bag half-filled with popcorn and as he languished in the passenger seat he munched from this in between sips from the canteen wedged in his lap. She'd been casting him sideways glances the whole way, Gerald hoping they didn't amount to anything more than mere curiosity. The only thing she'd said to him so far was, I thought you might be hungry, when she'd handed him the popcorn bag, and she didn't say another word until they were passing Hanna Avenue.

Hanna was a boundary of sorts leading into the town's east-ernmost residential neighbourhood. The street lights were on there too. The houses, mostly modest bungalows and simple two-storeys, all had their porch lights on and most of their win-dows effused a yellow glow and it didn't seem much like anything had changed since last he'd been here, except that there were more people about than he'd ever seen before. Older couples walking their dogs and families strolling along, kids on bikes and groups of others playing basketball on stand-alone nets in front of driveways loaded with cars and not a single vehicle out on the road other than a few quads weaving through the crowd, none moving faster than a brisk stroll.

You know, the woman said as Hanna Avenue fell behind, you look familiar. What did you say your name was?

He hadn't and had no intention of telling her now so he said the first name that popped into his head.

Clayton, he offered. Clayton Crisp.

She shook her head.

Doesn't ring a bell.

Gerald had finished the bag of popcorn and was washing the last mouthful of that down with the rest of the water.

You from Sudbury? she asked.

Elliot Lake. It was where his grandfather had been posted when he'd first joined the RCMP and he'd had only good things to say about it. But I've been living Midland way these past few years.

Elliot Lake, that's where you're going?

My parents are still there, figure it's as good a place as any.

You walking the tracks?

Yeah.

Well you've a ways to go yet.

She was looking at him like she didn't quite believe him and Gerald asked, What was the name of this town again?

Capreol.

Gerald shook his head.

Nope, he said. Never heard of it.

They were passing by the townhouse complex between Hemlock and Field Streets. There was a country rock song blaring in French from a speaker somewhere, adding the perfect accompaniment to the revelry taking place in the parking lot — a community barbecue it looked like, its good cheer embodied by a throng of kids racing about with sparklers upraised, chasing each other amongst the adults, their elders laughing in between sips from the tall cans of beer in their hands.

Field Street was so named because it ran along the perimeter of the old high school field and its approach added a sombre taint to the otherwise festive atmosphere. It was crowded with tents and several dozen RVs and camper trailers and swarming with a few hundred people milling about in between. It struck Gerald as similar enough to what he'd seen at the train camp that when a flare of red shot up from somewhere within, a pit carved its way into his stomach as he watched it shoot into the sky, his mounting dread hardly diminished as the flare exploded overtop a line of railcars parked on the tracks beside the road. It released a flower of sparks like an autumnal tree burst into life, its leaves floating on a lazy downward drift even as another flare, green this time, shortly followed its trajectory and exploded into the outline of a four-leaf clover.

The woman had slowed the quad to allow a father and two sons to cross the road, heading towards the field. All had skin the colour of coffee beans and fishing rods propped on their shoulders and the eldest of the boys, maybe twelve, was carrying a string of three fish on a metal chain. They looked like bass. The woman must have read something in Gerald's expression and the way his hand was clutching at the hilt of his knife as the clover dissolved and was replaced by a crackling sizzle of white streamers, one after the other seemingly without end.

Midland, huh? she said as she throttled forward. How's things down south these days?

Well they ain't got the power on yet, as far as I've seen.

It's only been three days since we got it on ourselves. You see those solar panels on your way in?

I was wondering about those.

They used to feed into the main grid and it was a heck of a time figuring how to get them back online. The circuits were all fried. Finally someone had the idea to feed them into the train engines. They're just big old batteries.

That so?

One of them is enough to power half the town and we got six of them now.

At the field's westernmost edge the town had built its children a splash pad. It was in full swing, thirty or so kids romping in its spray and lit up by the multicoloured halogens imbedded in the cement of its bowl, their laughter trailing its mirth after the quad as it approached the *Welcome To Capreol* billboard. Beneath the greeting was a painting of an old steamer train puffing three clouds of smoke above the inscription, *Established in 1918*. A banner reading *Capreol Days Now On!* was tacked below that. To this someone had added in black paint *Come Celebrate 142 Years of Train Power!* and hearing what the woman had said, it seemed fitting to Gerald that it was the trains which had brought Capreol back to life since it was those that had given birth to the town in the first place.

Up ahead he could see an unbroken stream of people crossing the highway at Kelly, a side street angling towards the downtown. He could hear the faint beat of a drum and the ecstatic whine of an electric guitar as the quad drove closer. The music was echoing down the canyon of houses on either side of Kelly and growing louder as the woman did a U-turn, bringing the quad to the curb a few yards from the intersection.

This is where I let you off, she said. Then pointing down Kelly Street towards Young: Downtown's that way. You can get something to eat there and there's a church across from the Foodland. You can ask if they still have any free beds.

I might just do that.

His knee felt like it had been hit with a hammer and his legs like they were filled with wet sand and as he slipped out of the seat they barely seemed to have the strength to support him.

You take care now, Clayton, Clayton Crisp.

She applied the gas and the quad shot away. Gerald watched after it until its taillights were but specks and its rumble only a whisper, then turned and walked towards Kelly Street. It was a couple of blocks to where it crossed the tracks, on the other side of which the road split into two one-ways. To the right, Bloor led past the railway museum and the old CN building before looping back towards Young at the foot of the block or so of stores lining either side of this, the main street. Even from his vantage he could see the festivities were in full swing. Young was lit up like the twelve days of Christmas all rolled into one and seething with a mass of people, could have been five thousand or more.

Most of the people crossing the tracks were headed away from the downtown, some of them eating hot dogs and others hamburgers, a smattering of kids among them holding popcorn bags and cardboard wands swirled with candy floss or drinking from bottles of pop. And here he was damn near starving, thinking that doing anything but taking the quickest route home would be nothing but a fool's errand.

It was a five-minute walk from where he was to Railway Avenue and from there it was only ten minutes to Stull. Twenty minutes at a brisk pace and he'd be walking up his driveway, though he doubted he could manage more than his weary trod and so it would probably take him the long side of forty-five.

Best get at it then.

He scanned down the river of people, looking for a break big enough to squeeze through and trying not to look anyone in the face for fear they might recognize him. He was just stepping into a gap and heard a voice raised in shrill sanction, What the fuck? I thought we were going to see the show!

He traced it to a woman standing with her back to him on the far sidewalk. She had a shock of synthetic neon-green hair to her shoulders and was wearing a matching spandex one-piece suit that lent her figure the appearance of a pear that had grown legs. She was shouting after a scruffy-looking man in ripped jeans and a black T-shirt, his hair a scraggled frazzle of curly brown tied into a ponytail lashing at his back. As he scurried away he threw a nervous glance over his shoulder, directed at none other than Gerald himself.

He didn't know the man but it was obvious the man knew him. As Gerald watched him barging heedlessly through the stream of people on Kelly Street in a mad rush to tell a certain someone whom he'd just seen, a clear image formed in his mind of what would likely happen next.

Slow down, son, I can't understand a word, Charlie Wilkes might be saying from his open front door in just a few short ticks. You just saw who?

The man repeating what he just said slower this time and Charlie shaking his head.

That's impossible. Gerald Nichols is in jail. And he ain't never getting out, I made sure of that.

The man frantic in his appeal, and that leaving old man Wilkes with little choice but to concede that it might at least be worth looking into.

Just let me fetch my piece.

Gerald telling himself, *They'll be looking for you on the main roads first. You ought to cut into the bush at the end of Vaughan, take the long way around. And you'll want to be quick about it too!*

But still he stood there as trenchant as a sapling whelmed in a spring flood while the stream of people jostled past on all sides, barely able to summon the energy to imagine himself fleeing through the woods much less actually doing it, his only hope of freedom reduced to a mad dash, likely with the hounds on his tail. The fact that he'd be running to something, maybe even towards his son, rather than away, seemed like a poor consolation.

Thinking then:

Fuck it. If they're going to come after you, you might as well have a full belly when they do. I'm about done with running anyhow.

And with that thought adding a spring to his limping gait, he started forward, swept at once into the ambling current of people drifting him in its languorous flow towards the downtown.

If there was one thorn in his grandfather's side about Capreol, it was that it hadn't died before he had.

When the old man had inherited the family homestead, the town's population had just dipped below one thousand and it seemed to be heading in that direction. The stores on Young were all boarded up and half the houses had simply been abandoned, the bottom having long fallen out of whatever real estate market had existed prior to his arrival.

After Gerald had come to live with him he'd often said with his characteristically sardonic smile, It won't be long now before it gives up the ghost altogether, and then I can finally die in peace.

But by the time he'd gone to check his trap-line that one last time, the population had surged to just over five thousand, a record of sorts, though a minor one in the grand scheme of things for sure. A bunch of new stores and a few restaurants had opened along Young and they'd even built a whole new subdivision off Ormsby, where before there'd only been a gravel field.

Gerald's grandfather had treated every grand opening or moving van unloading its wares as just one more cut in a death of a thousand, as if each new arrival was waging a personal vendetta against his dreams of ever finding peace.

If this keeps up, he quipped one time they were returning from Hanmer and saw a crew recalibrating the population sign to 5250, I ain't never goin' die.

That the blame for its revitalization could be attributed to the Northern Ontario Repopulation Act, which had allowed his mortal enemies to so prosper, was for him like salt poured into those thousand wounds. The influx of undesirables from the south into Sudbury was matched with a corresponding influx of medical personnel, social workers and PSWs at a government mandated ratio of four to one. Those of a status too low to qualify for housing in the "safe zone" had sought out the relative safety of the surrounding towns, Capreol acquiring a prominent place among them since it was the most isolated of them all.

Crossing the tracks, Gerald, confronted by the roiling sea of people wandering up and down Young Street, mused that his grandfather must have been rolling over in his grave. The densest conglomeration of them seemed to be about halfway down, centred on the vacant lot beside the Legion, which was where the music was coming from. They'd often had live shows there on Saturday nights and all of the bands sounded pretty much like the one he was hearing now belting out a rollicking blend of country and rock, the singer screaming something about a girl called "Mustang Sally."

The parking lot of the Foodland on his immediate left was almost as packed and everyone he could see was eating a hot dog or hamburger, the adults all drinking from tall cans of beer and the kids from bottles of pop. He could see wafts of smoke rising above the crowd from in front of the grocery store's sliding doors, carrying the aroma of grilling meat. He joined the end of the line, twenty people deep, and bided his time while he waited scanning people's faces, looking for someone he knew or rather someone who might have known him. He saw a few he wasn't entirely sure of but no one he truly recognized until he was only a couple of spots from the four folding tables separating the hungry masses from twelve propane barbecues, six loaded with hot dogs and the rest with hamburgers. There were bags of buns on the table and three older women and an older man wearing aprons and paper chef hats were filling them with an endless sizzle of wieners and patties. It was the man he'd recognized, none other than Rudy Mills.

Rudy had been Capreol's deputy fire chief, which Gerald had always found odd since he was the last person he'd have expected to see up on a ladder saving lives. He had a belly about as big and hard as a twenty-pound bag of flour and skinny little legs that always seemed to be on the point of buckling under his girth. He was pretty near the first person Gerald had met when he'd come to town on account he was one of his grandfather's most loyal customers, and then one of Gerald's too when he took over the family farm. When Gerald was a kid, if it had been him who'd gone to fetch his eggs, Rudy would always slip a folded-up ten dollar bill into his hand on the sly and whisper, Now don't let the old man find out. Stingy old bastard like that'd like to dock it from your pay, nudging him in the ribs as he said it so the boy would know he'd meant it as a joke.

As friendly a fellow as Gerald had ever met and no doubt he still was but that didn't stop Gerald from stiffening at the sight of him. Rudy had seen him too and was also standing statuesque, holding a hot dog halfway to a bun and staring at him with lips slightly ajar and quivering. Except that he used to have a few streaks of black in his beard and it was now all white, he didn't seem to have aged much since Gerald had seen him last, on the day he'd come by to pick up his weekly allotment of a dozen eggs and a roasting hen, not two days before Millie had been shot.

The person in front of him had shuffled off to the side carrying four hot dogs and two hamburgers stacked in a pyramid and there was nothing between Gerald and Rudy except the table. Rudy's gape had since relented into a tenuous smile, veiled and secretive. It struck Gerald as only slightly less foreboding and he turned to one of the women. She was short and plump with a powdery white face and was wearing a bright red smear of lipstick and so much perfume he could smell it over the simmer of meat. It was the latter more than anything that clued him in that she was Rudy's wife, he couldn't remember her name. If she recognized him she made no sign, offering him a sprightly if somewhat haggard smile as she asked, What can I get for you?

All of a sudden Gerald seemed to have forgotten what he was here for, and when he opened his mouth he was at a loss of what to say.

Do you want a hamburger or a hot dog? she prompted and that snapped Gerald back to task.

If it's all the same to you, he answered, I'll have one of both.

He ate his food leaning against the concrete barrier at the rear end of the parking lot, biding his time watching the minnow races they'd set up a few feet away.

The track was resting on another of the folding tables and fashioned out of six ten-foot lengths of PVC pipe halved length-wise and filled with water, exactly the same rig they'd used for the races they'd held every year during Capreol Days when he was a kid. The first year he'd lived with his grandfather he'd won a fishing rod after coming in second out of a field of twenty-two with a minnow he'd caught in the creek that bordered their property, and his grandfather had made a pretty big deal out of that. Here the kids could choose from a selection of minnows swimming about in clear plastic cups occupying a second fold-out table. As far as he could tell, the only thing the kids could stand to gain was the winning fish itself, the paucity of the reward hardly dampening the participants' enthusiasm one bit.

There were two other men leaning against the barrier, both with tall cans of Keith's India Pale Ale, chatting idly in between sips and cheering on their kids, a couple of three- or four-year-olds who never seemed to grow tired of waiting in line to have another go.

Have you been up to the rail museum? the one was asking. He was dressed in the standard summer garb of your average local — khaki shorts and a faded T-shirt — and had a beard almost as full as Gerald's, though it was comprised of black curls to Gerald's red.

The other man shook his head. He was clean shaven and wearing tan slacks and a blue golf shirt and his perfectly coiffed hair — chestnut — made him out to be some sort of professional, a doctor or maybe a teacher.

The lineup was too long, he answered.

It always is on Capreol Days. Though, of course, we've never had one quite as busy as this.

It's my first.

You don't say. How long you been in town?

Just a couple of months.

And you're coming from where?

Guelph.

Well, you picked a helluva time to make the move. Lucky, is what I'm saying.

You don't have to tell me.

They say there's enough food in them trains to last us at least the winter.

How many do they have now?

Three. But one of them is five kilometres long so it might as well be two all by itself.

I sure wish they'd find some diapers.

You got a baby?

Twins.

Ooooh, the local groaned. At least we got lots of beer.

Cheers to that.

They were clinking cans at the exact moment Gerald was taking the last bite of his burger and thinking, *An ice-cold beer sure would hit the spot right about now.*

Hey daddy, look what I won!

The local's son was standing in front of his father. He was holding up a Ziploc bag with a minnow thrashing about within and beaming with the pride of an Olympic gold medallist.

It's a fish, the boy's father said.

No. It's a minnow.

A minnow's a kind of fish, ain't it?

The boy scrunched his face, unsure of how he might reply to that.

I'm going to put it in the river, he finally said. Come on!

Grabbing his father's hand and pulling him away, the man making out like he was being dragged along behind a horse at a hard gallop, barely able to keep up.

Nice talking to you, he said over his shoulder to the man from Guelph, who responded by raising his can, bidding him a silent adieu.

Say mister, Gerald asked after the man had another sip, could you tell me where you got that beer?

The man raised his hand, pointing, and Gerald followed his finger to a freight container sitting on a narrow strip of grass across Bloor Street from the church on this side of the tracks. It was white and had an air conditioning unit on its rear end, under which someone had spray painted in five-foot letters *COLD BEER*.

But he might as well have been pointing at the two men standing right in front of it.

Both were clad in the blues of the Sudbury Police Service, the younger of the two bare-headed with a military crewcut, wearing shorts and a collared T-shirt, the older wearing a cap and in long sleeves and slacks and glassing over the crowd with a pair of binoculars. They passed over Gerald by an inch and then backtracked, fixing him in their lens.

Gerald already knew who the latter man was but it wasn't until he'd lowered the binoculars, revealing the pasty white of his skin and the glare of piercing hate in his eyes, that Gerald was willing to acknowledge his name.

Charlie Wilkes, he thought and that bringing the taste of bile into his mouth.

Until this moment he'd never even considered what he'd do if ever again he saw the man who was standing not thirty paces away from him now. He still didn't exactly know but his right hand seemed to have a clue, for it had just then settled in a death-grip on the hilt of his knife. His eyes too had a pretty good idea and had narrowed to slits. There must have been some sort of challenge inherent in them for Charlie Wilkes's hand too had sought out the butt of the sidearm in the holster at his belt. The younger cop, who might well have been another of his sons — he'd had two others besides the two Gerald had shot — was clutching at his arm and saying something into his ear. It could very well have been, *This isn't the time or the place*, even as Gerald was thinking that it was as good a time or a place as any, heedless of the fact both cops were armed with guns and him with only a knife.

To any reasonable man it would have seemed an unfair fight but seeing Charlie Wilkes hadn't put Gerald in much of a reasonable mood. It seemed plenty fair enough to him and after all he'd been through, he was giving himself better-than-even odds that he'd be the one coming out on top. Maybe the younger cop had got a sense of this from the way Gerald was advancing through the crowd on such a resolute course that the people were seemingly parting before him and how his hand was gripped at his belt, clutching at something, could very well have been a gun, he was still too far away for them to be able to tell with any certainty. Or maybe he simply didn't want to spoil the festivities by shooting a man down in the street.

Either way, his opinion must have carried some weight for as Gerald came to the edge of the parking lot, Charlie was letting himself be pulled backwards, telegraphing one last hateful glare at Gerald before he was swallowed into the throng of people shuffling to and fro across the tracks.

H ere now Gerald stands with a beer in his hand, watching the band.

It was made up of two men and two women, the former comprising the guitarist and drummer and both wearing garish cowboy shirts and the singer and bassist wearing no less colourful knee-long dresses embellished with a lasso design. What they lacked in finesse they made up for in enthusiasm and the crowd responded in equal measure, bobbing and bouncing and most of them screaming out along with the singer, testifying with an almost evangelical zeal every time she came to the refrain that it had indeed been a hard day's night.

They'd given out the tall cans in four packs. He'd already drunk three and had just fetched his last from the ground at his feet, telling himself that when he was done with that, he ought to be heading home. He hadn't seen Charlie Wilkes again nor the other officer but he had no doubt there was someone, none too far away, keeping an eye on him. And whenever his thoughts wandered to his house at the end of Stull, he imagined Charlie Wilkes along with his two remaining sons and a posse of six or eight of his friends hiding in the bushes, awaiting his return.

Let 'em wait! he thought with a rueful scowl as he cracked the tab on his fourth tall can, drinking that in parsimonious sips as if hoping that if he drank it slow enough the night might never end.

After they were finished with "A Hard Day's Night," the singer said they'd be taking a little refreshment break, adding with a good-natured wink, Don't y'all go anywhere now, ya hear.

Still, the crowd began to disperse, most of them heading back towards the tracks, no doubt to get a little more refreshment themselves. The man standing directly in front of Gerald was turning along with them but was stopped before he'd made more than a step by a woman holding up a four-pack of the tall cans. She was in her early twenties, same as the man, but that's about where any similarities between them ended. He was well over six feet and built like a linebacker and she was no more than five-foot-six with a waist about the same width as one of his arms.

I brought you some more beer, she said.

Golden, he replied and that earned him a wide grin from the girl.

He cracked open one of the cans without bothering to pull it from its plastic wrap, upending the four of them and draining the beer in one long gulping swig. The whole time the woman was watching him, her eyes were aglow as if she was witnessing a feat of derring-do the likes of which she'd never seen. When he was done he belched a deep rumble that foundered somewhere in his throat, and wiped his mouth with the back of his hand.

You're Shelley, right? he asked, cracking another beer.

She nodded exuberantly.

And you're Chris.

I sure am.

He took a sip from the can and it was clear to Gerald from the way he was glancing about that he was already looking for a way out of the conversation.

Well Shelley, he said, I got to (*burp*) take a piss. Maybe I'll see you around sometime.

Gerald had almost no memory of the night Millie had followed him home from the Legion. He couldn't exactly say how they'd met but it might as well have happened just like that. The first thing he did remember about her was coming into his kitchen the next morning — drawn by the smell of eggs and the burble of coffee percolating on the stove — and finding a strange woman at the sink, washing his dishes. His grandfather had never been overly meticulous about keeping a clean house and in the year since he'd died Gerald had rarely so much as touched the broom. But the floor had been freshly swept and the table wiped and on one side of the sink there was a full rack of clean plates and bowls, though they still paled in comparison to the mountain of dirties on the other side. He'd stood at the kitchen door, not exactly sure what he felt — a little irritated maybe that his morning routine would be thus disturbed — and after a while she'd turned to him, giving him the glimmer of a smile, too weak to hide her obvious chagrin.

There's coffee, she'd said curtly. And eggs.

Gerald had wandered off towards the stove, trying not to get in her way as he fished a clean plate and cup from the pile on the counter. He'd loaded the plate up with scrambled eggs and poured himself a steaming cup of the coffee, dosing that with fresh cream from a mason jar he kept in the fridge.

She wouldn't speak again until he was sitting at the table and was raising a fork to his mouth, about to take his first bite.

I don't know how a person can live like this, she'd said, the acrimony clear in her voice and the loud clatter of plates providing perfect punctuation. It's disgusting. Only an animal would live like this.

Millie had never been one to mince words and always spoke straight from her liver, as his grandfather might have said, meaning that as a compliment. And he knew exactly what she'd have said if she was standing there right now, watching him getting drunk when he should have been out there looking for their son, the acrimony in her tone as plain as the scowl that would be crimping her face.

And so, as he drained the last of his beer, it was her voice he heard once again ringing in his head.

Goddamnit Gerald, she said, *get your fucking ass home!*

A t long last he was stumbling down Stull Street.

As far as he could see, it had since been paved all the way to the river and on the right-hand side the sparsely treed meadow that turned into a swamp every spring when the creek flooded had also been paved over and filled with row after row of townhouses, the last of which bordered the line of cedar trees at the edge of his property. It was late, must have been past midnight, and the houses were mostly dark except for lights shining over front porches, their warm and yellow clashing against the harsh glow of the streetlights illuminating perfectly manicured yards and glinting off the lacquered sheen of the two or three cars parked in every driveway. As he crested the hill leading down into the river valley the sight had come as such a shock to Gerald that his gaze went instinctively to the street sign at the first intersection, even though he knew exactly where he was.

God, gramps really would be rolling over in his grave if he'd lived to see this.

That sounded a little odd for reasons he couldn't quite grasp and he stumbled on, passing by the two-storey house where Charlie Wilkes had once lived at the corner of Stull and Lloyd and hocking a spit into the driveway to mark that, though he knew the Wilkes family had been one of the first to buy a house in the subdivision off Ormsby. Searching ahead then for any sign that Charlie and his gang might be hiding in the bushes up ahead.

If they were they'd have to be on the left, crouching in the thin fringe of trees — mostly aspen and poplar — between the road and the mesh wire fence behind them. It was eight feet tall and topped with rusted loops of razor wire and encircled an area some twenty acres in all. It had always been a mystery to Gerald why someone would go to such lengths to guard what, ever since he could remember, had amounted to nothing more than an abandoned warehouse about the size of a football stadium looming over a vacant lot. There were train tracks running right up to the warehouse's loading dock and someone had since put those to good use. A line of freight cars spilled along them through the back gate. An excavator about the same size as the one he'd seen at the prison but equipped with a chain laced through its bucket's teeth was lifting the container off one of the cars, swinging the box over the heads of two men wearing bright yellow vests. One of them was motioning it forward with his hands and, when it had come abreast of another container, he held them both up to signal, Stop! The container lowered with a thudding clank and the two men immediately converged on it, prying open its doors even as a crane with a ball and hook picked up the container beside it. It swung on a hard left and motored off towards the stacks of freight containers piled in blocks, five and six high, now filling the lot's twenty acres.

Scanning past those, searching for any hint of movement that might tell him that someone was hiding in the shadows on the side of the road. Seeing nothing but the outlines of trees and hearing only the grumble of the crane's engine above the rustle of poplar leaves agitating against a slight breeze. Just beyond the last townhouse the asphalt did indeed give way to dirt. It hadn't been graded for some time and was studded with the rippling pockmarks that so often had him and his grandfather making a game of letting their jaws go slack for the last kilometre before reaching their driveway, the road's corrugation finding perfect expression in the fitful chattering of their teeth.

The equally familiar line of cedar trees still buffered the edge of the property and he could hear the creek gurgling through the culvert on either side of the road though the latter, he saw as he approached, wasn't really a creek anymore but a cement channel drawing the overflow away from the townhouse complex. As he came to the edge of his driveway, there arose the faint creak of the weather vane on the barn's roof vacillating in the wind and that more than anything telling him he was home.

How many times had he stumbled drunkenly back from the Legion, turning into the driveway and seeing the metal rooster cast against the night sky? He'd come to name it Max and he'd always call out to it as he lumbered towards the house, Thanks Max!, by which he'd meant for watching over the place while he was gone.

Feeling the same sort of weary resignation he often had then he walked onwards and up the drive on mincing steps, searching through the row of Jack pines bracketing the gravelled lane on the left-most side and finding the house's dark silhouette, scanning that for any sign that Evers might be waiting for him inside. Seeing nothing there and hearing nothing either except for the persistent murmur from the creek and the weather vane's wobbling squeak until he'd reached the last Jack pine before the driveway turned towards the porch, stopping at the sight of a familiar metal triangle.

It was a sign that had been hanging there since the morning of his third (or it could have been his fourth) Christmas on the farm, a present he himself had bought for his grandfather. It had been painted bright yellow and was a play on those highway hazard signs warning of a moose or deer crossing and instead had on it the silhouette of a chicken. He'd meant it as a gag but he would never see his grandfather more serious than when he'd nailed it to the Jack pine a few minutes after he'd opened it, all the while muttering under his breath, Maybe that'll finally get them bastards to slow down!

The paint had long since peeled off of it and the metal had rusted and bent out of shape and there was nothing really about it that warranted a closer look but still it coaxed him forward. Three steps from being able to reach out and touch it, he stepped on a pine cone. It crunched underfoot and that was immediately followed by the low growl of a dog spinning him on a quick axis towards the house. The dog was standing at the top of the porch steps — a hulking shape big enough to be a Rottweiler.

It let out a snarling bark as it stalked down the steps, the rattle of its chain raking against wood hardly enough to stop Gerald's hand from reaching for his knife. It made it halfway to the treeline before the chain snapped it back and stood there growling and barking as the porch light flared behind it, Gerald taking a step closer, holding his breath, waiting for Evers to appear.

But when the door opened it was an elderly woman who stepped out. She was wearing a white nightdress and shouldering a shotgun. Seeing that, Gerald dodged backwards scurrying for the cover of the cedars.

What is it Roxy? she called out in a thin and croaking voice. Is someone there? A brief pause then. Whoever it is, I'm warning you, you got to the count of five before I let her off her chain.

Gerald cowering amongst the cedars, telling himself,

Evers'll be at the lake then. You knew he would be anyway.

The quickest route to get there was to take the path behind the barn but the dog would make that a dicey proposition at best. He'd have to take the long way around after all.

D awn found Gerald perched on a boulder overlooking *Crique à Gros Orteil*, what his grandfather had always called the cove on Beausilake's southwestern shore where Hubert Beausoleil had built the cabins for himself and his wife and their six children.

The boulder was halfway up the lightly treed slope that encircled all but the lake's heel. It was the size of a compact car, flat-topped and furred with a thick cushion of moss such that it made a more comfortable mattress than the one he'd slept on these past five years. But Gerald wasn't tired enough to sleep. He'd never, in fact, been more awake in his whole life than he was peering through the finely feathered needles of a hemlock tree and finding ample evidence that someone — could very well have been Evers — was living in the middle cabin.

He could see the dark outlines of two towels strung on the porch's rail and there was an ember glowing orange in the indentation that formed a bowl in the granite at the foot of the

peninsula and which the Beausoleils had used for their camp-
fires over the hundred or so years they'd been coming up to the
lake. It was the lingering vestiges of the smoke from this that,
when he'd crested the slope leading downwards into *Crique à
Gros Orteil,* had steered him off the path, its once clearly delineated hard-pack of dirt and exposed granite overcome with
ferns, horsetail, patches of trilliums and fallen trees but his feet
nonetheless finding their way clear enough without any help
from his eyes.

Catching a faint whiff of the smoke as he crested the rise,
he'd ducked into the woods and stalked along the highlands
until he'd come to a V made by two birch trees growing out of
the same trunk. He cut down the slope and climbed onto the
backside of the boulder, sitting on its frontside, letting his legs
dangle over the four-foot drop, peering through the branches of
the hemlock the same way he had when he'd stumbled upon it
the very first time he'd followed his grandfather up to the lake.

It was five weeks after he'd moved onto the farm, a trial-some
five weeks to say the least, and a time Gerald had pushed to the
farthest reaches of his mind, ashamed of the way he'd treated his
grandfather, though he knew the old man never cast the blame
back upon him. He'd overheard him say as much to the social
worker from the children's aid who'd visited the farm once a
week during his first year living on Stull and then once a month
for the two years after. Mostly she wanted to talk to Gerald but
one morning when she'd knocked on the door Gerald had heard
her tell his grandfather that she'd like to speak to him for a few
moments alone.

Come on out to the barn, he'd told her, I've got to milk the
cows anyway.

Gerald was eating breakfast in the kitchen and had waited
for the front door to click shut before slipping out the back. He'd

hid around the rear corner of the house, sneaking quick peeks at the barn, seeing his grandfather disappearing inside and the woman from the children's aid holding up at the door, seemingly reluctant to follow.

I can get you a pair of boots if you don't want to get your shoes dirty, his grandfather had called back to her after a moment.

She was wearing high heels and a grey pinstriped pantsuit. It was what she wore whenever she visited and was also about the only thing he remembered about her except that she talked in a chalky near-whisper and always brought him a pack of Life Savers, asking in exchange only that he save her a green one.

She'd answered his grandfather that it was okay, she'd manage. She'd stepped delicately over the doorstop and Gerald had run across the yard, circling around behind the barn where his grandfather kept his Holsteins and pressing his ear against a hole left by a knot in one of the wooden slats.

It's been a trial all right, his grandfather was saying.

The social worker said something too low for Gerald to hear and to which his grandfather replied in the same gruff voice he always used when someone was telling him something he already knew.

I know it's not his fault, he said. A pause, then: Of course he thinks about his ma. I think maybe it's all he ever thinks about. After what he's been through . . . His voice trailing off and shortly replaced by the metallic thrum of milk squirting against the bucket's galvanized steel.

Relating as he worked the udders how Gerald would go all of a sudden quiet and freeze at whatever he was doing. He'd be like that for maybe a few seconds and then his shoulders would give out a sudden twitch, which his grandfather likened to the sputter of a plane's engine the moment before it went into a tailspin. His mood would spiral downwards from there into an explosion of rage and the old man took its brunt, in curses and kicks, as he tried to bring the boy back towards reason. Relating then how, one morning after five weeks of suffering through that, he was sitting at breakfast and saw the boy's hand stall mid-air with a spoonful of cereal, knowing he couldn't, he just couldn't, deal with one of the boy's fits today, not after yesterday when he'd come at him with a stick of firewood.

So I says to myself, Let him wreck the goddamn house, for all I care.

Gerald had a clear memory of that moment watching his grandfather pushing himself up from the table, a look of bitter resignation hardening his face.

I'll see you in a few hours, he'd said to Gerald on his way out of the kitchen, calling then back over his shoulder as he came to the front door: Careful to mind the farm while I'm gone!

Gerald watched him through the living room window as he fetched his rod and tackle box from the shed and right up until the moment he saw the old man disappearing into the woods beside the barn he was sure that his grandfather must have been bluffing about leaving a seven-year-old boy such as himself all alone.

The social worker expressed a similar concern.

You left him alone!

It was the first time she'd raised her voice loud enough for Gerald to hear what she was saying and her tone was one of genuine alarm.

I was pretty sure he'd follow me, his grandfather had countered. And, sure enough, I wasn't but halfway to the lake before I heard the crackle of leaves from somewhere to the left of the path and I knew the boy was tracking after me through the bush.

It was only a few moments later that Gerald had discovered the moss-furred boulder and had sat there watching from undercover of the hemlock as his grandfather slid his old aluminum canoe onto the lake and clambered in after it.

If you were going fishing, the social worker had asked at this point in the telling, why didn't you just invite Gerald to go along with you?

I figured it best if he made up his own mind about that, he answered, and that seemed to satisfy the social worker enough that her voice was softened somewhat when she asked, So what happened next?

After an hour or so his grandfather had returned to shore. He'd dragged the canoe to the middle cabin and leaned it up against a side wall, hanging his oar on two nails above it. He was just starting up the path, homewards bound, when he called out loud enough to make Gerald suspect that the boulder wasn't nearly as well hidden as he'd thought, Oh Gawd, I shore hope he ain't wrecked the place while I been gone!

Gerald had run all the way home and when his grandfather had come into the yard he was standing on the porch steps with his grandfather's spare rod raised at a drastic angle in his hand. The lure was snagged on a clump of scrub grass twenty feet from the house and Gerald was pulling on the rod like he might as well have been trying to reel in a shark.

Thereafter, whenever he'd see his grandson's sudden shudder he'd call out to him, See you in a few hours. Careful to mind the farm while I'm gone! Every time, without fail, he'd hear the crackle of leaves off to the side of the path as he had before except that they'd be moving through the woods at a hard run. And when he'd get to the lake Gerald would already be there, driving the çanoe on a quick line away from shore, doing his best to ignore his grandfather setting his tackle box on what Millie would later come to call the birthday rock.

The lake only had one island, a small outcropping of granite clustered with stunted pines in the middle of what would have been the foot's arch, and it was from there that Gerald would most often fish. He'd tie the canoe off to a tree and circle the island in stages, casting his line. By the time he'd got back to the canoe he'd have caught two or three walleye, which some people called pickerel but never his grandfather, who'd often said the latter was an inferior fish, though he could never explain exactly why. These he'd drag, still alive on a hooked chain, behind the canoe on his return trip. His grandfather would be waiting on shore. Whatever he'd caught he'd have thrown back, but still when Gerald fetched his fish he'd say, Looks like you had all the luck in the world. I couldn't have caught so much as a cold.

Together they'd drag the canoe up beside the middle cabin and Gerald wouldn't think twice about walking back home alongside the old man.

The years passed and it got to be that whenever he felt his own mood souring, Gerald would simply grab his rod and tackle box.

I'll see you in a few hours, he'd tell his grandfather on the way out. Careful to mind the farm while I'm gone!

The old man would pretend to ignore him but without fail, whenever Gerald returned he'd be sitting on the rocking chair on the porch, casting his own line into their yard, the hook most often caught in the scrub grass and the old man pulling on it like he was in a life-and-death struggle and it'd either be the fish or him. Gerald would unsnag the lure and as he reeled in the line his grandfather would say, Shoot, I thought I had that one fer shore. Then seeing his grandson's catch, he'd say, Looks like you had all the luck in the world. I couldn't have caught so much as a cold today.

Not so lucky after all, Gerald would counter. All I could catch was these damn pickerel. Don't know where all them walleye have gone.

Gerald would gut and fry up what he'd caught in butter with a pinch of salt and a little dill, which is how his grandfather preferred it. They'd eat together, often watching the news on their only channel, the old man shaking his head and grumbling all the while until he'd picked his fish clean. Then he'd click the TV off with an almost terminal resign and sometimes add, Gawd, it's goin' to take a miracle to fetch the world out of this mess.

That miracle had obviously never come and here was Gerald now waiting on another, no less divine.

Strains of light were leaking through the trees at his back, nudging at the dark and crystallizing the lake's opacity into a finely rendered mirror reflecting the clear blue sky as a cold steel-grey ringed with the inverted spires of the trees along its shore so that the water appeared to conceal an almost unfathomable depth. A strand of light had struck upon the middle cabin's front window before he'd seen a shade of movement from below: two hands drawing apart the window's drapes, punctuated with a sudden *bang!* — the front door slamming open.

A boy, couldn't have been older than five, burst onto the porch, hustling towards the steps. He had a mess of dark brown hair curled upwards into what almost looked like horns and was wearing a T-shirt like a rainbow had been melted over it. There was a fishing rod propped over his one shoulder and he was carrying a tackle box in the other hand. He hurried down to the peninsula, oblivious to the sharp censure of a woman's voice calling to him from inside, Zack, what did I tell you about slamming the door!

The woman emerged just as the boy was opening his tackle box at the foot of the birthday rock, though she was hardly a woman at all. She couldn't have been older than sixteen and had two long braids of reddish hair draped over her chest that made her appear a fraction younger than that. She was wearing a summer dress almost as colourful as the boy's shirt — a whirlpool of pinks and greens and oranges swirling around a blotch of grey centred at her navel. Her belly was swollen enough to be seven months pregnant and she had one hand propped under the bulge as she eased herself down the steps. In her other hand she was holding a silver metal coffee percolator, the same one that had sat on the potbellied stove in the middle cabin for as long as Gerald could remember.

When she'd got to the bottom of the steps, she called over her shoulder, Honeybear, can you bring me a lighter? I forgot.

She walked to the fire bowl at the foot of the peninsula and squatted there like she was about to take a pee, setting the coffeepot down on the iron barbecue grate Gerald himself had welded to four pieces of rebar some ten years earlier so he'd have a surface on which to cook. But Gerald wasn't watching her anymore. His eyes were locked in a vice grip on the front door. Honeybear was what Millie had sometimes called him, a term of affection she reserved for when her sister had stopped by to pay a visit. He'd never really quite figured out why she only called him that then, and hearing the woman calling the same back into the cabin seemed like a pretty big coincidence, unless . . .

That *unless* . . . hanging in his mind as he held his breath, waiting, he was sure, for Evers to appear in the door. But when someone finally did appear it was another girl, younger than the first, ten or maybe eleven. She was a little chunky and wearing skin-tight jeans and a black blouse with a heart outlined in purple sequins. Her skin was the colour of molasses and her hair a vibrant yellow so it made perfect sense that someone would call her Honeybear.

But still . . .

Watching her tread down the stairs and taking her time doing so, idly flicking the lighter in her hand.

I told you not to call me that anymore, she chided, padding barefoot over the pine needle–strewn ground with the delicate steps of someone walking on broken glass.

Call you what?

The pregnant girl had packed the bowl with crumples of birch bark and set over these smaller twigs, layering on top of them a lattice of split kindling taken from a pile stacked beside a dozen or so quartered logs just behind the pit.

Honeybear. I'm not a kid anymore, you know.

But you'll always be my little Honeybear. Now where's that lighter?

The younger girl clenched her hand and crossed her arms, staring back at the other with the wilful petulance of a spurned child.

Okay then, *Angela*, the pregnant girl conceded, drawing the name out with a smirk. Now can I please have the lighter?

She handed it over and stood again with her arms crossed, her face contorting to a grimace as she looked over at the lake.

Zack's pissing in the lake again, she said.

The pregnant girl looked up and Gerald followed her gaze towards the boy. He was standing on the birthday rock with his back to them, peeing a long arcing stream into the water.

The pregnant woman opened her mouth, about to chastise him, but it wasn't her voice Gerald heard but another: a man's voice, deep and booming.

What's this I hear about you not wantin' to be called Honeybear no more!

Swivelling his head on a quick lateral, Gerald tracked it back to the cabin, left of centre. And there he was — it couldn't have been anyone else: Evers stepping through the door, though he hardly looked anything at all like the boy Gerald had last seen. He stood just under six foot though the three inches of hair standing on end like a crown made him appear a shade taller. He was wearing only a pair of boxer briefs, exposing skin a deep shade of brown, his arms and legs gangly and long like his mother's and his beard almost as full, and red, as his father's. He had a slight paunch at his belly and he was picking at the downy channel of hair leading towards his pubis as he walked down the steps, carrying the same easy gait that Gerald himself had so often adopted coming out of the house and onto the porch, lazing down the stairs like he hadn't a care in the world even when it felt like it was crashing down all around him.

The girl had turned towards him too.

My name is Angela! she barked.

I guess we'll just have to see about that.

Hunkering low, his hands flexing to grab, he stalked after her. But she wasn't in a playing mood. She took a hard line towards the middle cabin, marching up the steps and pausing only once she'd reached the door, spinning back and screaming, Angela!

If her outburst bothered Evers at all, he didn't show it, and the lackadaisical meander returned to his stride as he approached the firepit.

What's got into her? he asked.

The pregnant girl was blowing at the flames creeping over the edges of the birch bark.

I guess she don't want to be called Honeybear no more, she said between puffs.

Well all she had to do was say so.

Evers had gone back to plucking at the hair on his belly though a certain wantonness had crept into his gaze as he let his eyes wander over the subtle curve of the girl's back.

The flames had taken hold and she was pushing herself up. Evers reached out to grab her by the arm and the girl shrugged him off too perfunctorily for him not to take it at least a little bit personally.

Tend the fire while I go take a pee, she said starting away. I'm about to burst. And tell Zack to stop pissing in the lake.

Zack, stop pissing in the lake! Evers yelled without skipping a beat, his gaze never once departing the girl until she'd disappeared into the space between the middle cabin and the next. We got to eat those fish too, you know!

The boy had already finished his business and had taken up his rod, casting his line a good twenty feet out.

But the fish piss in the lake too, don't they? the boy shouted back.

Evers knelt down at the fire, taking a quartered log from the pile and setting it on top of the rapidly keening flames, and Gerald knew exactly what he was going to say next, for hadn't he himself said it often enough when the boy's logic had defied him, though it rarely defied his mother.

Well, he said with Gerald mouthing the words right along with him, I guess you got me there.

H e watched their morning unfold, as patient as the sun cresting the tops of the trees at his back, harrying the shadows into a tenuous retreat.

They ate soup for breakfast. Evers had heated it in the old tin pot missing its handle and then ladled it into the blue metal bowls that had taken up permanent residence in the main cabin's lone cupboard. He ate sitting on an upended log and the boy on another sitting beside him. While they slurped at the soup they carried on a hushed discourse, Evers several times pointing out at the lake's lone island so it seemed to Gerald he must have been giving him fishing tips.

The pregnant girl sat on the porch's top step, Angela behind her, leaning against the wall of the cabin. She seemed to be in a better mood now and chattered happily away at the other, Gerald catching little of what she said except for the odd word, *town* being prominent amongst those, and the pregnant girl seemed to have caught even less. She didn't so much as speak a word the whole time, most of which she spent gazing down at Evers by the fire with an expectant expression as if she was just waiting for him to turn her way. When he finally did, she responded by sticking out her tongue in girlish spite and Evers answered that by calling over, You better watch yourself there, someone's liable to cut that off!

She frowned and then heaved herself up, leaving her bowl on the stairs and calling down to the boy, Come on Zack, you can help us pick some blueberries.

But I want to fish!

There'll be plenty of time to fish when we get back. Come on now, don't make me ask twice.

The boy scowling and Evers whispering something to him, reaching into his pocket and taking out a penknife, holding it out. The boy snatched for it but Evers held it firm, giving him instructions with the solemn countenance of a father sending his youngest son off to war. The boy nodded and Evers ruffled his hand through his hair then released the knife.

Ev'rett said I could check the traps! Zack hollered to the pregnant girl as he raced past the cabin and that gave her reason enough to frown again.

He'll be okay, Evers soothed.

If he cuts his finger off, it's on you.

He won't.

The girl smirked and turned back through the cabin's open door, calling out, Hon— and cutting herself off. I mean *Angela*, we're—

I'm coming, I'm coming already!

She came out the door carrying two empty four-litre plastic milk jugs, the both of them capless and stained purple. She handed one to the pregnant girl and then tromped down the stairs, banging the jug against her leg and hurrying along the same path as the boy, the pregnant girl following after her and calling over her shoulder to Evers, Mind you do them dishes while we're gone!

Watching his son crouched over at the end of the peninsula, rinsing out the pot and four bowls, the spoons and the ladle, Gerald felt a grave reluctance creeping out of the pit in his belly.

He seems to be making out fine by himself, he thought, though it wasn't Evers he was really thinking about, it was Charlie Wilkes. *You stick around it'll just mean trouble down the line. Best thing you can do for him is to just leave him alone.*

Yet still he sat watching Evers trundling back to the middle cabin, setting the pot holding the bowls and the cutlery on the porch and standing there arching his back and scanning over the lake. He'd been doing so for only a few seconds when a shudder all of a sudden ran through his body and an anguished expression blanched his face. He muttered something, sounded like, Motherfuckers!, and his hand clenched into a fist and his face into an angry mask, his teeth grit and his skin shading red, his eyes darting about, as if looking for something to smash. Taking a deep breath then. His hand relaxed and he shook his head, spitting at the ground and running both hands up over his face, weaving his fingers into his hair and digging his nails into his scalp, looking like he was about to scream out again. He didn't and after a moment he released his grip, slapped his hands against his cheeks and muttered something else, Gerald had no idea what.

Gerald was thinking about all he'd gone through to get here and wishing his son had had an easier time of it, seeing now that he probably hadn't and wanting nothing more than to run down to him right then, take him in his arms, tell him everything would be all right the same as he had after Evers had fallen off the cliff face, knowing even then that it was a lie.

It was that ever-present lie that had been foremost on Gerald's mind every time he'd tried to write Evers a letter from prison and here it was again keeping him away from his son, so close and yet in the five years he'd spent in a cell he'd never felt further apart from the boy than he did right then.

Y ou need a hand?

    He'd snuck up behind him without making a sound.

Evers was using a claw hammer to pry apart the boards on the backwall of the last cabin in the row and when Gerald spoke he lashed around, holding the hammer raised above his head, about to strike. There was hate in his eyes, same way there'd always been when Gerald had snuck up on him and startled him when he was a kid, but there was something else in them too. If Gerald had put a word to it that word would have been *murder* and seeing his son looking at him like that a half a tick from caving in his skull with a claw hammer, his legs wobbled, about to give out beneath him.

But shortly Evers's eyes softened into a familiar expression of grudging bemuse, though they stopped short of dazzling with that spark of tenacious remonstration that when he was a kid would tell Gerald he was already thinking about how he'd get him back. Instead he smiled wide enough that Gerald could see he was missing one of his two top front teeth, a healed over scar on both lips bearing testament to its abrupt removal and Gerald wondering how he'd come to lose that.

Son of a bitch, Evers said, drawing out the curse into a perfect expression of disbelief. Then shaking his head: I guess Wayne-Jay was right after all.

Wayne-Jay? Gerald asked, hardly able to suppress a grin of his own at the mention of maybe his only real friend in all the years he'd lived on the farm.

He said if anyone'd make it back, it'd be you.

He'd since averted his gaze and snuck a quick peek out of the corner of his right eye which told Gerald he still couldn't quite believe his father was standing right there.

When did you see Wayne-Jay? Gerald asked, happy they still had something to talk about after all these years.

Evers, too, seemed pleased about it.

First time was a week ago, he said. He dropped by on one of his wanders.

It was how Gerald had met him in the first place, a couple of weeks after his grandfather had died. He'd been practically living up in the cabins then, the house seeming too big and too empty and all too full of the old man. He'd been frying up a couple of walleyes over the firepit and Wayne-Jay, or so he'd said, had caught a whiff of that. They'd been friends ever since.

The second was just a couple days ago, Evers continued. Dropped us off a half roll of Typar for the cabins, said it'd get us through the winter anyway.

Boy, Gerald said, I'd sure like to see Wayne-Jay again.

You will. Said he'd be back before the snow to bring us a new wood stove, if he can figure how to get it up here.

If anyone can figure that out, it's him.

Evers nodded and they stood for a moment just looking at each other. A lump was forming in Gerald's throat and a glisten was appearing at the corners of Evers's eyes. He turned away, rubbing at it with the back of his hand like there was a piece of grit in it.

You were saying something about Typar? Gerald asked and Evers had to clear his throat before speaking again.

Wayne-Jay had a half roll left over from when he built his new house, he answered.

He finally got around to that? He's been talking about it for years.

I guess he must've. Evers then turned towards the middle cabin, looking almost embarrassed. Got gramps's cabin pretty much done before I realized it'd work better on the outside.

You put the Typar on the inside?

Evers nodded.

Stupidest damn thing.

Evers was shaking his head, looking sideways at Gerald, his cheeks flushing red.

It's an honest mistake, Gerald said.

I was leaving it up until I got the wood together to use as siding.

It'll be easy enough to get back off.

Evers was looking at him just short of relieved.

I was figuring on using a screwdriver, he offered.

All right then, well let's get at 'er.

Wayne-Jay had dropped off a staple gun and a box of staples and it was these that Evers had used to tack on the thin shield of protective sheeting. It didn't take much to pop them out with a flat screwdriver from the bag of tools Wayne-Jay had also left. Evers had gone back to stripping the wood from the other cabin and Gerald didn't see him again until an hour or so later.

Gerald was just coming onto the porch carrying the rolled-up Typar on his shoulder and he heard Zack's voice raised in jubilation.

We saw a snake! he was saying while Gerald draped the loose roll over the porch's railing.

Was it a rattler? he heard Evers ask.

There ain't no rattlers around, you said so yourself.

So what kind was it?

It was a big old garden snake.

You mean a garter.

No, it was a garden.

Was it green and black with a yellow stripe?

Yeah.

Then it was a garter snake,

Was it a garder snake we saw? The boy's voice had elevated some and he was calling his question to the pregnant woman. She'd just come to the steps of the middle cabin and had frozen stiff at the sight of Gerald.

Was it a garder snake we saw? the boy repeated when she didn't answer.

What? she asked, irritated.

The snake! He was clearly exasperated too. Was it a damn garder?

No, she said, unwilling it seemed to take her eyes off Gerald, even for a moment. It was a garden snake. That's what Rachel always called them anyways.

It was a garden snake.

You say so, Evers was saying as he and the boy came to the front of the cabin with Angela trailing behind.

Zack and Angela were both carrying milk jugs full of blueberries and when they saw Gerald standing on the porch they too stopped short, the boy gaping up at him in open-mouthed wonder and the girl wiping the blueberry juice from her mouth with the back of her hand, no less surprised.

Oh shoot, Evers said. Where's my manners? This here's Gerald. He'll be staying with us for a while. Gerald this here's Zack, Angela and Melody. He pointed off each in turn and they all stood there for a moment, saying nothing.

Then to Gerald:

We were all staying together at the home. After Milt and Rachel took off — they were the couple who owned the house — I figured coming here was as good a place as any.

The pregnant girl — Melody — was glowering at him with a sour look and Gerald didn't know what to say to that so he kept his mouth shut. Zack had got over his initial surprise and was now tugging at Evers's free hand, whispering upwards at him just loud enough for Gerald to hear.

Is he the one you told us all them stories about?

Evers whispering back, That's right.

Isn't he your . . . dad?

He sure is.

Then looking over at Melody and raising his voice a trifle so as to make his point loud and clear.

And you all are going to treat him real nice now, you hear?

I s it true you killed a bear one time with only one stab? Zack asked.

Melody had dragged Evers down to the lake and they were engaged in some sort of a hushed argument, the way she kept pointing her chin back at Gerald leaving no doubt in his mind it was about him. Angela had since gone inside, walking past Gerald with a shy smile as he nailed the Typar to the front of the cabin, but Zack had no such reticence, planting himself beneath the porch, gazing up at Gerald. It had only taking a few moments for him to summon the nerve to ask about the bear.

It's true, Gerald answered. With this knife right here on my belt, as a point of fact.

But I thought you left *that* knife in the bear's eye.

Oh, I did. A friend, he got it back for me.

He stole it from the police?

I guess he must've.

The boy nodded at that, believing the lie.

I thought you were supposed to be in jail, he said after a moment.

I was.

They let you out?

I'm here, ain't I.

Ev'rett said they weren't never going to let you out.

That's what he said?

Uh huh.

I guess I must've got lucky then.

The boy opened his mouth, about to say something else, but was cut off by Melody yelling out, angry:

Zack! Angela! We're going to town!

She was striding away from Evers and he was looking after her with a rough approximation of the expression Gerald had worn in that first birthday photo.

I want to stay, Zack protested, whereby Melody took a hard line straight towards him.

You're coming!

No!

Lashing out with her hand, she gave him a twisting pinch on the back of his arm.

You're going and that's final!

She landed a swat on his ass and the boy tromped away, rubbing the back of his arm and grumbling, You didn't have to pinch me.

You'll get more than a pinch, I hear another word out of you!

Angela came out of the cabin, slinging a large army-green rucksack onto her back, and seemed to have no compunction at all about going to town.

I hope they still have candy floss, she was saying, hurrying after Melody skulking up the path winding rootworn and serpentine on its way to the old farm on Stull.

Evers had since come to the foot of the steps, watching after them with his tongue prodding at the gap in his front teeth.

Don't mind her, he said after they'd disappeared among the trees. She's been pissed off ever since I told her we'd be living up here rather than finding a place in town. You'd have thought after what happened in Scuzzbury . . .

Shaking his head then. It was obvious that whatever had happened in Sudbury, he wasn't ready to talk, or maybe even think, about that.

Being so pregnant don't help much neither, he said by way of changing the subject.

How far is she along?

Seven months.

It yours?

Gerald had been wondering that ever since he'd first seen her. Evers shot him a look of startled bewilderment.

No, he said. God no! You know, she's only fourteen?

Sorry, I—

It was a boy she knew from school. He stopped coming around after she started showing and that sure as hell didn't help her mood none either.

Evers had taken to staring back down the path and was again tonguing the gap between his teeth.

She'll come around, he said, looking over at Gerald though it was plain he was really just talking to himself. All she needs is a little time. She'll come around, I know she will.

They finished tacking up the Typar together, neither speaking beyond the demands of the job until Evers had popped in the last staple.

I guess we'll call that lunch, he said. Prime rib and potato or spicy sausage? Soup, I mean.

Spicy's good, Gerald answered, his primary complaint about prison food being that it was mostly flavourless where he'd always preferred a bit of heat.

Spicy it is, Evers answered. I'll go fetch it if you'll get the fire started.

Will do.

There was still a good bed of coals and it didn't take more than a couple of blows to ignite the loose weave of birch bark and kindling he'd stacked over it. While Evers opened the cans of soup, Gerald stood, stretching out his back and gazing down at the lake.

Why don't you go on and take a swim while it heats up, Evers said, setting the second can on the rack and licking the juice off his fingers.

Do I smell that bad?

No. I mean— Evers's face was pinched and he'd clearly not meant it that way. You always said you liked nothing better than a cool dip on a hot day.

You're sure right about that.

Gerald peeled off his shirt. His back was to Evers and when he glanced over his shoulder the boy was staring at him with an expression of grim despair, seeing the scars the bear had left like lashes from a whip on either side of his spine, maybe blaming himself. When he saw he'd been caught looking Evers averted his gaze, idling his discomfort by rooting around in the pile of quartered logs, apparently searching for the perfect one.

Gerald stripped off his pants and set those on the closest upended log. When he placed the laminated photograph on top he looked back at Evers but he was prodding at the fire with a piece of kindling and didn't seem to have noticed.

A few seconds later, Gerald was taking a running dive off the peninsula. The lake was fed by a series of underground springs and even at the end of August the water was still cool enough to take his breath away. He came up with his skin riddled in goosebumps, wiping the water out of his eyes and up over his head, feeling more than a little like his old self. When his vision cleared, he could see Evers standing at the log where he'd left his clothes. He was holding the picture between both hands and gazing down upon it, Gerald watching him but too far away to tell of his expression.

He dove again and swam underwater all the way back to the steep slope of granite feeding onto the peninsula, his fingers running along the algae-slicked rock and finding the crack just below the surface of the water where it always was. Taking hold of that he thrust upwards, clawing his hands ahead and snagging hold of a lip in the stone, using that to drag himself onto dry land. Steam was rising from his skin as he walked back towards the fire.

Evers gave him a curious sideways glance while Gerald was reaching for his shorts.

I always wondered if you'd gotten that, Evers said, holding up the photo to make his meaning clear as Gerald got dressed.

It was the damndest thing, I tellya. It was Charlie Wilkes gave it to me. He visited me one time—

Oh, I know. I was the one who sent him.

Then seeing the look of confusion on Gerald's face.

He didn't tell you?

He didn't say a damn word. Just left it with a guard.

That son of a bitch.

He is that. When'd you see Charlie Wilkes?

He dropped by the foster home after your trial. Said he was just checking in. I gave him the picture then.

And you told him to give it to me?

Figured it was the least he owed you, after you'd done gone and saved his life and all.

It was true. It was only three days after Gerald had killed the bear that Charlie Wilkes had found it and tracked them to their cave. Gerald was laid up in their cubby, dying maybe. He'd got the fever and had been in and out of consciousness. He'd awoken one afternoon to find his face mashed into the floor of the cave, someone kneeling on his back, zip-tying his hands.

He didn't know it was Charlie Wilkes until after the cop had rolled him over and grabbed him by the scruff of his hair, wrenching his body up to a sit.

Where's Everett? he'd growled.

Gerald responded by spitting in his face and Charlie had given his hand a twist hard enough that Gerald could feel the roots of his hair snapping between the cop's fingers.

Where is he?!

That's when Gerald had heard the click of a gun cocking. Charlie had heard it too. He spun around and there he was staring down the barrel of that old Smith & Wesson — the same gun that had killed two of his sons. That veil of steely-eyed resolve had cemented itself on Evers's face and Gerald knew beyond a sliver of a doubt that the boy was less than a breath away from pulling the trigger. He'd have been a cold-blooded killer then too, and what kind of a father would he have been if he'd let that happen?

So he'd kicked out with all his remaining strength, striking Charlie in the back and sending him reeling forward, knocking into Evers and the gun going off, the shot *ping!*ing harmlessly off the cave's wall. The last thing Gerald remembered before he passed out was Charlie on top of Evers, punching him in the face. It was this memory of his son that he'd carried with him to jail and looking at Evers now he knew it was then that he must have lost his tooth.

And he's never had it fixed.

Knowing that meant something but he wasn't sure exactly what.

Gerald must have been staring at it for Evers had closed his mouth, hiding the tooth and maybe his own shame for the way things had played out. Gerald was trying to think of what he might say to ease his pain yet unable to see a way around all those years he'd spent believing Charlie had given the picture to him out of spite, to show him what he'd lost, while really it was just his son trying to reach out to him.

And here was Evers reaching out to him again.

You've been wearing it around your neck all these years? he asked.

I guess I have.

Evers looking down at the picture again, staring deeply into its depths as if trying to divine the hidden significance of that. He seemed to have reached some conclusion for when he looked back up at Gerald, he was holding it out and then seemed to reconsider.

You know, he said, I got the others inside.

The others?

The other twelve pictures Mo—

He choked on the word and shook his head, gritting his teeth and turning away, looking like he was about to cry.

She'd have wanted them to be together, Gerald offered and Evers forced a strained smile.

I'd bet you're right about that.

The photographs were lined up on a shelf tacked to the far wall in Marguerite, what they'd always called the cabin right of centre, that being the name of Gerald's great-grandfather's oldest daughter.

The shelf was made of a single slat of the same wood as the walls and had been secured with new roofing nails so Gerald knew Evers had built it himself. Otherwise, the cabin was empty except for a sleeping bag unfurled on the floor and a backpack spilling over with an odd assortment of shirts and pants.

It was Mr. Mills who brought them to me, Evers was saying as Gerald approached the shelf. Instead of a gap where the fifth picture should have been here was the familiar cover of *Savage Gerry: Canadian Outlaw* and the mad-dog eyes — his own — glaring at him through the prison door's slot were enough to check his step.

Rudy Mills? he asked, using that as an excuse to look away from the book.

He used to drop by every couple of months when I was at the foster home, Evers answered, stopping beside his father. Take me out to Burger King, the go-karts, stuff like that. Always gave me a folded-up ten dollar bill before he left just like he did after I fetched him his eggs.

That sounds like Rudy all right.

Funny, I ran into him the other day when I was in town. He's the one who gave us all that soup.

Hearing him say that a clear image formed in Gerald's mind of how Rudy had been smiling at him last night, veiled and secretive. It had seemed foreboding to him at the time but he now saw it was quite the opposite. Rudy had simply been revelling in his own personal delight imagining the reunion shortly to come.

Never did tell me where he got the photos from, Evers was saying.

Probably just took them from the mantel in the living room, Gerald offered.

That's what I figured.

They'd been standing there all the while they talked and finally Evers clued in as to why.

Oh, he said, sweeping forward. Let me get that.

He plucked the book from its place and Gerald took those last few steps to the shelf. Unstringing the shoelace from the picture, he set the photo in the open space and scanned over the lot of them, from youngest to oldest, as he always did. There'd been a time when it had seemed that when he was looking at them all together he'd be able to catch a glimpse of the man his son one day might become and he saw now that had only been wishful thinking. They were all taken in good times, not bad, when it was the bad, he now saw, as much as the good that had truly made Evers into the man he'd become, a thought which led him quite naturally to another.

It was also all the bad times you'd had which had a hand in bringing you to where you are right now too.

Standing there beside his son, all the violence and suffering and despair he'd seen and felt seemed a world away — a dark cloud receding on the horizon, leaving him with a deep and utter longing for the prospect of countless days again filled with only blue skies and sun.

So as he scanned down the line, coming back to the fifth in the row, it wasn't a sense of loss he felt but a renewed sense of hope. Seeing the picture returned to its proper place, he recalled how he'd so often passed it by on the mantel in their living room and had whispered to himself, *May he never lose that spirit.* He saw this quiet invocation hadn't been to his son at all, but to himself, for he knew now that it was only he who'd had the power to shape the boy into the man he'd hoped he might yet one day become. And while he might have forsaken him in his hour of greatest need, their story was far from over. There was still plenty of time for his son to become the man Gerald had always wanted him to be. That thought drawing his attention back to the first picture, seeing his younger self standing there looking lost and forlorn and Evers full of reckless abandon, about to take that one step too many.

It was the first time Gerald had failed him, not so much because he'd almost let him fall but because of the uncertainty he'd felt at the time — about being a father and a husband — and he made a solemn promise to himself that he'd never fail his son like that again.

Shoot, Evers was saying behind him, I forgot about that.

When Gerald turned, Evers was bending down, picking up what appeared to be a flattened joint from the floor. It must have been in the book and had just fallen out. Evers caught him looking and, with consternation turning his father's face into a question mark, was all of a sudden just another teenage boy whose father had discovered him trying to hide a bit of mischief.

Wayne-Jay left it, he said a little too quickly. He said you'd probably appreciate a puff if you ever did make it back.

That right? Gerald answered as if he didn't believe a word.

Evers passed it over, grimacing. It was dry and crinkled between Gerald's fingers. He wet it between his lips and stuck it in his mouth, reaching into his pants for a lighter. While he touched flame to its end, Evers walked the book over to the lone window and propped it on the sill. He stepped back, appraising it, and then glanced over his shoulder at Gerald as if he was trying to reconcile the man's eyes on the cover with the ones staring back at him now.

But it wasn't that.

You mind if I have a puff too? he asked.

Gerald motioned to pass it over and then reconsidered.

Your mother said she'd skin me alive she caught me sharing a puff with you even a day before you turned eighteen.

Well then I guess it's lucky I turned eighteen in June.

You sure about that?

Pretty sure.

What year is this anyway?

Evers told him and Gerald made a play at counting the years out on his fingers, Evers never looking more like his mother than he did right then, scowling at him.

Shoot, Gerald finally said, I guess you really are eighteen.

He passed the joint over and Evers took a couple of clipped tokes before passing it back.

In the meantime Gerald's gaze had wandered over to the book on the window's sill.

You read that? he asked handing Evers the joint again.

Evers nodded.

It was mighty inspiring, he said and took another puff.

Funny, I heard another fellow say the exact same thing.

Evers was holding out what was left of the joint. It wasn't much more than a roach and Gerald waved it off.

Well, it's true, Evers said as he took one last short nip and flicked what was left out through the door. Got me through quite a few rough times, I'll tellya that.

The downcast reflection in his eyes while he spoke testified well enough to those and that and the slowly creeping buzz lent Gerald a conciliatory mood.

I guess maybe I'll have to get around to reading it some day, he said.

What, you never did?

Gerald shook his head.

I think you'll be surprised, Evers offered. Then smiling wise: I know Mr. Wilkes surely was.

How's that?

Mr. Asche made him out to be the bad guy.

That right?

He almost lost his job on account of it, way I heard. Falsifying evidence and whatnot. Roughing up people he thought were helping us. He even broke Wayne-Jay's jaw with the butt of a rifle after he found out he was leaving us those packages of food over the winter.

He broke his jaw?

Uh huh. And he used to beat his wife too. He was rotten to the core, way Mr. Asche made him out.

Gerald thought about that and it led him to thinking about something else too.

You know I saw him yesterday, Gerald said after a moment.

Who? Mr. Wilkes?

When I was in town.

He see you?

He did.

Evers expression blanched.

You think he's going to come after us again? he asked.

There was fear in his eyes pleading with Gerald, begging him to tell him it wasn't so. But that'd mean lying to his son and so he took a moment for himself, passing his thoughts over what had happened since he'd got out of jail and then tracking backwards to all the years he'd spent on the farm, trying to come up with a few true words to start things anew, all over again.

At last, his thoughts settled on the first time he'd ever seen Charlie Wilkes, the day he'd come to take Gerald away from the farm for beating his son half to death. He heard his grandfather growling in his faux-western drawl and that lent Gerald, as it so often had, a measure of the old man's unfailing resolve.

Well, I'll tellya one thing, he finally said with the terminal deliberation of a voice calling out to him from beyond the grave, Id'a shore like to see him try.

with gratitude to

tanja, anyk & kai, for the continuing adventure

jack david, for "it's wonderful!"
emily schultz, for the light at the end of the tunnel
&
david birnbaum, as always

and extra special thanks to

the good people of capreol who shared their stories
and sometimes their lives with us

the del papa family, matthew, bob & cookie
shawn robichaud
larry & chris (next door)
melissa, james, braxton & brody
janet gibson & lee ann ducharme
terry & his dog, mia
the real gerry i met while snowshoeing
&
clayton crisp

and to

craig "shag" beattie, rick leipert, nick black
paul hettinga (who i should have thanked before)
craig from guelph (for coming to visit us)
trevor hodgson, jenn gauthier & darren kaliciak
nicholas ruddock & stephen henighan
denis stokes & everyone at the conspiracy of 3

ron, dale, jill, guy & richard
roger & chris nash, rene trudeau, tom leduc & waub rice
george "robert" jackson (who knows why)

&

all the fine folks at ecw press
(but especially)
david, peter, samantha, michel, emily (f.), elham, aymen &
adrineh

and lastly in memory of

earl wallace brazier
(1970-2013)

may we *never lose* his *spirit*